797,885 Books
are available to read at

Forgotten Books

www.ForgottenBooks.com

Forgotten Books' App
Available for mobile, tablet & eReader

ISBN 978-1-331-48465-3
PIBN 10196462

This book is a reproduction of an important historical work. Forgotten Books uses state-of-the-art technology to digitally reconstruct the work, preserving the original format whilst repairing imperfections present in the aged copy. In rare cases, an imperfection in the original, such as a blemish or missing page, may be replicated in our edition. We do, however, repair the vast majority of imperfections successfully; any imperfections that remain are intentionally left to preserve the state of such historical works.

Forgotten Books is a registered trademark of FB &c Ltd.
Copyright © 2015 FB &c Ltd.
FB &c Ltd, Dalton House, 60 Windsor Avenue, London, SW19 2RR.
Company number 08720141. Registered in England and Wales.

For support please visit www.forgottenbooks.com

1 MONTH OF FREE READING

at
www.ForgottenBooks.com

By purchasing this book you are eligible for one month membership to ForgottenBooks.com, giving you unlimited access to our entire collection of over 700,000 titles via our web site and mobile apps.

To claim your free month visit:

www.forgottenbooks.com/free196462

* Offer is valid for 45 days from date of purchase. Terms and conditions apply.

Similar Books Are Available from
www.forgottenbooks.com

The Chief Legatee
by Anna Katharine Green

The Return of Sherlock Holmes
by Arthur Conan Doyle

Twenty Years Experience As a Ghost Hunter
by Elliot O'Donnell

The Leavenworth Case
A Lawyer's Story, by Anna Katharine Green

A Millionaire's Love Story
by Guy Boothby

The Woman in the Alcove
by Anna Katharine Green

The Technique of the Mystery Story
by Carolyn Wells

X y Z: A Detective Story
by Anna Katharine Green

The Millionaire Mystery
by Fergus Hume

The Man in the Corner
by Baroness Orczy

Memoirs of a Great Detective
Incidents in the Life of John Wilson Murray, by John Wilson Murray

The Mystery of the Hidden Room
by Marion Harvey

The Veil Withdrawn
A Novel, by Berton J. Maddux

The Siege of Lucknow
A Diary, by Inglis

The Secret House
by Edgar Wallace

The Secret Adversary
by Agatha Christie

The Yellow Claw
by Sax Rohmer

The Piccadilly Puzzle
A Mysterious Story, by Fergus Hume

His Last Bow a Reminiscence of Sherlock Holmes
by Arthur Conan Doyle

The Curse
by Fergus Hume

THE MAELSTROM

THE MAELSTROM

BY
FRANK FROEST

AUTHOR OF
THE GRELL MYSTERY

NEW YORK
GROSSET & DUNLAP
PUBLISHERS

COPYRIGHT, 1916, BY
FRANK FROEST

COPYRIGHT, 1916, BY
EDWARD J. CLODE

THE MAELSTROM

2129530

CHAPTER I

HALLETT blundered into an unlit lamp-post, swore with fervour, and stood for a second peering for some identifiable landmark in the black blanket of fog that muffled the street. Where he stood, a sluggish dense drift had collected, for following the treacherous habit of London fogs, it lay in patches. About him he could hear ghostly noises of traffic muffled and as from afar, but whether the sounds came from before or behind, from right or left, was more than his bewildered senses could fathom.

For the last ten minutes he had been walking in a spectral city among spectres. A by-street had trapped him and no single wayfarer had come within his limited area of sight. He lifted his hat and rubbed his head perplexedly as he came to the conclusion that he was lost. It was as though London had set out to teach the young man from New York a lesson. The fog had him beat.

"Guess I shall fetch somewhere, sometime," he muttered and strode doggedly on.

He had gone perhaps a dozen yards when from ahead a quick burst of angry voices broke out. Then there came a running of feet on the sodden pavement. Hallett came to a stop, listening. The fog seemed to thin a trifle.

THE MAELSTROM

Out of the thickness the outlines of a woman's figure loomed vaguely. She was running swiftly and easily with lithe grace. As she noted the motionless figure of a man, she swerved towards him and he caught the hurried pant of her breath—caused rather, he judged, by emotion than by exertion. She halted impetuously as she came opposite to him and he caught a glimpse of her face—the mobile face of a girl, with parted lips and arresting blue eyes. She was hatless, and though Hallett could not have described her attire, he got an impression of some soft black stuff, clinging to a slim figure. She surveyed him in a quick, appraising glance, and before he could speak had thrust something into his hand.

"Take it—run," she gasped, and tore forward into the fog.

It had all happened in a fraction of time. She had checked rather than halted in her flight. An exclamation burst from Hallett's lips, and he was almost startled into obedience of the hurried command. Then heavier footsteps thudding near brought him to himself. He moved to interrupt the pursuer. As a man came into view, Hallett's hand fell on his shoulder.

"One moment, my friend——"

An oath was spat at him as the man wrenched himself free and was blotted out in gloom. Hallett shrugged his shoulders philosophically, and made no attempt at pursuit.

THE MAELSTROM

"Alarums and excursions," he murmured. "Wonder what it's all about?"

In nine and twenty years of life Jimmie Hallett had acquired something of a philosophy that made him content to accept things as they were, save only when they affected his personal well-being. Then he would sit up and kick with both feet. His lack of curiosity was almost cold-blooded. There was indeed a certain inoffensive arrogance in his attitude towards the ordinary affairs of life. He was the sort of man who would not cross the road to see a dog-fight.

Yet he always had a zest for excitement, providing it had novelty. A man who has scrambled for a dozen years in a hotch-potch of vocations retains little enthusiasm for commonplaces. When Hallett Senior had gone out from the combined effects of a Wall Street cyclone and an attack of heart failure, his son and heir had found himself with a hundred thousand dollars less than nothing. Young Hallett went to his only surviving relative—an elderly uncle with a liver—and with the confidence of youth rejected the offer of a cheap stool in that millionaire's office. He believed he could get a living as an actor—but a five weeks' tour in a fortieth-rate company, which finally stranded in the wilds of Michigan convinced him of the futility of that idea. Thereafter he drifted over a wide area of the United States. Farm-hand, railwayman, cow-puncher, prospector, and one very vivid voyage as a deck-hand on a cattle boat. It was inevitable that of course he should eventually drift into that last refuge of the unskilled intellectual classes—journalism. Equally of course it was inevitable that fate, who delights to take a hand at unexpected moments, should interfere when he showed signs of making a mark in his profession. His uncle died intestate and Jimmie leapt at a bound to affluence beyond his wildest dreams.

He had stayed long enough in New York after that to realise how extensive and variegated were the acquaintances who had stood by him in adversity. They took pains that he should not forget it. And forthwith he had taken counsel of Sleath, the youthful-looking city editor of *The Wire,* who breathed words of wisdom in his ear.

" Go to Europe, Jimmie. Travel and improve your mind. Let the sharks forget you."

So Jimmie Hallett stood lost in a fog, somewhere within hail of Piccadilly Circus, with an unopened package in his hand and the memory of a girl's voice in his mind. A less observant man than Hallett could not have failed to perceive that the girl was of a class unlikely to be involved in any street broil. The man flattered himself that he was not impressionable. But he retained an impression of both breeding and looks.

He dangled the package—it was small and light—on his finger, and moved forward till an electric standard gave him an opportunity of examining it more

THE MAELSTROM

closely. It was closely sealed at both ends with red sealing wax, but the wrapping itself had apparently been torn from an ordinary newspaper. He hesitated for a moment and then tore it open. He could scarcely have told what he expected to find. Certainly not the thirty or forty cheques that lay in his hand. One by one he turned them slowly over, as though the inspection would afford some indication of why they had been so unexpectedly thrust upon him. A bare possibility that he had been made an unwitting accomplice in a theft was dismissed as he noticed that the cheques were dead—they all bore the cancelling mark of the bank. Why on earth should the girl have been running away with the useless cheques? And why should she have so impulsively confided them to a stranger to avoid them falling into the hands of her headlong pursuer?

Not that Hallett would have worried overmuch about these problems had the central figure been plain or commonplace. She had interested him, and his interest, once aroused in any person or thing, was always vivid.

Keen-eyed, he scrutinised the cheques, in an endeavour to decipher the signature. They were all made out by the same person, and payable to " self." The name he read as J. E. Greye-Stratton. Whoever J. E. Greye-Stratton was he had drawn within three months, in sums ranging from fifty to three hundred pounds, an amount totalling—Hallett reckoned in United States terms—more than fifteen thousand dollars.

THE MAELSTROM

He stuffed the cheques into his pocket as an idea materialised in his mind. An opportune taxi pushed its nose stealthily through the wall of fog and halted at his hail.

"Think you can fetch a post-office, sonny?" he demanded.

"Get you anywhere, sir," assented the driver cheerfully.

"Find your way by the stars, I suppose," commented Hallett, the tingle of fog still in his eyes.

Nevertheless, the driver justified his boast and his fare was shortly engrossed with the letter "G" in the London directory. There was only one entry of the name he sought, and he swiftly transcribed the address to a telegraph blank.

"Greye-Stratton, James Edward, Thirty-four, Linstone Terrace Gardens, Kensington, W."

Shortly the cab was again crawling through the fog, sounding its syren like a liner in mid-channel. All that the passenger could make out was a hazy world, dotted with faint yellow specks, which now and again transformed themselves into lights as they drew near them. Later the yellow specks grew less as they swerved off the main road, and in a little while the car drew to a halt.

The driver indicated the house opposite which they were standing, with a jerk of his thumb, as Hallett descended.

"That's the place, sir."

THE MAELSTROM

It was little that Hallett could see of the house, save that it was a big old-fashioned building, with heavy bow-windows, and a basement, protected by wrought-iron rails. There was no light in any part of the house, not even the hall. Twice the young man wielded the big brass knocker, arousing nothing apparently but an echo. As he raised it a third time, the door was thrown open with disconcerting suddenness, and he was aware of someone standing within the blackness of the hall. Hallett could distinguish nothing of his features.

"I wish to see Mr. Greye-Stratton," said Hallett, and tendered a card.

The other made no attempt to take it. "He won't see you," he declared with harsh abruptness, and only a sudden movement of Hallett's foot prevented the door being slammed in his face.

His teeth gritted together, and he thrust the door back and himself over the lintel. He was an easy-tempered man, but the deliberate discourtesy had roused him to a cold anger. "That will do, my man," he said, clipping off each word sharply. "I want ordinary civility, and I'm going to see that I get it. My name is Hallett—James Hallett, of New York. Now you go and tell your master that I want to see him about certain property of his that has come into my hands. Quick's the word."

There was a pause. When the man in the hall spoke

again his tone had changed. "I beg your pardon, Mr. Hallett. It is dark—I mistook you for someone else. I am sure Mr. Greye-Stratton would have been happy to see you, but unfortunately he is ill. If you will leave whatever you have, I will see that it reaches him. By the way, I am not a servant, I am a doctor. Gore is my name."

Hallett thrust his hand in the pocket that contained the cheques. He had no intention of handing them over without some information about the girl in black. And he fancied he detected a note of anxiety in the doctor's voice, as though, while forced in a way to civility, he was anxious for the visitor to go.

"I quite understand, Dr. Gore," he said coldly, "I will call at some other time. I should like to return the property to its owner in person—for a special reason. Good-night."

"Then you will not entrust—whatever you have to me?"

"I would rather see Mr. Greye-Stratton at some future time." He half turned to go.

"One moment." The doctor laid a detaining hand upon his sleeve. "I did not wish to disturb my patient unnecessarily, but if you insist I will arrange you shall see him. Will you come with me? I am afraid it is rather dark. The electric light has gone wrong—frightfully awkward."

Hallett groped his way after his guide, his brain

busy. It was queer that the light should have given out—queerer still that no apparent attempt had been made at illumination, either with oil or candles. The place was deadly quiet, but that was only natural with a sick man in the house. He wondered why some servant had not answered the door. A man of less hardened temperament would have felt nervous.

The doctor's footsteps falling with ghostly softness on the carpet in front of him ceased.

"Here we are, Mr. Hallett. Keep to your left. This is the room. If you will wait here a second, I will see if I can get a light. Where are you? Give me your hand."

Slim delicate fingers gripped Hallett's hand as he followed the direction. He passed through a doorway and for a moment his back was turned towards the doctor. He heard something whirl in the air and a blow descended with crushing force on his right shoulder. He wheeled with a cry, but there was no question of resistance. A second blow fell, this time better directed, and a million stars danced before his eyes. He dropped like a felled ox.

CHAPTER II

PUNCTUALLY at half-past six, the little plated alarm clock exploded and Weir Menzies kicked off the blankets. Punctually at seven o'clock he had breakfast. Punctually at half-past seven he delved and weeded in the square patch of ground that was the envy and despair of Magersfontein Road, Upper Tooting. Punctually at twenty-past eight he left his semi-detached house and boarded a car for Westminster Bridge.

There were occasions when the routine was upset, but it will be observed that on the whole Weir Menzies was a creature of habit. He had all that respect for order and method that has made Upper Tooting what it is. From the heavy gold watch-chain that spanned his ample waist, to his rubicund face and heavy black moustache, he wore Tooting respectability all over him. It was a cause of poignant regret to him that circumstance prevented him taking any part in the local government of the borough. Nevertheless, he belonged to the local constitutional club, and was the highly esteemed people's warden at the Church of All Saints. The acute observer, knowing all this, might have judged him a deserving wholesale ironmonger.

And the acute observer would have been wrong.

Punctually at half-past nine, Weir Menzies would pass up a flight of narrow stone stairs at the back of

THE MAELSTROM

New Scotland Yard into the chief inspector's room of the Criminal Investigation Department. From his buttonhole he would take the choice blossom—gathered that day at Magersfontein Road, Upper Tooting—place it carefully in a freshly-filled vase, exchange his well-brushed morning coat for a jacket of alpaca, place paper protectors on his cuffs, and settle down on his high stool —he preferred a high stool—to half an hour's correspondence.

Mr. Weir Menzies, churchwarden of Upper Tooting, was in fact Chief Detective Inspector Menzies of the Criminal Investigation Department, New Scotland Yard. Not that he made any secret of it. There was no reason why he should. It is only on rare occasions that a detective needs to conceal his profession.

Although the residents of Magersfontein Road, Upper Tooting, knew that Mr. Weir Menzies was an admirable churchwarden, they had to take his reputation as a detective on trust. And being constant subscribers to circulating libraries, they knew him as an innocent fraud. A man something over forty, with an increasing waist-line and a ruddy face, was obviously against the rules of all the established authorities. It was only understandable because he was at Scotland Yard. Everyone knows that official detectives are heavy, dull, unimaginative fellows, always out of their depths, and continually receiving the good-natured assistance of amateurs, by whom they are held in tolerant contempt.

THE MAELSTROM

Magersfontein Road, Upper Tooting, would have smiled broadly had anyone remarked that Chief Detective Inspector Menzies held an international reputation—that he was held one of the subtlest brains in the service; that he was a man who had time and again shown reckless courage and audacity in bringing off a coup; that he, in short, had individuality and a perfect knowledge of every resource at his disposal in carrying out any purpose to which he was assigned.

He looked a commonplace business man; he was a commonplace business man with many of the traits of his class. He hated the unexpected and protested that he loathed with a fierce abomination those cases in which he was engaged that meant a departure from the ordinary routine. But yet those cases, when they arose, there was no man more capable of dealing with their baffling intricacies than he. He had a faculty of adjusting himself to an emergency, of ruthlessly discarding the superfluous that in twenty-three years had carried him to within one rung of the top of the ladder.

It was shortly before midnight. He had returned from a remote suburb where with a corps of assistants he had made an entirely successful raid upon certain pickpockets, who had been too well acquainted with the resident detectives to give them any chance. It had been a triumph of organisation and vigilance, and Menzies had gone back to headquarters to arrange that the histories of the birds he had caged should be ready before the police court proceedings in the morning. He was struggling into his overcoat when he was summoned to the telephone. He picked up the receiver irritably.

"Hello," he said.

A musical buzz answered him, and Menzies allowed himself an expression that should be foreign to a churchwarden. Then far away and faint he caught a voice. "That Mr. Menzies?"

"Yes," he answered impatiently. "Speak up. Who is it? What do you want?"

A prolonged buzz reached him. He was conscious of someone speaking, but only intermittently could he hear what was said.

"Pretty done up—buz-z—come at once—buz-z—at thirty-four—buzz-z—Gardens, Kensington—buzz-z."

"Number, please?" said a new and distinct voice.

"Blast," said Menzies simply, and put down the telephone. This addiction to forcible language on occasions of annoyance was a constant regret to him in his more reflective moments.

Jimmie Hallett's first impression on awakening had been that someone was swinging a sledge-hammer irregularly on to his temples. He lay still for a little, wondering why it should be. By and by he sat up and tried to piece together the events of the evening. His head ached intolerably, and he found consecutive thought painful.

THE MAELSTROM

It was totally dark, and he could make out nothing of where he was. Then the whole thing flashed across his mind and he staggered rather uncertainly to his feet and, steadying himself against the wall, struck a match.

The feeble flicker showed him a blue papered apartment, furnished as a dining-room. He had been lying just inside the door, which he now tried. It refused to answer to his tug, and he realised how weak he was as he all but toppled backwards. The match went out and he struck another.

Then it was that he noticed an electric switch and pulled it over. A rush of light flooded the room and he tottered to one of the Jacobean armchairs at the head of the table. The sledge-hammer was still swinging at his temples and things swayed dizzily to and fro before his eyes. He made a resolute effort to pull himself together. His eyes roved over the room, and he noticed a pedestal telephone on a small table in the corner furthest from him.

" What was the name of the chap Pinkerton gave me an introduction to," he muttered, and drawing a bundle of papers from his breast pocket, sorted them till the envelope he needed lay at the top.

Chief Detective Inspector Weir Menzies,
New Scotland Yard, S. W.

THE MAELSTROM

Cautiously the man began to move across the hearth-rug towards the telephone. Four shambling steps he took, then something that had been hidden by the table tripped him and he sprawled on all fours. He gave a little gasp of horror, and steadying himself on his knees, held his hands a foot in front of his face, gazing at them stupidly. They were wet—wet with blood, and the thing that had tripped him was the body of a man.

It is one thing to be brought in association at second-hand, so to speak, with a crime, as are doctors, reporters, and detectives, but quite another to be so closely identified with it as to be an actor in the drama. Hallett had seen violence, and even death in his time, but never had cold horror so thrilled him as it did now. In ordinary condition, with nerves previously unshaken, he would have been little more moved than a spectator at a play—perhaps even less so, for real life tragedies are rarely well stage managed.

Circumstances, however, had conspired to bring home to him the last touch of terror. The sudden assault, the locked room, and now the dead man, had played the mischief with his nerves. He could have shrieked aloud.

He wiped his hands on his handkerchief, but the stain still remained. Carefully he stepped over the body and made his way to the telephone. His imagination was beginning to work, and he recalled cases where per-

THE MAELSTROM

fectly innocent men had been the victims of circumstantial evidence that had convicted them of hideous crimes. The story of the cheques thrust upon him in the fog seemed to him ridiculously unconvincing. Had his mind been less overwrought, had he been able to take a calmer survey of the matter, he would probably never have given his own position a thought. He fingered the telephone book clumsily and his mind reverted to the coincidence that he should hold a letter of introduction to one of the senior detectives of Scotland Yard.

"Queer that it should come in so handy," he grinned feebly, and then weakness overcame him.

He gave the number. Hours seemed to elapse before he got Menzies. In a quick rush of words he made himself known to the detective and recited the happenings of the evening. He did not know that barely a dozen disconnected words had reached him. His strength was waning and he wanted Menzies to know everything before he gave way. As he finished the receiver dropped listlessly from his hand, and for the first time in his life Jimmie Hallett fainted.

At the other end of the wire Weir Menzies was left with one of those harassing little problems that he hated. It was an irregular hour—an hour when he had reckoned on being safely on his way home. For all the insistence of the voice at the telephone, it might be quite a trivial affair. Menzies did not like losing

THE MAELSTROM

sleep for trivialities. People in trouble are apt to take distorted views of the importance of their difficulties. That is why private enquiry agencies flourish.

He was impatient with ambiguous messages. He thought of his well-aired bed and sighed. But the fact that he had been appealed to by name ultimately swayed him.

In two minutes he had set in motion the machinery which would reveal the point from which the voice originated. It needed no complex reasoning, no swift flash of inspiration: merely to look up in the Kensington directory a list of thoroughfares ending in " Gardens," and the names of persons who resided at the respective thirty-fours.

" And get a move on," he said to one of his men. " I don't want to hang about all night. Ask Riddle to come up and 'phone 'em through to the local people as you check 'em off. Tell 'em they'll oblige me by sending out as many spare men as they've got to ask at each address if anyone rang me up."

He adjusted his coat with precision, lit a cigar, and sauntered over to the underground station opposite. Barring accidents, the address would be ready for him by the time he reached Kensington.

He was not disappointed. One of the advantages which the Criminal Investigation Department has over the individual amateur detective, beloved by Magersfontein Road, is the co-operation at need of a prac

THE MAELSTROM

tically unlimited number of trained men. True, the detective staff at Kensington had long since gone home, since there was no extraordinary business to detain them, but in this case a dozen ordinary constables served as well. Nine of them had returned when Menzies walked in. There was only one who interested him. He had reported that he could get no reply from Linstone Terrace Gardens.

"Did you find who lives there?" questioned the chief inspector.

The reply was prompt. "Yes, sir. Old gentleman named Greye-Stratton. He lives alone. Had two servants until last week, when he sacked 'em both because he said they had been bribed to poison him."

"Ah!" Menzies nodded approval. "You've got your wits about you, my lad. Where did you get all this from?"

The constable flushed with pleasure. He was young enough in the force to appreciate a compliment from the veteran detective. "The servant next door, sir," he answered.

"That will do. Thank you." Menzies rubbed his hands with satisfaction as he turned to the uniformed inspector by his side. "It begins to sound like a case," he muttered. All his petulance had gone. When it came to the point, the man was an enthusiast in his profession. "I'll get you to come along with me, inspector. It sounds uncommonly like a case."

CHAPTER III

THE eminent Tooting churchwarden, perched on the stalwart shoulders of his uniformed colleague, wriggled his way on to the roof of the porch with an agility that was justifiable neither to his years nor his weight. He was taking a certain amount of risk, if there were no serious emergency within the place, for even a chief detective inspector may not break into a house without justification.

He worked for a while with a big clasp knife on the little landing window, with a skill that would have done credit to many of the professional practitioners who had passed through his hands, and at last threw up the sash and squeezed himself inside.

"Wonder if I'm making a damned fool of myself, after all?" he muttered with some misgiving as he struck a match and softly picked his way along the corridor. He was peculiarly sensitive to ridicule, and he knew the chaff that would descend on his head if it leaked out that he had elaborately picked out and broken into an empty house.

There would be no way of keeping the matter dark, for every incident of the night would have to be embodied in reports. Every detective in London keeps an official diary of his work.

He burned only one match to enable him to get his

bearings. Noiselessly he descended the stairs into the hall, and his quick eye observed a splash of light across the floor. It came from under a doorway. He turned the handle and pushed. The door resisted.

"Locked," he murmured, and knocked thunderously. "Hello in there! Anyone about?"

Only the muffled reverberation of his own voice came back to him. Frowning, he strode to the doorway, slipped back the Yale lock, and admitted the uniformed man.

"If I had nerves, Mr. Hawksley, this place would give me the jumps," he observed. "There's something wrong here and I guess it's in that room. See, there's a light on."

"That's queer," commented the other. "It could only just have been switched on. I didn't notice it outside."

"Shutters," said Menzies. "Shutters and drawn curtains. Come on. I'm going to see what's behind that door."

There was no finesse about forcible entry this time. Half a dozen well-directed kicks shattered the hasp of the lock and sent the door flying open. Menzies and his companion moved inside.

For the moment the blaze of the electric light dazzled them. Menzies shaded his eyes with his hand. Then his glance fell from the overturned telephone down to the prostrate figure of Jimmie Hallett. He was across

THE MAELSTROM

the room in an instant, and made swift examination of the prostrate man.

"Knocked clean out of time," he diagnosed. "Help me get him on the couch. Hello, there's another of 'em." He had observed the body on the hearth-rug.

He bent over the murdered man in close scrutiny but without touching the corpse. His lips pursed into a whistle as he marked the bullet wound that showed among the grey locks at the back of the head. He was startled but scarcely shocked.

He straightened himself up. "This looks a queer business altogether, Hawksley. You'd better get back to the station. Send up the divisional surgeon and 'phone through to the Yard. They'd better let Sir Hilary Thornton and Mr. Foyle know. I shall need Congreve and a couple of men, and you'd better send for Carless and as many of his staff as can be reached quickly. They'll know the district."

The faculty of quick organisation is one of the prime qualities of a chief of detectives, and Menzies was at no loss. The first step in the investigation of most great mysteries is automatic—the determination of the facts. It is a kind of circle from facts to possibilities, from possibilities to probabilities, and from probabilities to facts. But the original facts must be settled first, and for any one person to fix them single-handed is an impossibility.

There are certain aspects that must be settled by

specialists; there may be a thousand and one enquiries to make in rapid succession. Menzies had no idea of playing a lone hand.

For a couple of hours a steady stream of officials and others descended on the house, and Linstone Terrace Gardens became the centre of such police activity as it had never dreamed would affect its austere respectability.

Men worked from house to house, interviewing servants, masters, mistresses, gleaning such facts as could be obtained of the lonely, eccentric old man, his habits, his visitors, friends, and relations. Inside the house the divisional surgeon had attended to Hallett ("No serious injury. May come round any moment"), and waited till flash-light photographs of the room had been taken from various angles ere examining the dead man. Draughtsmen made plans to scale of the room and every article in it. A finger-print expert peered round searchingly, scattering black or grey powder on things which the murderer might have touched. In the topmost rooms Congreve, Menzies' right-hand man, had begun a hasty search of the house that would become more minute the next day.

Menzies occupied a morning room at the back of the house and was deep in consultation with Sir Hilary Thornton, the grizzled assistant commissioner, and Heldon Foyle, the square-shouldered, well-groomed superintendent of the Criminal Investigation Department.

THE MAELSTROM

There was little likeness between the three men, unless it lay in a certain hint of humour in the eyes and a firmness of the mouth. A detective without a sense of humour is lost.

Now and again Menzies broke off the conversation to issue an order or receive a report. Thornton observed for the first time the characters in which he made a few notes on the back of an envelope.

"I didn't know you knew Greek, Menzies," he remarked.

The chief inspector twiddled his pencil awkwardly. "I use it now and again, Sir Hilary. You see, if I should lose my notes by any chance it's odds against the finder reading them. I used to do them in shorthand, but I gave it up. There are too many people who understand it. Yes, what is it, Johnson?"

The man who had entered held out a paper. "Addresses of the cook and housemaid, sir. One lives at Potters Bar, the other at Walthamstow."

"Have them fetched by taxi," ordered Menzies curtly.

"Couldn't you have statements taken from them?" asked Hilary mildly. "It's rather a drag for women in the middle of the night."

Menzies smoothed his moustache. "We don't know what may develop here, sir. We may want to put some questions quickly."

While thus Menzies was straining every resource

THE MAELSTROM

which a great organisation possessed to gather together into his hands the ends of the case, Jimmie Hallett awoke once more. The throbbing in his head had gone and he lay for a while with closed eyes, listlessly conscious of the mutter of low voices in the room.

He sat up, and at once a dapper little man was by his side. "Ah, you've woke up. Feeling better? That's right. Drink this. We want you to pull yourself together for a little while."

"Thanks. I'm all right," returned Hallett mechanically. He drank something which the other held out to him in a tumbler, and a rush of new life thrilled through him. "Are you Mr. Menzies?"

"No, I'm the police divisional surgeon. Mr. Menzies is in the next room. Think you're up to telling him what has happened? He's anxious to know the meaning of all this."

"So am I," said Hallett grimly, and staggered to his feet. "Just a trifle groggy," he added as he swayed, and the little doctor thrust a supporting shoulder under his arm.

The three in the next room rose as Hallett was ushered in. It was Foyle who sprang to assist Hallett and lifted him bodily on to the settee, which Menzies pushed under the chandelier. The doctor went out.

"Quite comfortable, eh?" asked Foyle. "Let me make that cushion a bit easier for you. Now you're

THE MAELSTROM

better. We won't worry you at present more than we can help, will we, Menzies?"

The three great detectives, for all that their solicitude seemed solely for the comfort of the young man, were studying him keenly and unobtrusively. Already they had talked him over, but any suspicions that they might have held were quite indefinite. At the opening stage of a murder investigation everyone is suspected. In that lies the difference between murder and professional crime. A burglary, a forgery, is usually committed for one fixed motive by a fixed class of criminal, and the search is narrowed from the start. A millionaire does not pick pockets, but he is quite as likely as anyone else to kill an enemy. In a murder case, no detective would say positively that any person is innocent until he is absolutely certain of the guilt of the real murderer.

Hallett, whose brain was beginning to work swiftly, held out his hand to the chief inspector. "Pleased to meet you, Mr. Menzies. I've got a letter of introduction to you from Pinkerton. That's how I came to ring you up. My name's Hallett."

Menzies shook hands. "Glad to know you, Mr. Hallett. This is Sir Hilary Thornton—Mr. Heldon Foyle."

"And now," said Jimmie decisively, when the introductions were done. "Do you people think I killed this man, Greye-Stratton?"

THE MAELSTROM

The possibility had been in the minds of everyone in the room, but they were taken aback by the abruptness of the question. Weir Menzies laughed as though the idea were preposterous.

"Not unless you've swallowed the pistol, Mr. Hallett. We've found no weapon of any kind. You were locked in, you know. Now tell us all about it. I couldn't hear a word you said on the telephone."

They all listened thoughtfully until he had finished. Thornton elevated his eyebrows in question at his two companions as the recital closed.

"Where are those cheques?" asked Foyle. "They may help us."

Hallett patted his pockets in rapid succession. "They're gone!" he exclaimed. "They must have been taken off me when I was knocked out."

"H'm," said Foyle reflectively. "Can you make anything of it, Menzies?"

The chief inspector was gnawing his moustache—a sure sign of bewilderment with him. He shrugged his shoulders. "There's little enough to take hold of," he returned. "Could you recognise any of the people you saw again, Mr. Hallett? the girl, the man who was running after her, or the chap in the house."

"I haven't the vaguest idea of what the face of either of the men was like," said Hallett.

"But the woman—the girl?" persisted Menzies.

Hallett hesitated. "I—I think it possible that I

might," he admitted. Then an impulse took him. "But I'm sure she's not the sort of person to be mixed up in—in——"

The three detectives smiled openly. "In this kind of she-mozzle you were going to say," finished Menzies. "There's only one flaw in your reasoning. She is."

Wrung as dry of information as a squeezed sponge, Hallett was permitted to depart. The courtesy of Sir Hilary Thornton supplied him with a motor-car back to his hotel, the forethought of Menzies provided him with an escort in the shape of a detective sergeant. Hallett would have been less pleased had he known that that same mentioned detective sergeant was to be relieved from all other duties for the specific purpose of keeping an eye upon him. Weir Menzies was always cautious, and though his own impression of the young man had been favourable enough, he was taking no chances.

All through that night Weir Menzies drove his allies hither and thither in the attempt to bring the ends of the ravelled threads of mystery into his hand. No one knew better than he the importance of a first hot burst of pursuit. An hour in the initial stages of an investigation is worth a week later on. The irritation at being kept out of bed had all vanished now that he was on the warpath. He could think without regret of a committee meeting of the Church Restoration Fund the following day from which he would be forced to absent himself.

THE MAELSTROM

Scores of messages had been sent over the private telegraph and telephone systems of the Metropolitan Police before, at seven o'clock in the morning, he took a respite. It was to an all-night Turkish bath in the neighbourhood of Piccadilly Circus that he made his way.

At nine o'clock, spruce and ruddy, showing no trace of his all-night work beyond a slight tightening of the brows, he was in Heldon Foyle's office. The superintendent nodded as he came in.

"You look fine, Menzies. Got your man?"

The other made a motion of his hand deprecatory of badinage. "Nope," he said "But I've got a line on him."

Foyle sat up and adjusted his pince-nez. "The deuce you have. Who is he?"

"His name is Errol," said Menzies. "He's a prodigal stepson of Greye-Stratton, and was pushed out of the country seven years ago."

"Menzies," said Foyle, laying down his pince-nez. "You ought to be in a book."

CHAPTER IV

WEIR MENZIES fitted his form to the big armchair that flanked Foyle's desk, and dragged a handful of reports secured by an elastic band from his breast pocket. Foyle snipped the end off a cigar and leaning back puffed out a blue cloud of smoke.

"It's been quick work, though I say it myself," observed Menzies complacently, "especially considering it's a night job. This night work is poisonous—no way of getting about, no certainty of finding the witnesses you want, everyone angry at being dragged out of bed, and all your people knocked out the next day when they ought to be fresh."

Foyle flicked the ash from his cigar, and a mischievous glimmer shone in his blue eyes. "It's tough luck, Menzies. I know you hate this kind of thing. Now there's Forrester—he's got nothing in particular on: if you like——"

Menzies' heavy eyebrows contracted as he scrutinised his chief suspiciously. Untold gold would not have induced him to willingly relax his hold of a case that interested him. "I'm not shifting any job of mine on to anyone else's shoulders, Mr. Foyle," he said acidly.

"That's all right," said Foyle imperturbably. "Go ahead."

THE MAELSTROM

Menzies tapped his pile of statements "As far as I can boil down what we've got, this is how it stands. Old Greye-Stratton was a retired West Indian merchant—dropped out of harness eight years ago, and has lived like a hermit by himself in Linstone Terrace Gardens ever since. It seems there was some trouble about his wife—she was a widow named Errol when he married her, and she had one son. Five years before the crash there was a daughter born. Anyway, as I was saying, trouble arose, and he kicked his wife out, sent the baby girl abroad to be educated, and the boy—he would then be about twenty—with his mother. Well, the woman died a few years after. Young Errol came down to Greye-Stratton, kicked up a bit of a shindy, and was given an allowance on condition that he left the country. He went to Canada, and thence on to the States, and must have been a bit of a waster. A year ago he returned to England and turned up in Linstone Terrace Gardens; there was a row and he went away swearing revenge. Old Greye-Stratton stopped supplies, and neither the lawyers nor anyone else have seen anything of Errol since."

Foyle rolled a pencil to and fro across his blotting-pad with the palm of his hand. He interrupted with no question. What Menzies stated as facts he knew the chief inspector would be able to prove by sworn evidence, if necessary. He was merely summarising evidence. The inference he allowed to be drawn, and so

THE MAELSTROM

far it seemed an inference that bade fair to place a noose round young Errol's neck.

"We have got this," went on Menzies, "from people in Linstone Terrace Gardens, from Greye-Stratton's old servants, from the house agents from whom he rented his house, and from Pembroke, of Pembroke and Stephens, who used to be his solicitors. Greye-Stratton was seventy years old, as deaf as a beetle, and as eccentric as a monkey. I don't believe he has kept any servant for more than three months at a stretch—we have traced out a dozen, and there must be scores more. But it is only lately that he has taken to accusing them of being in a plot to murder him. The last cook he had he made taste everything she prepared in his presence.

"He had no friends in the ordinary way and few visitors. Twice within the last year he has been visited by a woman, but who or what she was no one knows. She came evidently by appointment and was let in by him, himself; remained half an hour and went away. Praetically all his business affairs had been carried on by correspondence, and he was never known to destroy a letter. Yet we have found few documents in the house that can have any bearing on the case, except possibly this, which was found in the grate of the little bedroom he habitually used."

He extracted from the pile of statements a square of doubled glass, which he passed to Foyle. It contained several charred fragments of writing paper with a few detached words and letters discernible.

"J. E. Gre. . . . Will see . . . ld you . . . ues . . . mother to her death . ous swine . let me hea. . "

"Errol's writing?" queried Foyle.

"I haven't got a sample yet, but I've little doubt of it. Now here's another thing. It was Greye-Stratton's custom to lock up the house every night at dusk, himself. He would go round with a revolver and see to every one of the bolts and fastenings, and no one was allowed in or out thereafter. It was one of the grievances of the servants that they were prisoners soon after four o'clock each day in winter. And though he always slept with that revolver under his pillow, we can't find it.

"There's another thing. Greye-Stratton had a little study where he spent most of the day, and there was a safe built in to the wall. It may mean nothing, or anything, but the safe was open and there was not a thing in it. Now we have been able to discover no one who has ever seen that safe open before. It's curious, too, in view of Hallett's story about the cheques, that we have not been able to lay our hands on a single thing that refers to a banking transaction—not so much as a paying-in book or a bunch of counterfoils.

"The doctors say the old man was shot about three hours before we got there. That would be about half-past nine. I don't know how Hallett struck you, Mr. Foyle, but according to his own account he must have arrived at Linstone Terrace Gardens at nine."

Foyle rubbed his chin thoughtfully. "You mean he may have been there when the shot was fired."

Menzies made an impatient gesture. "I don't know. I own freely I don't quite take in this yarn, and yet the man struck me as genuine. He's got good credentials, and if he's mixed up with the murder, why did he 'phone to me?"

"Search me," said Foyle. "What about the daughter? You said there was a girl."

Menzies stuck his thumbs in the sleeve holes of his waistcoat. "That's another queer point. She was brought up abroad, and scarcely ever saw the old man. Pembroke says she spent her holidays with an old couple down in Sussex, to whom he had instructions to pay three hundred pounds a year. When she left school he had the allowance paid to her direct. She had a taste for painting and was apparently quite capable of looking after herself. For two years she has not called or given any instructions about it. He wrote Greye-Stratton, who retorted it was none of his business— that the allowance would be paid over to his firm, and that if the girl did not choose to ask for it, it could accumulate. He did not seem at all concerned at her disappearance. Take it from me, Mr. Foyle, we shall run across some more damned funny business before we get to the bottom of this. There's not even a ghost of a finger-print. If only we can find Errol——"

Foyle was too old a hand to offer conjecture at so early a stage of the case. Nor did Menzies seem to expect any advice. Hard as he had driven the investigation during the night, the ground was not yet cleared. Until he had all the facts in his possession it was useless to absolutely pin himself to any one line of reasoning. There was now one man who, on known facts, might have committed the murder. But plausible as was the supposition that Errol was the man, the detectives knew that at best it was only a suspicion. And suspicion nowadays does not commit a man. It does not always justify an arrest. There must be evidence, and so far there was not a scrap of proof that Errol had been within a thousand miles of Linstone Terrace Gardens on the night of the murder.

Menzies went away with his bundle of documents, to have them typed, indexed, and put in order, so that he could lay his hand on any one needed at a moment's notice. He was in for a busy day.

Two advertisements he drafted in the sanctuary of his own office. One was to check Hallett's own account of the evening before, and to identify, if possible, the street in which the cheques had been forced on him.

"£1 REWARD. The taxi-cab driver who, on the evening of ————, drove a fare from the

THE MAELSTROM

West End to 34, Linstone Terrace Gardens, Kensington, will receive the above reward on communicating with the Public Carriage Office, New Scotland Yard. S. W."

The other ran differently, and seemed to give him more trouble. Several sheets of note-paper he wasted, and discontentedly surveyed his final effort.

"If James Errol, last heard of at Columbus, Ohio, U. S. A., will communicate——"

He crushed the sheet up, flung it in the waste-paper basket, and lifted a speaking-tube "Any newspaper men there, Green? Right. Tell 'em I'll see 'em in half an hour. Send me up a typist."

The newspaper press, if deftly handled, may be a potent factor in the detection of crime. Moreover, the ubiquitous reporter is not to be evaded for long by the cleverest detective living. The wisest course is to meet him with fair words—to guide his pen where there is a danger of his writing too much, and put him on his honour on occasion. Many a promising case has been spoilt by tactless treatment of a pressman at a wrong moment.

Menzies dictated an account of the murder, in which he said just as much as he wanted to say and not a word more. The conclusion ran:

THE MAELSTROM

"The stepson of the deceased gentleman, a Mr. James Errol, left England for the United States many years ago, and his present whereabouts are unknown. The police are anxious to get in to touch with him, in order that certain points in connection with his father's career should be cleared up."

The chief detective inspector knew that the simple paragraph would throw into the search for Errol the energies and organisation of every great newspaper—an aid he did not despise. It was not intended as an official statement. The Criminal Investigation Department does not issue bulletins officially. It was an act of courtesy, and incidentally a stroke of policy to maintain the good-will of the Press. The reporters might paraphrase it as they would.

He received the newspaper men pleasantly, parried their chaff and too adroit questions with unruffled good-humour, and told them little anecdotes which had not the slightest bearing on the murder or Greye-Stratton. They read the typewritten sheets he handed them greedily and cross-examined him as mercilessly as ever he had been cross-examined at the Old Bailey. A clerk brought a card to him and he read it without a change of countenance.

"In a minute," he said to the waiting clerk, and put the card in his waistcoat pocket. "Well, gentlemen, you know as much as I do now. If there's anything else you want to know, just drop in and see me when you like. Good morning."

They accepted their dismissal, and he took another glance at the card. "Miss Lucy Olney," he read; and underneath, written in pencil: "Peggy Greye-Stratton."

CHAPTER V

THE early evening papers were on the streets before Jimmie Hallett rose, and the inevitable reporters had established a blockade of his hotel. He cursed them while he shaved. As an old newspaper hand himself, he had little taste to be served up again all hot and spiced for the delectation of a morbidly hungry public.

He surveyed a salver full of cards that had been brought up to him with a scowl. Vivid recollections came to him of the way in which he had himself dealt in " personal sketches," and " personal statements " on big stories, and he began to conceive a certain fellow-feeling for his long-forgotten victims. But his chin grew dogged.

" I'll see 'em in hell before I'll talk. Go away and tell 'em I'm dead."

The liveried functionary who had brought the cards gave as near an approach to a grin as his dignity permitted " Yes, sir," he said quietly; " they'll not believe it, sir."

Hallett swung his eyes sideways to the man, and his hand slipped to his trousers pocket. It was no use getting angry. " Say, what are you getting out of this, sonnie? " he demanded. " It's all right. You needn't answer." A bank-note crackled between his fingers.

THE MAELSTROM

"If you can clear out the gang below this is yours. It's more than they'll give you."

"Very good, sir. There'll be no harm in telling them you're in a very critical condition, sir, I suppose?"

"Not in the least. If they've any bowels of compassion they won't worry a dying man. It will stave 'em off for a while, perhaps."

As a matter of fact, beyond a mild headache and some stiffness, he felt scarcely a trace of the attentions of his overnight assailant. He was uncertain whether that was a tribute to the skill of the divisional surgeon or to the hardness of his skull. He inwardly congratulated himself that the injury was not a particularly noticeable disfigurement. Indeed a skillful brushing of the hair almost hid it.

He descended to breakfast with an appetite that of itself was proof that his general health remained unaffected, and discovering that there was a back entrance to the hotel, decided to make use of it, lest some pertinacious reporter might still be lingering in the reception hall. He wanted to know something of what the police were doing, and a visit to Scotland Yard seemed the best way of finding out. In the background of his thoughts there was perhaps less concern that a murderer should be brought to justice than curiosity in regard to the lady of the fog.

There is a way, mostly used by tradesmen, at the Palatial Hotel, which leads through a narrow alley for

THE MAELSTROM

fifty yards on to the Embankment. Through this Hallett sauntered. He was halfway through when a tap on the shoulder caused him to wheel. He confronted a slim-built, shallow-faced man, of lank moustache and burning black eyes.

"Pardon," he said. "Your name is Hallett?" He spoke silkily and the extremely correct pronunciation of his words showed that he was neither English nor American.

"Well?" demanded Hallett shortly. He feared that he had been run down by a reporter after all.

"You were at the place where this man was killed yesterday—eh?" The man shook a newspaper under his face.

"Well?" said Hallett again. He had resumed his walk but the other was keeping pace with him.

A hand caught at his arm. The burning black eyes were within three inches of his face. "You know who killed heem, eh?" The English had become a little less correct under stress of some excitement. "You have not told the pol-lice yet. You will not tell them?"

Hallett shook himself free angrily. "Look here, my man," he said. "I don't propose to answer your questions, so you can put that in your pipe and smoke it. Now git."

The foreigner's hand dropped to his pocket. He did not remove it, but pressed something hard through the

THE MAELSTROM

cloth against the young man's ribs. "You are hasty, Mr. Hallett," he remonstrated. "You don't know what it is you say—what you're up against. This is a pistol you can feel"—he pressed it close—"and unless you listen quietly I shall keel you dead. Understand?"

"Well?" said Hallett quietly.

"You were at the house. You saw who killed the old man? You would know him again?" The man did not wait for an answer. "You must keep your mouth shut. This is for a warning. If you see him again you not tell—eh? There are many of us. You will be watched. And if you split——" A prod with the pistol finished the sentence.

The theory that his molester was a reporter had long ago been abandoned by Jimmie Hallett. It was evidently thought that he had seen the face of the man at Linstone Terrace Gardens and he was to be terrorised into silence. He had sense enough to reflect that for all the audacity of the hold-up, the threat of surveillance was bluff—perhaps even the concealed pistol was bluff. Not that his actions would have differed much even had he supposed them real.

He took a quick step backwards and sideways and a bullet that tore its way through the cloth of the other man's pocket told that that part of the story was reliable. Then Hallett's knee was in his back and Hallett's arms were woven in a strangle-hold about his throat. The man collapsed, gurgling.

THE MAELSTROM

The whole business had occurred in barely two seconds of time. As they fell there was a third arrival.

"Hold him down a minute, Mr. Hallett. That's all right." The third man possessed himself of the squirming captive's wrists and twisted them behind his back to Hallett. Then he methodically and quickly ran his hands through the prostrate man's clothing, possessing himself of a still smoking Derringer and a formidable sheath-knife.

"Thank you, sir. Now this gentleman might get up. We'll run him along to King Street station and see what Mr. Menzies has to say about it."

Then Hallett noted that the man who had come to his assistance was the liveried functionary who had accepted his five-pound note to put off the press men less than an hour ago. But he no longer wore livery. He was in quiet, unassuming tweeds and his manner was not exactly that which might be expected from a waiter to an hotel guest—even in the circumstances.

He surprised Hallett's look of enquiry and smiled as he locked his arm into that of the prisoner. "Detective Sergeant Royal, sir," he explained. "I'll let you know all about it later. What's your name, my man?" He shook his captive slightly.

"Smeeth—William Smeeth," said the man sullenly, and Royal winked at Hallett.

"That's a good old Anglo-Saxon name," he said. "Come along."

THE MAELSTROM

It was in the Criminal Investigation office at King Street, while they were awaiting Menzies, that Royal gave his explanation with a certain apologetic tone. "It was this way, Mr. Hallett. You see, Mr. Menzies asked me to keep an eye on you when you were sent home yesterday. Of course he thought you were all right, but it doesn't do to take anyone's say-so in our trade. This is murder, you see, and though it seemed all right, you might have forged or stolen the introduction you had. We couldn't be sure your name was really Hallett."

"And sandbagged myself on the back of the head," interpolated Hallett with irony.

Royal gave a shrug. "Mr. Menzies doesn't take any risks, sir. It couldn't do you any harm. They know me at the hotel and that's how it was I was able to get into livery and walk into your room pretty well as I liked."

A new light broke upon Hallett. "I get you. I thought perhaps I was a bit fogged when I got up and had forgotten where I put things. You've been searching my room."

Royal's face never shifted a muscle. "I don't admit it, sir. That would be illegal without your permission."

"Illegal or not, you did it," retorted Hallett. "I hope you're quite satisfied."

"Oh, there'll be no more trouble about that. Mr.

Menzies told me on the telephone just now that he'd cabled to the States and they've put your reputation straight. Besides, there's what I learned about you."

"I suppose you read my letters," ventured Hallett. "No. Don't worry to soothe me down. I'd probably have half killed you if I'd caught you at it, but I'm quite calm now. By the way, there was a fiver——"

A flush mounted to the temples of the detective and he shook his head in vehement denial of the implication contained in the broken sentence. "I had to take it or you might have suspected something. I passed it on to the servants and told 'em what to do. I never saw the press people myself. Some of 'em might have known me. When you went down to breakfast I changed my clothes and slipped a 'phone message through to headquarters. They told me to hang on to you till Mr. Menzies had seen you. You'd never have known a word about it if it hadn't been for our bird down below." He jerked his head in the direction of the cells.

Hallett began to appreciate some of the realities of detective work. Before he could make any comment, Menzies came in. He nodded affably to the young man.

"Morning, Mr. Hallett; not much the worse for last night, I see. I've got a little job for you presently. Meanwhile I want to see your friend down below. Like to come along?"

He made no apology for the espionage he had set on foot and Hallett did not think it worth while to thrash out the subject again.

"William Smith," it seemed, had already been searched with care and thoroughness. Royal explained to his chief that nothing which would serve as a hint to who he was had been found on him—nothing but the pistol, nine cartridges, and some money.

"Have you looked for the name of the tailor on his clothes—the brace buttons, the inside of the breast pocket, the trousers band?" demanded Menzies.

"Of course, sir," said Royal. He was a trifle offended that it should even be thought that he had neglected so elementary a precaution. "There's nothing —nothing at all."

Preceded by a uniformed inspector they went down to the cells. Smith looked up sullenly from the bench on which he was seated and met Menzies' gaze squarely. The detective chief was no believer in Lombroso's theories of physiognomy, but he studied the face intently. In point of fact he was analysing the features to discover if he had seen the man before. He wanted, too, to get some clue as to the manner he should adopt—authoritative and official, or familiar and persuasive.

"Well, sonny," he said gently. "You've tumbled into a mess. Attempted murder is a serious business in this country."

THE MAELSTROM

Smith glanced at him blackly over his shoulder. Menzies went on: " Of course we don't believe the cock-and-bull story you told Mr. Hallett of there being a gang of you——"

" You don't, eh? " exclaimed the prisoner, wheeling in sudden passion to face his visitors. " Then you are —what shall I say—wooden blockheads." He pointed a long slender forefinger at each of them in turn. " You! and you! and you!—I tell you, you will be marked. I failed—but there are others who will not fail, if you persist."

Royal turned away to hide a snigger. This kind of melodrama failed to impress him.

No doubt, no doubt," assented Menzies soothingly. He might have been calming down a headstrong questioner at a vestry meeting " But there are a good many police officers in London. It will take a long time to kill 'em off. Now why don't you be reasonable, Mr. Smith? "

" Pah! " interrupted the prisoner. He spat on the cell floor to indicate his contempt.

" You've shown you know something about this murder," went on Menzies. " The judge is pretty sure to take that into account one way or the other at your trial. I, of course, should tell him if you helped us. It would probably make a difference, you know."

The prisoner showed two rows of yellow teeth in an unmirthful, contemptuous grin. " Go away, wooden-head. I shall not go to prison, but you will die. You don't know what you call—what you are up against."

"Perhaps I've got an idea," said Menzies. His voice changed. "I don't know whether you're playing the fool, my man," he said sternly, "or whether you really believe that kind of wild talk. Perhaps your friend Errol will be able to enlighten us."

"Errol?" said Smith blankly. "I know him not."

"I hear you," said Menzies. "You think over what I've said, my lad. Meanwhile, we'll have a doctor to look at you."

CHAPTER VI

MENZIES let an unparliamentary expression slip from his lips as the cell door clanged behind them. It is tantalising to have a piece of evidence drop into one's lap, so to speak, and then refuse to be evidence. He was annoyed because his efforts to unlock the lips of the prisoner had failed. He knew that if only the man could have been induced to talk, days, possibly weeks, of heart-breaking labour would be saved.

This fresh development had him guessing, as Jimmie Hallett might have said. Who was " William Smith "? Why had he threatened Hallett, and even gone so far as to try to carry his threat into execution? The hint of an organised conspiracy to save the murderer of Greye-Stratton would have excited his derision if it had not aroused speculation. The secret societies in England may talk murder at times, but they never seriously plot murder or carry out a murder. A man who perils his neck has invariably some strong, personal motive. And when others actively shield him they also have some motive other than pure altruism.

One person may commit an irresponsible act for no reason; it is even conceivable that two people may act in concert in some insane crime. But here were at least three people concerned and possibly more—the woman who had passed the cheques to Hallet, the murderer of

THE MAELSTROM

Greye-Stratton, and "William Smith." What was the link that bound them all together? That each was acting from some powerful self-interest he felt confident. It might be that there was a community of interest, but he was sceptic enough to think that accidental.

The chief inspector checked his flow of thought with a jerk. Speculation without materials spelt a fixed theory—and to a detective too early a theory may be fatal. He is apt to try to prove his theory rather than the truth.

He laid a hand on Hallett's arm as the gaoler inserted a key in the big steel door that led to the charge room.

"Wait a minute. There are a dozen people the other side of the door waiting for us. I want you to have a good look at them when you go in. If you recognise any of them I want you to go up and touch her."

"*Her*," repeated Hallett. His pulse throbbing unaccountably faster. Menzies eyed him keenly.

"You said last night that you would probably know the woman again who planted the cheques on you. I'm relying on you, Mr. Hallett. You're a man of the world. Don't run away with the idea that a pretty face can't be mixed up in crime."

"So you've run her down. Why didn't you tell me before? Who is she? Does she admit passing the cheques?"

Menzies shook a forefinger blandly at the young man. "I'll answer your questions some other time. Only play the game, Mr. Hallett" He was a shrewd judge of men, and all along he had been doubtful whether Jimmie's chivalry would be proof against the test to which he proposed to put it.

And Jimmie himself was doubtful. A week—a day—ago he would have ridiculed the idea that a pair of blue eyes, seen only once, could have swayed him in any degree. He did not put his thoughts into form, but he wondered what the effect to her of an identification might be. Had Menzies any suspicion against her? Jimmie found himself arguing illogically enough that it was impossible. Menzies' words braced him as they were intended to—come what would, he would point her out if she were in the charge room.

And then the door swung back. The charge room, lofty and bare, was tenanted by a little group of women seated in a row, at the lower end. Apart from them, in the centre, by the inspector's tall desk, were a couple of officers. A third was leaning against the dock. The chatter of voices ceased.

"Take a good look at these ladies," said Menzies' suave voice.

Jimmie had not needed more than one glance. There was a sufficient general resemblance among the army of women, but *she* was unmistakable. She was the second from the right. He had taken one pace towards her when her gaze met his. There was nothing in it of appeal. It was indifferent, cold, impassive. Yet Hallett's resolution wavered. He walked past her along the row and back again. He felt himself a fool. There was not the faintest reason why he should not identify her. She was a stranger. She was at least indirectly responsible for the unpleasant experiences that had beset him. She was possibly concerned in a deliberate murder. And then out of the tail of his eye he saw her moisten her dry lips. That was the only trace of emotion she gave.

"It's no good, Mr. Menzies," he said quietly. "I don't recognise anyone here." He had played poker in his time and his face and voice were absolutely expressionless.

Menzies tapped a forefinger thoughtfully alongside his nose and smiled ruefully.

"All right," he said, and Jimmie fancied there was an inner shade of meaning to the words. "That will do, ladies, thank you."

The women—wives and daughters of police officials for the most part—separated. Only the girl of the cheques remained behind. As the room emptied she walked towards Menzies.

"That's over, Miss Greye-Stratton," he said cheerfully. "I am ever so much obliged to you. I want you to know Mr. Hallett—the gentleman who first called our attention to the death of your father."

Jimmie concealed the surprise that the name gave him. Although there was a certain touch of melancholy in the oval face, there was none of that grief which might have been expected in a girl who had suddenly learned of the murder of her father. For a moment he was repelled. He murmured some conventional phrase of sympathy, but she swept it away as though aware that her manner needed explanation.

"Yes, this is very dreadful, Mr. Hallett, but not so dreadful to me as it might have been. You see I scarcely knew my father. We were almost complete strangers."

"Miss Greye-Stratton called on me at the Yard as soon as she heard of the murder," interposed Menzies. "I thought it as well in the circumstances that there should be no ground for misunderstandings. You see your story of the way the cheques came into your possession is bound to make talk when you give evidence at the inquest. I wanted it to be definitely clear that Miss Greye-Stratton was not the lady and she was good enough to consent to this arrangement."

Hallett wondered how the diplomacy of the detective would have got over the difficulty if the girl had refused. That she had consented showed nerve, for she had not known that he would not identify her. He was curious, too, as to what would have happened if he had picked her out. Would she have been arrested on suspicion?

"If it had been Miss Greye-Stratton she would hardly have sought you out," he remarked.

"No, no, of course not," said Menzies soothingly. "I never thought for a moment that she was the woman.

THE MAELSTROM

One likes to save anything in the nature of scandal, though. I remember a case where two elderly ladies—sisters—living in a country house were attacked by someone with a hammer. One was found dead, the other unconscious—she remained unconscious for weeks. The hammer was found in an outhouse a hundred yards away. Now there was a considerable amount of gossip and the theory was firmly held by dozens of people that the living sister had attacked the dead one. They overlooked the fact that to have done so she must have walked to the place where the hammer was found *after* her own injuries had been inflicted. That's an example of what I mean."

The girl nodded. " I am quite sure you only meant to save me possible future unpleasantness. Is there anything else? You have my address."

" There is no other way at the moment in which you can help. As matters develop I may call on you. It has been very good of you——"

She stretched out her slim gloved hand to Hallett. But he was not inclined to let her escape so easily. She owed him something, if only an explanation. " I am going your way," he said unblushingly. " Perhaps if you don't mind——"

" You are very kind, Mr. Hallett," she said formally.

Menzies stroked his moustache and his eyes roved sideways to his aide-de-camp, Royal, who, after an ab-

THE MAELSTROM

sence of two or three minutes, had now returned. Royal nodded almost imperceptibly, and the inspector said good-bye.

"By the way, you had better be at the police court at two, Mr. Hallett. We shall charge this man Smith today. I don't expect you'll be kept long. It will be purely formal. We shall apply for a remand."

Hallett and the girl went down the steps to the street. He was conscious that though she appeared to be gazing serenely in front of her that she occasionally scrutinised him with curious eyes.

Not till they were a hundred yards away from the police station did either of them speak again. Then Jimmie ventured on the ice.

"Perhaps now you will tell me what it's all about?"

"Oh!" she stopped and turned full on him with the wide-open, innocent blue eyes of a child. "So you knew all the time. I wasn't sure."

"Wasn't sure that I knew you as the girl in the fog?"

"Yes. Shall we walk on? We might attract attention standing here. Why did you do it? Why didn't you denounce me?"

Jimmie twiddled his walking-stick. "Hanged if I know," he confessed. Her self-possession rather daunted him. "I thought—that is—if you wanted to you would have explained the incident yourself."

"That's no reason. You didn't know me. There

THE MAELSTROM

was no earthly motive. All the same I am grateful to you, Mr. Hallett—sincerely grateful." She sighed.

A porter with a parcel under his arm loitered three yards behind them. Ten yards behind him a "nut," scrupulously dressed and seemingly conscious of nothing but the beauty of his attire, swaggered aimlessly. Menzies, as has been said, was not a man who took anything for granted. His arrangements for "covering" Peggy Greye-Stratton in the event of Hallett not recognising her had been completed long before he had confronted them in the charge room.

Hallett might have guessed—if he had thought about it at all. The girl certainly did not. Jimmie caught at her last words.

"You can prove that. Although we have only been formally introduced in the last five minutes, we are not exactly strangers. Come and lunch with me. Then we can talk. There are several things I want to know."

She assented, it seemed to him somewhat indifferently. He hailed a taxi-cab and gave the name of a famous restaurant. As she sank back in the cushions it was as though a mask had dropped from her face. It had suddenly become utterly weary. She gasped once or twice as if for breath. Only for an instant had the mask dropped, but Hallett had seen and understood. The girl was strained to breaking point, supporting her part only by strength of will.

What that part was, and why she was playing it, he

was fixed in the resolution to learn. He spoke on indifferent subjects till lunch was over and coffee was brought. Then he leaned a little forward across the table.

"I shall be glad if I can be of any help to you, Miss Greye-Stratton," he said.

A smile, palpably forced, appeared on the girl's face. She twisted a ring on her finger absently. "That is a polite way of bringing me to the point, Mr. Hallett. You have a right to ask."

A sigh trembled on her lips, and her eyes became absent. The man said nothing, but waited. Very dainty and desirable did Peggy Greye-Stratton seem to him then. Yet he would not have been human if he had not had misgivings. Her very reluctance to speak aroused a little spark of suspicion which he deliberately trampled under foot. A beautiful face, a high intelligence, and courage—and all these he knew she possessed—are not necessarily guarantees against crime.

She appeared to come to a resolve. "I will tell you what I told Mr. Menzies," she said looking up. "Knowing what you know it will seem incomplete to you, but you"—she looked him full in the face—"are a gentleman. I trust you not to question me too far. There are—other people."

He, too, had come to a resolve. "Tell me," he said levelly, "before you say anything else. Did you have act or part in the murder of your father?"

She stared at him whitely and half rose. Her shapely throat was working strangely. "Do you think——" she began. And then tensely: "No! no! no!" Her voice fell to a strained whisper. "Why do you ask me that—if I had known—if I could have prevented——" She was rapidly becoming distraught.

He felt himself a cur, but he pressed home the question relentlessly. "Do you know who it was that murdered your father?"

Her fair head fell to her arms on the table. Had Hallett known, he could not have put his questions at a time more likely to wring an answer from her. All that morning she had borne herself before the keen eyes of Menzies and his assistants, conscious that the slightest falter might betray what she did not wish known. Her nerves were now paying the penalty. She raised a face torn with emotion towards Hallett.

"God help me," she moaned. "I believe I do."

CHAPTER VII

HE had expected the answer, and yet it came to him as a shock. She was regarding him with an expression, half defiant, half appealing. His eyes wandered round the room. He had engaged a table that stood in a recess behind one of the marbled pillars and they were thus separated from the general company in the room. Their voices had been low, but he was afraid they might have attracted attention. But no one seemed to have observed them and he turned once more to her.

Somehow she had repressed her weakness. He signalled to the waiter and ordered a liqueur. As she took it he observed that her hand was perfectly steady. And yet but a moment before she had been on the verge of hysterics.

"Tell me just what you like," he said simply. "Just as much or as little as you like. You can trust me."

"Thank you," she said; "you are very good. Let me think. . . . To begin with, you must know my father was a very strange man. When I was quite a baby he quarrelled with my mother and I was sent down into the country, where I lived with an old gentleman farmer and his wife named Dinward. I always understood that I was their child until a few years ago—they never spoke of either my father or my mother. Once—just before I went to school—he came to see me. I, of course, did not know who he was.

"I was sent to a convent school at Bruges, where I was brought up, coming home for the holidays—home, of course, being in Sussex. Occasionally I was brought to London. I won't go into all the detail of my life until I left school—it wouldn't interest you. All this time, remember, I had no knowledge of any relations but the Dinwards. When I left school I learnt for the first time that I was not their daughter. Mr. Pembroke, a solicitor, came over to Bruges and told me very nicely. But—acting on instructions, he said—he could give me no clue to my parents. There would be three hundred a year payable to me quarterly by his firm. I was no longer to look to the Dinwards for support.

"Mr. Pembroke was very nice, but he had his instructions. I asked him what I was expected to do. 'I presume,' he said, 'that your benefactor intends that you shall have enough to support you respectably. Think over your plans to-night, my dear young lady, and we will talk it over in the morning.'

"I did think it over. You may imagine that I slept little that night. I have a certain facility for painting and that seemed to me to offer an outlet to ambition. I told Pembroke next day. He expressed neither approval nor disapproval. A cheque he said, would be waiting for me at the offices of his firm on the first day of every quarter. He offered to give me introductions

THE MAELSTROM

in London, but I answered that the only introduction I needed was to my parents. He shook his head at me a little doubtfully and that ended the conversation.

"I wanted to see the world a little before I settled down in London. I went to see the Dinwards, but no word could I get from them as to who I really was. They would tell me nothing.

"The Dinwards were troubled about me—naturally. Of course I promised to keep in touch with them. I changed my name. I had been called Peggy Dinward. I became Lucy Olney. That, by the way, Mr. Hallett, is the name I still keep.

"The allowance I was to receive seemed a tremendous fortune to me. I went abroad—to study art, I told myself. I went to Paris, to Rome, to Venice, and other places. But the money did not prove so ample as I expected. Perhaps I was extravagant. Anyway, in about eight months I was in London, determined to make my fortune—and I still thought that my art pointed the way.

"You will guess that I had some troubles. Art for art's sake is one thing, but I am afraid I haven't the true temperament. I wanted recognition, and though I could have existed without the money I wanted money as a proof that I was recognised. But no one seemed to appreciate me as a genius. It was difficult enough to get dealers to take my pictures at a price that barely paid for canvas and paint. Then I drifted into magazine and book illustration work and in that I found my metier. I earned much more than I really needed—even without my allowance."

She fingered a serviette absently for a moment. There was an abstraction in her eyes. Hallett waited without interruption for her to resume.

"I have not told you that I have a step-brother," she went on " Indeed I did not know it myself till two years ago. He is my mother's son by her first marriage and is much older than myself. He was sent abroad at the time that I was handed over to the Dinwards. As I say, two years ago he traced me out—I believe he got my assumed name and my address from the Dinwards. It was from him that I first learned who I was, who my father was, who my mother was. He told me the whole terrible story of Mr. Greye-Stratton's—I can't call him my father—break with my mother. He swore that she was innocent—that it was a madman's fit of jealousy that broke up the home. I—I——"

Her throat worked and it was some moments before she took up her account again. " My brother had only recently returned to England, and he told me that his first step had been to find me. He wanted me to go back with him to Canada. 'You're my baby sister,' he said, ' I have a right to look after you. There's only you and I now.'

"I can't express how I felt. My quick anger against my father was less intense than his long-nursed hatred.

THE MAELSTROM

We talked long. I refused his offer to go back to Canada and told him that I would never take another penny from my father. He was against that. He argued that it was the least Mr. Greye-Stratton could do for me. When he saw I was determined he pointed out the possibility that I might be Mr. Greye-Stratton's heiress, and that to refuse the allowance might embitter him against me." She flamed for a moment into passion. "As if I wanted anything—*anything* from that man.

"When he left me I scarcely knew what to do—what action to take. I resolved to do nothing. After all, when I was in a colder mood, I could see nothing that I could do. I could not or would not attempt a reconciliation with my father. I could not attempt the vindication of my mother. I renounced the allowance and things went on as they were before—except that I had my brother.

"He went back to Canada and the United States. Now and again I had letters from him. He had a hard struggle to make ends meet."

Hallett nodded mechanically. Something in her tone made him begin to see the brother in a less sympathetic light. He blurted out the question on the spur of the moment. "He bled—I mean he wrote to you for money?"

She winced. "Yes. He wrote to me for money. A little more than a year ago he was in England again."

THE MAELSTROM

Her words came more slowly. "He has stayed here ever since. He called on Mr. Greye-Stratton and something happened—what I don't know. I suppose there were recriminations, but my brother told me little but that he was now entirely without resources. Mr. Greye-Stratton"—Hallett noted that she persisted in the formal mode of reference—"had cut off all help from him. I don't know if Mr. Menzies has said anything to you about my brother?" She flashed the question at him suddenly.

"Not a word. This is the first I have heard of his existence."

"I ask because he questioned me closely about him. My brother is a hard man, Mr. Hallett, and his outlook on life is different from that of the ordinary person. Circumstances have been against him. He was driven to find a living as he could. I want you to remember that if he was desperate he was driven to it. I helped as far as I could, but he had heavy expenses. He signed my father's name to some cheques."

"He committed forgery?"

"Yes. The cancelled cheques came into the hands of —someone else who knew that Dick Errol was my brother. He threatened to pass them on to Scotland Yard and give evidence against Dick unless I paid. Last night there was an appointment made at my flat. The price he demanded was greater than I could pay. When he went I followed him. I knew he had the cheques

THE MAELSTROM

on him and I hoped that I might find some way to get them from him. Just before I met you I had appealed to him again. He refused. He had the cheques in his hand. I snatched them, and when I ran into you I passed them to you on the impulse of the moment. That is all, Mr. Hallett."

"But there is something more," he said; "something you have not said."

She shook her head, her lips pressed tightly together. "I have said all I can—all I dare. You helped me, Mr. Hallett, and I have told you more even than I have the detectives. It has been a relief "—she sighed—" to tell anyone."

Jimmie was silenced. Yet a score of questions trembled on his lips. Trained to see the weak points in a narration, he could not fail to realise that there were gaps in the story—gaps that needed filling before one could come to full judgment. She had passed no hint of the blackmailer, the man from whom she had the cheques. That he was closely linked with her in some manner he felt confident.

And then speculation was lost in a rush of pity for the girl who had been so unwittingly dragged into a maelstrom from which he could see no way of escape. That the man Errol was a scoundrel was certain on her own showing. He glimpsed through her reticence the fresh tragedy that his advent had meant to her life. Vainly he tried to see for what purpose she was being used. Of course Errol had been bleeding her, but there was something more. It came to him suddenly. She knew the murderer—she had said so. Here was a motive for Errol—a motive more powerful than revenge or passion. She would stand to gain a fortune by Greye-Stratton's death and Errol would look to dabbling his fingers in it.

Yet this was the man for whom she was playing with fire. He was not very clear about English legal methods, but he conceived that in trying to shield him she was laying herself open to suspicion. He had judged Menzies acutely. If Greye-Stratton's fortune were to come to her that detective would leave nothing undone to be absolutely sure that she had no hand in the crime. Points would arise, actions be revealed that would look black against her by the very reason that she had carefully concealed them.

"Miss Greye-Stratton," he said gravely, "forgive me for what I am going to say. I believe it is a crime here to be an accessory after the fact. Do you realise that? Don't you think it would be wiser for your sake —for your brother's sake—to be candid with the police? Believe me, all that you have told me is sure to be known sooner or later."

Her face was irresolute. "You think they will find out? That it will be worse because I tried to conceal it?"

"I do. If you will take my advice you will come

with me to Menzies now. Understand me. I shall not betray a word of our conversation without your permission."

She placed her elbows on the table and rested her chin in her cupped hands, staring across the room in reverie. Presently she stood up.

"I will think of it," she said. "I will think of it."

CHAPTER VIII

No effective detective organisation is dependent on one man. Co-operation is the essence of all successful detective work exactly as it is in the carrying on of any great business. Scotland Yard will throw a score, a hundred, ten thousand men into an enterprise, if need be, and everyone of them from the supreme brain downwards will have an understudy ready at any moment to pick up a duty abandoned from any cause. No individual is vital, though some may be valuable. Every fact, every definite conclusion arrived at is on record.

That is why Weir Menzies found time to cover the case against the pickpockets he had captured the preceding evening and to return to headquarters to smoke a quiet pipe and consider things in general. He stuck his feet on a desk, leaned back in his chair, and began serenely to go through the reports that had accumulated from every point where information, however remote, might have been gathered on the Greye-Stratton affair.

He liked to have the salient facts of an investigation clear-cut in his mind. That often saved time in an emergency, as well as being an aid to definite thinking. Presently he began to make his Greek notes with a stubby pencil on the back of an envelope. Some of them would have surprised Hallett had he chanced to see them:

THE MAELSTROM

"Statement of P. Greye-Stratton clearly incomplete. Knows much more than she says. Certain that Errol has been for many months constant visitor at her flat in Palace Avenue. (Goulds report interview with maid at her flat.) Yet she denies that she has spoken to or been in communication with her brother for nearly a year. Lift attendant remembers man calling on her the evening of the murder. Left after short interview and immediately after she went out hatless in a hurry."

He commenced a string of question marks across the paper. "I'll see that lift man myself," he murmured, and continued:

"It was the maid's night out. Lift attendant does not remember having seen man before, but he knows Errol. Description vague. Think possible P. G.-S. alarmed. Must handle cautiously and keep under constant surveillance. If can induce Hallett to cultivate her may learn something."

A sharp tap at the door interrupted him. He snapped an irritable "come in," and, pencil in hand, surveyed frowningly a young man with a badly bruised eye.

"Well, Jakes," he demanded impatiently; "who's been decorating you? What's the trouble?"

THE MAELSTROM

"I got this from Hallett, sir. He———"

Menzies' feet dropped from the table with a crash. "What the blazes! Some muddle, I'll be bound. Where's Gordon?"

"Down below, sir. We———"

"Then you've lost the girl?" He smacked an angry fist down on the table. "Oh, *damn* your explanations. I beg your pardon—you confounded idiot." He sprang to the door and roared down the green-painted corridor: "Royal! Royal!"

That individual popped out of a door like a rabbit out of a hole. "Come here, Royal. These two cabbages have let Miss Greye-Stratton dodge 'em. Take Smithers and get along to her flat, No. 74 Palace Avenue, and see if you can pick her up. She may have gone straight home, or she may not. I've got to come there myself presently, but I'll hear what this dough witted jackass has got to say."

Ordinarily Menzies was courteous to his underlings, but when anything like stupidity interfered with his plans he let himself go. "They remembered it and it's better than putting 'em on the M. R.," he explained once to a colleague, which was his way of saying that he preferred a few hot words to putting the culprits on the morning report for judgment and punishment. "Only I sometimes wish that I didn't swear so much at them."

Royal had slipped away to carry out his instructions with the swiftness of the well-trained man. Menzies turned with a snarl to the young detective, who was trembling nervously and as ill at ease as any young clerk " carpeted " before his departmental chief for the first time.

"Let's have it," he said shortly.

The young man squared his shoulders. "They lunched at Duke's in Piccadilly, sir. I went in with them but could not get near enough to hear what was said. The lady did most of the talking. When they came out they walked towards Regent Street. I was close behind. Gordon about twenty paces behind me. They turned into Regent Street and then sharp back along Jermyn Street. When they reached St. James Street he said something to her and came back towards me. I would have passed him, but he caught me by the shoulder and asked what I meant by molesting a lady.

"I pulled myself free and told him I was a police officer. She had turned the corner by this time. I would have gone on, but he pulled me back again, and Gordon came up——"

"And stopped to see what the matter was instead of going straight on," commented Menzies bitterly. "I know. Go on."

"He stopped to help me. Mr. Hallett was giving me a fair rough house. It took the two of us to tackle him properly. He kept it up for about three minutes and then gave in."

"And by that time the girl might have been in Timbuctoo. He put up a plant on you and you both fell into it."

"Yes, sir."

"Did you arrest him?"

"No. We thought it ought to be reported to you before we did anything."

"That's the only gleam of common sense you showed in the whole business. Go away. I'll think it over. And the next time you're shadowing, young man, remember you've got to stick—if the heavens fall you've got to stick."

He whistled softly to himself when the other had gone. "I thought as much. She's put the comether on him—and Hallett is a brainy man."

He revolved the matter steadily in his mind as he walked to Palace Avenue. Hallett, if he could be persuaded, would be a valuable ally in discovering what information Peggy Greye-Stratton had withheld. Menzies used the instruments to his hands; and there was no reason why he should have scruples. If he had troubled at all to formulate the ethics of the question he might have argued that when a crime was committed a person who deliberately withheld or evaded giving information could not fairly object to any means adopted to break her taciturnity. That the rôle he proposed allotting to Hallett was actually that of a spy did not concern him. That would be Hallett's own affair if he accepted the commission.

Royal appeared out of nowhere as he neared the corner of Palace Avenue. "Not come back yet," he reported laconically.

"Well, there's plenty of time yet," said Menzies with a resignation that had been conspicuously absent in his talk with the delinquent officer. "She's bound to turn up. You'd better 'phone for Gould to relieve you and get down to the court to charge Smith."

He strolled on to the block of flats, sent his card in to the manager in a sealed envelope, briefly explained as much of his errand as was necessary, and was presently confronted with a weedy, pale-faced youth who nervously twisted his cap in his hands as the detective questioned him. His story varied nothing from the statement Gould had put in.

"Now don't get flustered, old chap," said Menzies with that suave air he knew so well how to assume. "Are you sure you wouldn't know the man again? Try and think for a moment. Was he tall or short, fat or thin?"

"Just an ordinary-looking man," said the attendant. "I didn't pay any notice."

"No, of course not. Do you remember if he had a beard or moustache, or was he clean-shaven?"

The youth wrinkled his brows, and after a moment's

THE MAELSTROM

thought shook his head. "Couldn't say, sir. I rather believe he was clean-shaven."

It was hopeless to try to extract a description from him. Menzies had expected as much. Observation is not often a natural gift; it is a matter of training, and many and laborious are the hours spent in teaching recruits to the C. I. D. staff the art. He switched to another point.

"When the man came out of her flat did he seem in a hurry?"

"No, sir, not particularly. He rang for the lift."

"Didn't say anything?"

"Not to me. At least he had something in his hand. He dropped it and when it rolled down the shaft he swore. I offered to go and get it, but he said it didn't matter—it was only a halfpenny."

"H'm!" Menzies stuck his thumbs in the armholes of his waistcoat and tapped his toe on the floor. "You went and made sure it was only a halfpenny afterwards, of course."

The man's eyes had hitherto not met his. Now they were fixed boldly on his face. "No," he declared. "I didn't think it worth while."

A man may fail to look one in the face and be perfectly honest and truthful. But when such a man does do so it is because he has become conscious that an averted gaze may arouse suspicion. Menzies smiled under his moustache and stretched out a hand. "Where is it?" he added quietly. "Give it to me."

THE MAELSTROM

The lift attendant flushed and drew back. The directness of the demand had disconcerted him. "I don't know what you mean," he said. "I haven't got anything."

"That so?" said Menzies smilingly. And then, with a swift change of voice: "Now, sonny, don't let's have any monkey business. You can't play with me."

Reluctantly, as though hypnotised, the attendant thrust two fingers into his waistcoat pocket, slowly drew something out, and placed it in the detective's hand.

It was a plain, heavy circlet of gold—a wedding ring!

CHAPTER IX

JIMMIE HALLETT had run into Weir Menzies in the police court corridor after the magistrate had formally remanded "William Smith." The detective threw up his hands quickly in the attitude of one parrying a blow.

"Don't hit me, Mr. Hallett," he implored. "I've got a weak heart."

Jimmie grinned a little shamefacedly. He had not been quite sure how the detective chief would take the assault on the shadowers of Miss Greye-Stratton. He brazened it out. "Well, what are you going to do about it?" he demanded.

Menzies caught him through the arm and pulled him into a small room set apart for consultations between lawyers and clients. "I suppose you know that men have got six months for less than you did this afternoon. You can't knock police officers about with impunity, you know."

There was an underlying current of seriousness in his jocular tone which Jimmie could not fail to perceive. He ran his hand through his hair "I'll see you," he said, adopting the language of the poker table. "What are you driving at?"

"This." The detective laid a thick forefinger on the palm of his left hand. "You've got sense, Mr. Hallett, and you've had experience. Now I've gone into your credentials and I believe you're straight. But I'm not going to stand for any funny business. I'm investigating a case of murder and anyone that stands in the way is liable to get hurt. Now don't interrupt. Let me finish. I don't know whether you were putting up a grand-stand play after lunch to win the girl's confidence or if she talked you over."

He paused enquiringly. Hallett pressed his lips together firmly. "Go on," he said.

"Right. You were butted into this at the start and I've tried to treat you fairly. Don't you forget murder's a dirty thing, however you look at it. I don't say Miss Greye-Stratton's not straight, but she knows a deuce of a sight more than she ought to—or than she's telling us. She's got something up her sleeve. She's no fool, for all her pretty face. She seems to have taken a fancy to you. Do you know why?"

The other shook his head, although he had a very good idea what Menzies was going to say. His face was impassive.

"For the same reason that the man we've got below tried to get you this morning. You're an important witness. She wants to shut your mouth and to find out how much you really do know."

Jimmie laughed outright. "You're wrong there. She's not asked me a single question. All the talking was on her side."

THE MAELSTROM

Then he realised that he had fallen into a trap. Not that Menzies gave any obvious indication of triumph. He merely stroked his moustache serenely. "Well, I don't know that I'm far wrong. She wouldn't be too quick. So she talked, did she? What did she say?"

The young man was not to be caught off guard a second time. "It will all be stale to you. She repeated what she said she had already told you."

"All the same, there may be something new," persisted the detective. "Let's have it."

"If you like to let me have a look at her statement I'll tell you if there's anything fresh I can add," parried Jimmie.

Menzies raised his eyebrows. "I think I see," he said. "I'd consider this a lot if I were you. Why, man, can't you see she's playing with you. Confidence for confidence is an old trick. She has known you a matter of hours, and here she is pitching a tale to you as though you were an intimate friend. I trust you—you trust me! That's what it comes to. Now why not play our game instead of hers. If she's innocent you won't hurt her, but if she's got her pretty fingers in the tar——"

Hallett became conscious of a smouldering rage at the innuendo of the comfortable, ruddy-faced detective. He did not realise that he was being deliberately provoked for a purpose. Menzies wanted to discover without doubt his attitude to the girl.

"Cut it out," he advised curtly. And then more quietly: "I think you entirely misjudge the lady. If I've only known her for a few hours, I guess I'm a better judge of her type than you."

"Bearings a bit hot, eh?" smiled Menzies. "It's no good getting angry with me. I'm clumsy, but I mean well. I hate to see a man stepping into trouble. And you'll find trouble on your hands pretty soon, believe me. If I were you I think I'd carry a life-preserver or advertise that you didn't see the man who killed Greye-Stratton."

Hallett had taken a quick turn or two about the room, his hands thrust deep in his trousers pockets. He came to a sudden halt. "What do you mean by that?"

Weir Menzies had a well-worn briar pipe in one hand and a tobacco pouch in the other. He methodically filled the pipe before answering. "Only from what I have gathered the lady's in with a tough mob. I'll know more about 'em by to-morrow, but I don't want you laid out before I've picked up all the ends. I've warned you. You must do as you like. Only don't go believing she's a little blue-eyed saint, that's all."

Jimmie's temper, held in till now, continued to rise. Whether it was the implication that he was being made Miss Greye-Stratton's cats-paw, or the suggestion that the radiant girl was the willing accomplice of a gang of criminals, he did not stop to analyse. He was wroth with Menzies because he did not know by intuition what was plain to him—that if she was acting a part it was for the sake of someone else. He regretted now that he was bound not to divulge anything she had told him.

"I guess you're a fool, Menzies," he sneered. "You're barking up the wrong tree."

Menzies took the handle of the door. "You think so, do you? Well, we'll let it go at that." He swung the door open. "I suppose the lady told you she was married?"

He spoke casually as though by an after-thought, but he was quick to observe the change that passed over Jimmie's face. "That's a lie," he blurted out. "You've got something at the back of your head."

The detective swung the door to again and took something from his pocket. "Look at that," he said, and smoothed a sheet of paper before Hallett's eyes.

Jimmie read it over twice, unable at first to completely grasp its significance. It was an attested copy of a marriage certificate between Peggy Greye-Stratton and Stewart Reader Ling.

"She didn't tell you about this," went on the detective levelly. "That may alter your idea that she intends to play straight with you."

Jimmie was struggling with a tangle of thoughts. "Who is Ling?" he demanded.

"A crook of the crookedest. He ran a wholesale factory for forged currency notes in the United States ten years ago. That was broken up and he did five years in Sing Sing. He has been at the back of a lottery swindle since he came out and Lord knows what else. We'd lost sight of him till I happened to get hold of this copy. That's the kind of man who's the husband of Miss Greye-Stratton."

"How did you find this out?"

Menzies puffed reflectively. He had no intention of completely exposing his hand. He was certain that Peggy Greye-Stratton was the woman who had given Hallett the cheques and that the latter had deliberately refrained from identifying her. Moreover, he was also convinced that she had told the young man something at lunch, though whether she was, as he affected to believe, using him as a tool he was not in his own mind certain. The more he considered the more he felt that she held the key to the mystery if only she could be induced to speak. With him, with any official of police, she would be on her guard. Hallett, if he could be persuaded, was the one man who might win her confidence without exciting suspicion. So long as his sympathies remained with her he was unlikely to be persuaded. Therefore, if possible, his sympathies had to be alienated.

"Just common sense," growled Menzies, "ordinary common sense. I learned that she had a wedding-ring —though she didn't wear it—sent up to Somerset

THE MAELSTROM

House to inspect the registry of marriages, and got this half an hour ago." He laid a hand gently on the young man's shoulder. "Better do as I advise. Anyway, take care of yourself."

He did not wait for an answer, but moved softly out of the room. He was wise enough to know when to stop. To say more might be to spoil things. Hallett might safely be left to his own reflections.

Hallett was a man whose brain as a rule worked very clearly. But now he was confused, and he strove vainly to reconcile reason with inclination. It seemed ages since the episode of the fog, years since he had looked into the pale oval of Peggy Greye-Stratton's face at lunch. Spite of the convincing proof of the marriage certificate, he could not think of her as a married woman. Anyway, he told himself, if Menzies was right in that it did not follow that all his inferences were right. He had felt the ring of honesty in the story she had told him. And yet the idea of the detective was plausible enough. He could see where things dovetailed. If she were stringing him she had been acute enough to tell him a series of half-truths. If she were a willing accomplice, as Menzies supposed, there was reason enough why she should mislead him. He had met female adventuresses before—pretty, cultivated women, some of them—but he had not been impressed by them as he had been by her. But then the circumstances were different.

THE MAELSTROM

He pondered the matter as he drove back to his hotel. Suppose he did accept Menzies' version—and he admitted to himself that there was a considerable weight of probability in that point of view. He could not see, however, why in that event he should become an unpaid amateur detective. The thought of spying on Peggy Greye-Stratton, adventuress or not, was entirely distasteful to him. He had no interest in the investigation. He had been dragged into the affair entirely by accident. Let the police do their work themselves.

It was in this mood that he arrived at his hotel and repulsed the newspaper men who were still blockading the entrance. He avoided the public rooms. He wanted to be alone. He went up to his private sitting-room.

There it was that a note was brought to him. He tore it open and glanced at it mechanically. But at once his interest was aroused. It had been scribbled in pencil, apparently in haste:

> "I am in trouble. For God's sake come and help me. I don't know to whom else to appeal. Call at 140 Ludford Road, Brixton, as soon as you can, but alone. Ask for me."

There was no signature, but Hallett needed none. He had never seen Peggy Greye-Stratton's writing, but the small, neat characters were beyond doubt to him.

THE MAELSTROM

His resolution to stand aside was already being put to the test. He held the note in his hand while he recalled Menzies' warnings. He was an important witness. Already one attempt had been made to secure his silence. Was this a trap?

Yet, on the other hand, if the girl was being used to secure his silence, she could not know that he had changed his decision to stand by her. She must suppose—the conversation at lunch would have made her believe—that he had allied himself on her side. No, the letter was certainly genuine.

He impressed the address on his memory, and tearing the letter into little bits, dropped them into the wastepaper basket. Then he searched in his kit-bag till he found, at the bottom, a small automatic revolver and a packet of cartridges. He loaded the weapon carefully and dropped it in his jacket pocket.

He had no idea where Brixton was, but a study of a street map gave him its location. He did not want to have to ask questions. He had come to have too much respect for Menzies' methods in following up a trail for that. For the same reason, when he went out into the Strand he turned abruptly in his walk once or twice.

The useful little book of maps issued by the Underground railways helped him on his next course. He went into a tube station and booked for Hampstead. At Leicester Square he changed for Piccadilly Circus.

THE MAELSTROM

There he changed for Kennington Oval. By the time he emerged into the sunlight he was satisfied that if there had been any shadowers on his trail he had thrown them off.

He had selected the Oval Station because the map had shown him that the district lay on the verge of Brixton. He was about to hail a taxi when his eye caught the label on one of the big electric cars swinging by. He jumped aboard.

Ludford Road proved to be a quiet road of small houses buried away at the back of Brixton Town Hall. It was a street that might very well have been inbahited solely by moderate salaried city clerks—retired, unobtrusive, and respectable semi-detached villas with neat squares of gardens behind iron railings. It was no street of mystery.

Hallett walked to the door of No. 140 and pressed the bell. It opened promptly, revealing a plump, pleasant-faced little woman with shrewd eyes and a strong mouth. Jimmie, whose right hand had been gripped round the automatic in his jacket pocket, removed it hurriedly and lifted his hat.

"I wish to see Miss Olney, if I may," he said.

The woman shook her head. "You have made a mistake. There's no one of that name lives here," she said, and Jimmie's last shred of suspicion vanished. If the note had been sent for a trap there was evidently no anxiety for him to walk into it.

"Pardon me. Miss Greye-Stratton, I should have said. My name is Hallett."

She smiled and flung the door wide. "Oh, yes. She is expecting you. Will you come in?"

Jimmie passed into the narrow little hall and the door shut.

CHAPTER X

WITH the satisfied feeling of a man who knew he had earned his salary, Weir Menzies betook himself homewards. As he boarded the Tooting electric car at the corner of Westminster Bridge he automatically shut out from his mind all thought of Greye-Stratton. He had ceased to be Weir Menzies, chief inspector of the Criminal Investigation Department. He was Weir Menzies, Esq., of Magersfontein Road, Upper Tooting, who, like other gentlemen of business, left his business worries behind him at the office.

He ate his dinner, while Mrs. Menzies, a motherly little woman who never asked questions, retailed the latest domestic gossip. He added his own quota. He was afraid that Browns, the new butcher in the High Street, was not doing too well. As he pushed his chair back and lit a cigar, Mrs. Menzies seized the opportunity to tell of a calamity.

"Bruin's been in mischief. He dug a big hole under that Captain Hayward rose today."

This news roused Menzies. He kicked off his slippers and began relacing his boots. "That da—shed dog. I'll bet he's ruined it. We'll have to chain him up. Ring the bell and ask Nellie for a candle, will you, dear?"

Candle in hand, he led the way to the garden, muttering discontentedly as he cast its glow on the damage. He raised his voice. "Bruin, here, Bruin," and a heavy bobtailed sheep dog came lumbering over the lawn. Weir Menzies regarded him sternly and pointed an accusing finger at the hole. "What do you mean by that?" he demanded. "You wicked, wicked dog." Bruin sprawled with downcast head, his whole attitude one of penitence and shame. "Where's the whip?" asked Menzies. "Go fetch it."

Reluctantly, with slow step like a boy sent by his school-master for a cane, Bruin recrossed the lawn, returning in a few seconds with a dog whip between his teeth. He cowered while Menzies administered a couple of light blows—blows so light that they were rather symbolic of disgrace than actual punishment. His master slipped the whip into his pocket. "Now go and see that the house is safe."

The dog, now that retribution was over, slipped away. Detectives, for all their profession, are no more immune from burglary than ordinary mortals, but Menzies had little fear of his house being looted while Bruin was abroad. To and fro over the house he trotted, pushing open doors or whining till they were opened by the maid, and inspecting windows and fastenings with an intelligence almost uncanny. By the time he had finished his inspection Menzies was in his own room. The dog trotted in, sat on his haunches, and made a low crooning noise in his throat.

THE MAELSTROM

"All correct, eh?" said Menzies. "Good dog. Go to bed."

He himself was asleep almost as soon as his head touched the pillow. Yet it seemed to him that he had not been asleep five minutes when the deep boom of the dog's bark and an insistent ringing of the bell aroused him. He looked at his watch as he slipped out of bed. It was four o'clock. He had slept seven hours.

He shivered as he shuffled downstairs in his slippers and opened the door. "Why, it's you, Congreve," he exclaimed. "What the devil is the matter? Come in."

Detective-Sergeant Congreve (graded first-class at headquarters) was too wise a man to say anything at an open door with a taxi-driver within earshot. He followed his chief into the dining-room and Menzies switched on the light. "The lady's come back," he interrogated.

"No, sir. I wouldn't have worried you for that. It's Hallett. He's gone, too."

Menzies muttered a little comminatory service—in a low voice, because Mrs. Menzies was probably awake. "That's awkward," he said at last. "I ought to have him kept under observation, but I guessed I could rely on the hotel people to let us know. I didn't want to have to arrest him for putting any more of our men on the sick list, but I wish I'd taken a chance now. He'd have been safer for us and safer for himself under lock and key. What's the point?"

THE MAELSTROM

"He came back yesterday afternoon, went to his room, found a note waiting him, and went out without saying anything. He has not come back. The hotel people rang me up an hour ago and I went round there. I found the note." He shook an envelope on to the table and a shower of torn fragments dropped. "I didn't wait to put it together. I came straight on here."

The chief inspector became unpleasantly conscious that his pyjamas were an inadequate protection against the bite of the cold. "I suppose this means that I've got to turn out," he grumbled. "I seem to get all the jobs where there's no rest. It's enough to make a man turn it up and take a cottage in the country. Have a go at that note, Congreve, like a good chap, while I go and get some clothes on."

By the time he was dressed Congreve had the note ready for him.

"It looks as if the girl had got him," he commented as he passed the copy over to the chief inspector. "Anyway, there's an address."

Menzies laid the copy down on the table. "That's something," he agreed cautiously. "But it looks to me as though we're right up against it, old man: Somebody'll have to stand from under when the thud comes. What do you make of it?"

"Empty house, likely," said Congreve laconically. "They've shut Hallett's mouth. If you're right about Errol, Ling & Co., sir, they'll not stand on ceremony.

THE MAELSTROM

They're up to their necks already. We'll find a dead man in Ludford Road. They won't let Hallett do any talking."

He spoke in the matter-of-fact way in which a surgeon might contemplate the result of a dangerous operation—not with the shudder with which the average man would speak of a cold-blooded murder. The case with which they were dealing concerned men who he believed would be desperate now that one life had been sacrificed in their efforts to cover their trail.

"I don't know," said Menzies thoughtfully. "They might go to extremes if they were forced, but they won't make the pace too hot. We've got nothing concrete against 'em yet—nothing even to suggest that one of them was near Linstone Terrace Gardens when the old man was killed. You bet they'll have alibis all right, all right. If we could lay our fingers on 'em this minute they'd brazen it out."

"You see," he went on, "unless we prove these other people accessories there is only one person whose neck is in jeopardy. That's the actual murderer. He probably wouldn't object to save himself by another murder. But the others are not going to that length if they can help it. They intend, I imagine, to try and bottle him up till Smith is discharged and the whole boiling of them make a clean get-away."

"But," objected Congreve, "Royal's evidence alone will convict the man."

THE MAELSTROM

"Maybe they don't understand that," retorted Menzies. "Anyway we won't worry yet. I'm going on to Ludford Road. I shall want you to go back and swear out a search-warrant in case it's wanted. Also have that note properly done up and photographed. You might get a paper merchant to examine a piece of the paper. There's just a chance we might find out when it was bought and who bought it. You can get an all-night tramcar at the end of the road. Leave the taxi for me. I'll have to change again."

An hour later a plump, ruddy-faced man, smoking a clay pipe, and with his hands thrust deep in his trousers pockets, slouched along Ludford Road. The loosened shoulders, the shambling gait, the unpolished down-at-heels boots (one of them laced with string), all told of the practical vagrant. Yet Weir Menzies had not disguised himself in the sense that disguise would be understood by those whose knowledge of Scotland Yard is derived from books and newspapers.

His face was untouched by grease-paint, he wore no wig nor false beard. He was just Weir Menzies as he might have been if fortune had made him a tramp. Yet he bore little superficial resemblance to the Weir Menzies, Esq., churchwarden of All Saints, Upper Tooting, or the Mr. Weir Menzies, chief inspector of the Criminal Investigation Department. His hair had been rubbed up until it looked as if it had not seen brush or comb for a month, and was surmounted by a battered

THE MAELSTROM

Trilby hat. He had rubbed his hands on a doormat and then on his face to prevent any suspicion of unnatural cleanliness. His neat moustache had been combed out till it hung down ragged and bristly. His clothes were shabby and no two garments matched. They might have been given him at different times by charitable householders.

There was nothing which could go astray and betray that he had assumed a character. Indeed, any accident to clothes or person would but increase the disreputability of his looks.

Twice he shuffled up and down the street, the second time meeting a policeman, who paused and without saying anything watched him out of sight. The two met again a quarter of an hour later and this time the constable was not so forbearing. He turned his bull's-eye full on the tramp and surveyed him up and down. It was at the back of his mind that he might have a charge " loitering with intent to commit a felony "

" What's the game, Isaacstein? What are you hanging around for? " he demanded. And because he had been trained not to take risks, his hand gripped the greasy collar of the nondescript and administered a slight warning shake.

One hundred and eighty pounds of trained policeman took the pavement with a thud. He sat up ruefully and with wrath. One does not expect a rickety, middle-aged tramp to have a working knowledge of ju-jitsu. And

THE MAELSTROM

it astonished him still more that his assailant remained instead of taking advantage of the opportunity and making a dash for freedom.

"All right," he growled and advanced cautiously.

"Don't make a fool of yourself, my man," said the tramp authoritatively. "I'm C. I. Walk on quietly to the corner and I'll show you my warrant card."

The constable hesitated. He was young and this was beyond his experience. But the authority of the voice shook him and he obeyed the order. Within five minutes he learned how near he had been to committing a bad mistake.

"I'm sorry, sir," he apologised. "I didn't know."

"That's all right," said Menzies. "Of course you didn't. I'm not blaming you. Now you hang on to this corner for half an hour. I'll be responsible to your superiors. Just stand here and keep your eyes and ears open in case I should want you."

He had straightened up during the conversation, but now he became again the shambling hobo. A clock somewhere had just chimed six, and he judged that there might be a chance to commence operations. He moved furtively up to the door of number one hundred and forty and rang the bell. Twice he had to repeat the summons before there was any movement within. Then a window was flung up above and a woman's voice demanded the business of the intruder.

THE MAELSTROM

Menzies' answer was to press the bell again. He had no very definite plan in his mind. His was merely a reconnoitring expedition. He wanted the door opened and had no intention of carrying on a conversation with the lady upstairs, whoever she was, at the top of his voice. He was shielded from her sight by the porch and he did not offer to step out.

The window closed with a bang and there were sounds of someone moving. Presently the door opened, and the pleasant-faced woman who had met Hallett confronted the detective.

" 'Ave you got a bite you could spare a pore man, lidy," he whined. " I've been walkin' all night an' nothin' 'as passed my lips since yesterday."

The pleasant-faced lady frowned. She had a dogged chin and a wide mouth and was quite obviously not the sort of person to be played with. " I've got nothing for you," she snapped, perhaps with excusable viciousness for one who had been dragged out of bed by a beggar. She flung the door to forcefully. Menzies' foot, however, was a shade the quicker as he thrust it in the opening.

" Why, Gwennie," he said smilingly, in his natural voice; " this is a nice welcome for an old friend. " Don't you remember me? I'm Weir Menzies.'

She gave a quick exclamation and pulled the door back. Her face did not for a moment bear any very noticeable expression of delight at the reunion. That, however, was only for a second. The next instant she had thrust out her hand with a bright smile.

"Why, so it is. Who'd have thought of seeing you here—and in a rig like that. Come right in, Mr. Menzies. I am glad to see you."

"After you, Gwennie," said Menzies politely but firmly "Lead the way. Never mind the door. I'll shut it."

CHAPTER XI

GWENNIE LYNE was a lady with a reputation—or without one. It depended on the point of view. As far back as Menzies could remember she had been a notable figure in the little coterie of master criminals who know no nation and to whom the world is a hunting ground. Long, long ago, in the days when bank robbery in the United States had been a profitable pastime, she had organised and even played an executive part in exploits any one of which ought to have made her fortune.

Menzies knew her record almost by heart, for she was one of the very few "Classic" criminals who brought to bear on an undertaking an ingenuity, enterprise, and audacity that had won her through in a score of tight places. At ten years of age she had assisted her mother to pick pockets in Philadelphia. At twenty she had married Jim Lyne, bank burglar and gunman. At twenty-one she had effected a particularly daring escape from Sing Sing. At twenty-five she had held a pistol to a watchman's head at a bank in New Jersey while her companions ransacked the vaults. At thirty she had probably more experience in every grade of professional crime—short of murder, which is not professional crime—than any person of her own age, male or female. Opportunely enough, her husband, always too much of a swashbuckler for his trade, was shot in

THE MAELSTROM

a drunken brawl in Wisconsin at this time. Thereafter she held her way undisputed, always ready to become a partner in any department of the higher walks of crime, from receiving, to organising a bogus bank.

She had of course met with checks. There were few civilised countries where she had not tasted prison for longer or shorter periods. All that was in the day's work.

It is a myth that there is a distinctive criminal physiognomy. Fifty years or more of crime had left Gwennie Lyne untouched by any outward mark. Hers was a face which none could dream of distrusting on sight—she had been a handsome and was still a comely woman. The mouth was perhaps a trifle wide and it curved downwards at the edges. Her hazel eyes were shrewd, but with the apparent shrewdness of years, not the cunning of the outcast. She spoke softly, with a slight drawl, but her voice was the voice of a cultivated woman.

Menzies had recognised her with something of a thrill. Her presence in the combination against him was singularly unwelcome, for he knew her fertility of resource and her daring. On the other hand, the mere fact that he knew she was with the other side was something gained.

His right hand dropped to his trousers pocket as he followed her, to make sure that the little baton he had placed there before leaving home was in place. He rarely carried a pistol for fear that he might be tempted to use it before it was absolutely necessary.

She took him into one of the two small front rooms of the house and pulled up the blinds to admit the now growing daylight. He observed "The Stag at Bay" and a "View of Naples" on the vivid yellowish-green wall-paper, and it needed not the faded, worn horsehair Victorian furniture, the pile of books on a table in the window, to tell him that Gwennie had had no hand in furnishing the house. She had the virtue of taste, at any rate, and probably the place had been taken already furnished—and for a purpose. He wondered whether its purpose had been entirely fulfilled or not.

"Sit you down, Mr. Menzies," she said briskly. "It's early hours for a call, but I guess you've got some reason at the back of your head. You'll have some breakfast. I'll go and see about it and make myself tidy."

The detective's broad figure blocked the doorway. He smilingly shook his head and with one hand behind him felt for the key. There was none in the lock. He jerked a chair towards him with his foot, placed it against the door, and sat down.

"No breakfast for me, Gwennie, thank you. And you look very charming as you are. Suppose we talk."

She made a graceful gesture of resignation and sat down, her hands in her lap. "I guess I wouldn't poison you," she said.

THE MAELSTROM

"Aren't you a deportee, Gwennie?" countered the man. "Surely my memory isn't playing me tricks. Wasn't an order of deportation made against you—let me see—six years ago now? You will remember a diamond tiara in Bond Street."

She faced him placidly. "You've got a good memory. What are you going to do about it?

"Mind if I smoke?" he asked. "Oh, nothing much. I needn't tell a lady of your experience it would have been wiser to stay where you belong."

"See Section 4, Vagrancy Act, 1824," she laughed. "That's it, isn't it. Oh, I've been there before. You can't alarm me any by talking." And Menzies knew the astute old lady was trying to make him lose his temper.

He lifted his clay pipe from his lips. "I've always admired your talents, Gwennie"—she rose and swept him a mocking curtesy—" and we've been pretty good pals—business apart."

"Lord bless the man," she cried. "Is this a proposal. I do believe he's making love to me." She shook a well-manicured finger at him. " I warn you—I might accept you."

He grinned appreciatively at the thrust but shook his head reprovingly. "I'm out for business, Gwennie. Let's cut out the funny business and get down to hard tacks. If you won't listen I'll have to take you along, that's all."

THE MAELSTROM

"And if I do?" she interpolated quickly.

"I'm making no bargains. Will you sit tight?"

"I'll be as good as gold," she promised, a demure half smile still lurking about her lips.

Menzies was too old a hand to make the mistake of despising such an antagonist. The woman knew every trick in the game as well as he did. An experience that went back to the cradle, and a cunning and brain power by which the organised detective forces of the world had often been defeated, had placed her chief among the very few criminals who can plan and successfully carry out great coups. On his side, however, Menzies had one factor on which he placed hopes. There is no such thing as honour among thieves. Sometimes there is a community of interest which forces them to keep faith one with another, but very rarely will one run a risk to save another. The detective had to stir Gwennie to alarm for her own safety—but whether she would allow herself to be alarmed or not was a doubt in his mind.

"Where is Mr. Hallett?" he asked bluntly.

If a person, ignorant of the elementary principles of arithmetic, was suddenly asked to solve a problem in algebra he might have looked as Gwennie did then. Her air of bewilderment was an education. Had Menzies been less sure of his ground even he might have been deluded. She stared at him blankly. "Mr. Hallett?" she repeated. "I never heard of him."

The man's face set grimly and his eyes grew hard.

THE MAELSTROM

"Or of Reader Ling, or of Errol, or Miss Greye-Stratton, or William Smith?" he demanded.

"I know Ling—some," she said artlessly. "But I haven't seen him for two or three years. Why don't you tell me straight what you're driving at, Mr. Menzies? I'm always willing to help you if I can."

"I aim to take you to pieces and see what makes you tick if you're not careful, Gwennie," he said "You'd better listen. You know of the murder at Linstone Terrace Gardens." He tapped out the bowl of his pipe against the heel of his boot and menaced her with the stem. "I'm not saying you had anything to do with it—but you know something." She met his eyes steadily. "You're going down, Gwennie, don't make any error about it. But I'd hate to be hard on you. I know you've never liked gun-play and I'm willing to believe that it was an accident, so far as you were concerned—that someone got out of hand. You know we've got this chap—Smith he calls himself. He's likely to get loose-lipped, you know."

The last hint was sheer bluff, and Menzies saw it was of no avail even before she replied. She was not to be bamboozled into an acknowledgment that she knew anything of Smith. "You believe I've had something to do with the Greye-Stratton murder," she answered. "If you've made up your mind I'll not argue. You'll have to find a better fairy-story than that to get me down to the Old Bailey." She rose and walked over to a seat nearer to the window.

"I should have thought a lady of your penetration could have put two and two together from seeing me here," he remarked.

She looked through the window. "I want to know," she said indifferently.

"There was a note sent to Mr. Hallett, you know. It asked him to come to this address. We have got the note, which is quite enough for me to act on if I want to charge you on suspicion of being concerned in this murder."

He thought that her cheek went a trifle paler but he could not be certain. Mrs. Lyne was not a lady who was likely to show her emotions by any physical change. She seemed deep in thought. She watched through the window for two or three minutes before replying. Her white fingers played an imaginary piano on her lap. Then she jerked her head abruptly as though she had come to some decision. "Where do I come in?" she asked. "I'm not admitting that I know anything, but *if* I did, would it be worth my while to tell you? What should I stand to gain, anyway? Let's talk plain business. You don't expect something for nothing. As far as I can see all you promise is your best thanks if I'll kindly supply you with evidence to get myself convicted."

There was reason in her point of view. There are

countries where a certain amount of elasticity is allowed to detectives in the matter of bargaining with guilty persons. But Scotland Yard holds very strict views on that point. The slightest resemblance of partiality in its men is rigorously condemned. Menzies was in a difficulty and knew it.

"There's something in what you say, Gwennie," he argued easily. "Only don't lose sight of this—I've got enough to act on in regard to you." He placed his hands on his knees and leaned forward. "It isn't as if we weren't bound to get the rest of our evidence sooner or later. You would be only saving time. You know if I put in a word for you at a trial——"

She interrupted him. "I'll climb down," she said. "You've got me docketed and I know when I'm beat." Her bright face relapsed into a momentary scowl. "I was foolish to send Hallett that note. I thought he might not take any notice of a verbal message. After all I guess you'll search this house, and you'll be bound to find him."

"He's here?"

She nodded. "He's here. He's had a tiring night if I'm any judge. If you'll stand out of the doorway we'll get along and drag him up. We stowed him in the cellar."

He had too much knowledge of Miss Lyne's resourcefulness to take any chances. She had the reputation of being a bitter fighter when hardest pressed and he

THE MAELSTROM

was alert for any indication that she meant to throw him off his guard. He gripped her wrist as he opened the door. "I'm going to hold tight," he warned.

"Oh, if you like it," she retorted, and they passed side by side into the passage.

In the semi-darkness by the kitchen door she stopped and pushed open a cupboard under the stairs "It's here," she said. "Have you got a match? There's a trap-door."

"We'll have to do without a match," he remarked. "I like clinging to you, Gwennie."

She made no answer, but he felt her stoop, and himself bent and groped on the floor. The fingers of his right hand came in contact with a heavy bolt, which he withdrew. She in turn flung back the trap-door and both peered down into the square of blackness which marked the opening.

"You there, Mr. Hallett?" he cried.

A muffled, inarticulate sound reached him. The woman raised herself almost upright. "He's tied and gagged. We'll need that match, after all, Mr. Menzies. There's a ladder somewhere."

He felt in his pocket with his free right hand and passed her a box of matches "You'd better strike it, then. Hurry up."

She fumbled with the matches clumsily enough, which was only natural. There was a quick burst of flame as the whole box flared up, and then Menzies gave a

THE MAELSTROM

cry as she brought round the flaming box with all the force of her left hand full in his face. His grip on her wrist involuntarily relaxed and the moment she had been waiting for arrived. She flung her full weight sideways upon him and he collapsed down the open trap-door.

She flung the door swiftly to, pushed home the bolt, and daintily brushing the dirt from her dressing-gown, withdrew, closing the cupboard door behind her.

CHAPTER XII

WEIR MENZIES, bruised in body but more battered in his feelings, was on his feet in a flash. Only the need for instant action kept him from expressing in unchurchwardenly terms his opinion of the trick that had been played him. A ladder which had made itself painfully felt in his descent he now ascended with a rush. He scarcely hoped that the trap was still unsecured, but he was a man who rarely took anything for granted. His fingers pressed against the rough surface of the boards and he gave one futile heave. Then he sat down on the top step to consider matters quietly.

It is an elementary principle continually dinned into the ears of junior members of the service that never in any circumstances must a prisoner upon whom hands have once been laid be permitted to escape. A captain who has lost his ship feels little more agony of mind than a Scotland Yard man who has lost his prisoner. It is always difficult to define the difference between negligence and ill luck.

True Gwennie had not been technically under arrest, but that was small consolation. He had intended to arrest her and she had outwitted him. That was the galling part—a part that could admit of little explanation or extenuation when he came to submit his report

THE MAELSTROM

to headquarters. He—a chief inspector of the C. I. D. —had dropped into this muddle.

He put the personal aspect aside for the moment while he sought to disentangle motives and probabilities. Gwennie could have no hope that his imprisonment would be more than temporary. She was too old a hand for that. Even if he were eliminated altogether, the investigation would still go on. His progress was recorded at Scotland Yard and there were able men ready to take it up where he had left off. Also she could scarcely suppose that he had ventured unsupported into the house. She would realise his colleagues would not be far away.

It needed no great reasoning power to conclude that her little effort against him was meant merely as a diversion to afford her time to make a get-away. And more, it seemed likely that she would succeed.

"I'd like to wring her neck," mused Menzies aloud and stabbed a hand viciously into his pocket to see whether he had a spare box of matches.

Down below in the darkness something stirred. The detective more than ever regretted the absence of matches. He cautiously descended the ladder and groped his way towards the sound. The cellar had seemingly been used as a depository of useless lumber and more than once he stumbled before, laying on a heap of coals, he placed his hands on a warm form. The figure moved under his touch and he felt the cords that enwrapped it. He slipped his pocket-knife under the bonds and the man moved stiffly, sat up, extracted a gag from his mouth, and spat.

"That you, Hallett?" said Menzies.

"Yes." The young man broke into a cackling laugh. "They've got you, then, Menzies. If I wasn't so sore this would be funny."

"You've a keen sense of humour," retorted Menzies grimly. "I don't see anything funny about it. Here—hold tight. Don't go falling about yet. I'll give you a rub-down and you'll be all right in a jiffy."

He chafed the numbed limbs until Hallett groaned with the exquisite agony of returning circulation. "Matches are what I want more than anything else at the moment," he went on. "Do you happen to have any?"

"I think there's some—right-hand vest pocket," groaned Hallett. "Easy—you're murdering me."

Menzies extracted a small silver box of vestas and struck a light. "You'll do now," he said. "Better keep quiet for a little while I have a look round. We'll talk when there's more time."

The light showed a low-pitched cellar such as is used for the storage of coals in many suburban houses. Hallett, indeed, had been lying upon a heap of coals and almost immediately above was an iron plate which Menzies supposed opened out on to the pavement. He pushed it upwards and a slash of light showed that he was right.

"By James!—I'll do Gwennie yet," he exclaimed. "This hole was not built to fit me, but I guess you'll be able to wriggle through, Mr. Hallett. You're slimmer than I. Feel you'd like to have a walk about now? Here, let me give you a hand?"

Supported by the chief inspector, Hallett took two or three uncertain steps. His strength was rapidly returning to him and by the time they had been twice round the cellar he declared himself fit for the undertaking. Menzies lifted him bodily and he wriggled upwards through the manhole. It was a tight squeeze and he sat gasping and exhausted on the pavement by the time he was through.

"What next?" he asked.

"There should be a constable at the corner to the right. Get him and break into the house if you can't do it any other way. Tell him to come and speak to me if he won't take instructions from you."

The policeman proved amenable, and within ten minutes Menzies had the pleasure of hearing the bolts of his prison withdraw and he heaved a sigh of relief as he emerged into comparatively open air. "That's better," he declared. He turned sharply on the constable. "Have you seen anyone leave the house since I came in?"

"There was a lady and gentleman about twenty minutes or half an hour ago, sir. I could have stopped 'em, but I didn't know whether you might want me to. I had no instructions. The gentleman was carrying a bag and the lady asked me where they were likely to find a taxi-cab."

"Did you direct them?"

"I told them the town hall was the nearest rank."

"Hump yourself down to that rank," said Menzies, "and find out if they took a cab. Get the number and hurry back, bringing a cab with you. Come on, Hallett. We'll make sure that all the birds have flown before we have that talk. And a wash wouldn't be amiss for either of us," he added, surveying the other's coal-blackened face.

"You've burnt yourself," said Jimmie.

"That," commented Menzies. "Oh, that's nothing—only Gwennie's trade-mark. She's a regular little spit-cat, isn't she?"

A room to room search of the house satisfied Menzies that it was empty save for themselves. He postponed a more detailed search until Congreve should arrive and led the way to the room in which Gwennie Lyne had received him. He dropped into a chair and looked Hallett up and down.

"If it hadn't been my duty to get you out of this hole," he said, "I'd have felt inclined to let your friends stew you in your own juice. You're a little too inclined to go off at half-cock for my taste."

THE MAELSTROM

Hallett flushed a little. He remembered that but for the detective he would probably have been still in the cellar, and he had passed no word of thanks. He tried to overlook the reproof in Menzies' tone. "I'll own I blundered, if that will satisfy you." He held out his hand. "If it hadn't been for you I'd have still been sweating my soul out down below. I take it all back. You're a good man, Menzies."

"The girl played you up, did she? You're not the first that's been made a fool of by a woman, my lad."

Hallett's teeth gritted together. Menzies seemed to have the faculty of invariably smoothing him up the wrong way. "Can't you leave that end alone," he said coldly. "You may be right or wrong, but you know my opinion. Miss Greye-Stratton isn't a criminal. Your judgment's warped."

Menzies smiled and made a gesture as of one indulging a child's whim. "All right, my son. Have it your own way. I know"—he cocked one leg over the other —"if I'd been lured into this shanty by the lady and bundled down to keep company with the coals, what *I* should think. I'm not blaming you for jumping to help a lady in distress—but if you'd gone to the Yard with that note instead of playing knight-errant, it would have been the sensible thing."

"That note was forged. I'll swear she had no hand in it."

Weir Menzies was whistling a tune softly to himself.

THE MAELSTROM

He stopped in the middle of a bar. "My dear young friend, for a man who's knocked about the world you're the most verdant sprig I've run across for a long time."

"How'd you know I was here?" demanded Jimmie.

"You left the fragments of the note in your room and we put them together. That's all. Suppose you let me know what happened. We'll want your statement, anyway."

Jimmie Hallett felt his unshaven chin absently "It's no good explaining to you why I fell into this frame-up. You wouldn't understand and you can call me all the names you like if it relieves you any. You've got to take it that I felt I had to do something when I got back to the hotel and found the note. That was how I came out here. I guess I led any of your men who were shadowing me a little dance. I hopped all over the old village."

"If you went to any trouble to avoid my men," said Menzies drily, "it was waste of time. There was no one following you. If there had been you wouldn't have thrown them off. That doesn't matter, though. Go on."

"Well," said Jimmie, "there isn't much more to it. A nice, gentle old lady—it's she who you call Gwennie, I suppose—opened the door to me. I was on the lookout for tricks, but she pretty well threw me off my guard when she denied that she knew Miss Olney—although when I mentioned Miss Greye-Stratton's name she was as nice as pie and asked me right in—into this very room.

"She asked me to sit down and went away—as I supposed—to fetch Miss Greye-Stratton. She was back in two or three minutes and she pitched me a little tale—I suppose while things were being got good and ready for me. She told me that she was an old friend of Miss Greye-Stratton——"

"Didn't that strike you as curious, seeing she hadn't recognised the name of Olney?" asked Menzies.

"It didn't occur to me—then," admitted Hallett. "I never gave it a thought. As I was saying, she declared that she was an old friend and that the girl had sought her advice in her difficulties. You can laugh, but I gulped it all down. Then there came a tap at the door. 'Peggy is ready to see you,' said she, and we got up. I held the door open for her and passed through close behind. The passage isn't well lighted, as you may have noticed, and as I half turned to close the door after me someone dropped a bag over my head and shoulders.

"I did my best but I didn't stand a dog's chance. If I'd had my arms free I might have done something, but that smothering bag prevented anything like an effective struggle. I had a gun but I couldn't get at it. There were three of them—Gwennie and two men— and I was dragged back into this room and handled.

THE MAELSTROM

"At last the two men managed to get hold of my wrists and held me while Gwennie drew the sack off. Then I was lashed and gagged as you found me.

"'Sorry to put you to this inconvenience, Mr. Hallett,' said Gwennie, 'but we just had to make sure of you.' I glared at her. Of course I couldn't answer. Laying as I was I couldn't see the faces of the two men—they seemed to be purposely keeping out of my line of sight, but one of them struck in.

"'Think yourself lucky that we haven't put you right out.'

"'All right,' thinks I to myself, 'I know that voice.' It was that of the man who let me in at Linstone Terrace Gardens.

"'You keep quiet,' said Gwennie—she seemed to be boss of the show. 'Now just listen to me, Mr. Hallett. You've been jolted into a business that is no concern of yours, and we're not the sort of people to allow our plans to be interfered with. It's up to us to keep your mouth shut about what you've seen or know, but you won't come to any harm unless our hands are forced. I'm afraid you'll have to put up with some discomfort for some hours, though, until we can make arrangements.'

"They lifted me up and carried me down that cellar—and anything harder than the coal they laid me on I've never known. There was a clock I could hear striking somewhere, so I was able to keep track of time.

THE MAELSTROM

At about half-past ten last night Gwennie came down and loosened the gag and gave me something to eat and drink. She didn't forget to put it on again afterwards, though. After that I was left alone till I heard your voices above the trap-door—though I never thought then that she'd diddle you as she has done."

"I've not finished yet, Mr. Hallett," said Menzies. "We're going to play this game out. It's one thing gained to know that Gwennie Lyne's in it—— Hello, there's a cab. That must be my constable back. Ah, and there's Congreve and a couple more men. It doesn't look as if we'd have stayed long in that cellar even if there hadn't been the coal-shoot. I'll have to decide what's to be done."

CHAPTER XIII

THE only man who appeared at all hurried or excited was the constable. He had gained not only the number of the cab in which Gwennie and her companion had driven away, but the name of the driver and the location of his garage. He was visibly proud of his success, though perhaps a little disappointed that Menzies should accept it as a matter of course. Still there was the thrill not often encountered in street duty of feeling that he was at work side by side with one of the best-known Scotland Yard detectives. It was none the less felt, although he had little idea of what was happening or what had happened.

His palpable excitement was in contrast to the imperturbable attitude of the detectives to whom the routine was familiar. They waited while Menzies swiftly scribbled a message to headquarters.

A definite stage had been reached in the investigation. The motive and identity of the murderer of the old man were still in doubt, but no longer was there any necessity for questing a trail. The law holds every person innocent until proved guilty, but common sense has at times to reverse the rule. No experienced police officer of any nationality would hesitate for a moment in forming an opinion even had the facts against Gwennie Lyne been much slighter than they were. Her mere reputation as an organiser of criminal coups was enough.

It might be difficult to bring home any proof of complicity in the murder, but there was now a legitimate reason for holding her (once she was caught) in the abduction of Hallett or even as a returned deportee. A suspect under lock and key has few opportunities of clouding a line of investigation. Menzies felt the elation of one who had viewed his quarry and could now run it down in the open. Once she and her friends were under arrest it would be easier to piece together the links connecting them with the murder.

He finished his despatch and folded and blotted it methodically. "Take that along to the station and have it wired off to the Yard at once," he ordered.

So he sent a warning that within an hour or less would reach each one of the six hundred odd detectives of London, to say nothing of the watchers of the ports. Not a single man of those six hundred going about his ordinary business but would shortly carry a photograph of Gwennie and be alert for any hint of her whereabouts. It was to that relentless, unceasing vigilance that Menzies pinned his faith rather than to the wearying task of following her up through the cabman who had driven her away. The cabman would only be able to say where he put her down, and she would have had ample time to cover her tracks.

THE MAELSTROM

"Did you get that search-warrant, Congreve? Right you are. You'd better start running over the house. I'll get some clothes and come back. What do you think about things, Mr. Hallett? Would you like to come along with me?"

Jimmie's lips were firm-pressed. "What are you doing about the girl?" he said. "She may be in danger. Isn't there something I can do?"

"You can't do anything but keep cool," said Menzies. "It's no good over-running ourselves. That young lady's a lot more capable of taking care of herself than you seem to think. We're getting on as fast as we can. Something might turn up in searching the house that will give us a fresh start, seeing that Gwennie hustled out of it in such a hurry."

Even if Jimmie had been still resolved to chip in on a lone hand, he recognised that he was helpless. He could not act by himself. He had no organisation to back him and no means of following up the girl unless he stood in with the detectives. He nodded in token of his acquiescence in Menzies' dispositions and the latter led him to the taxi-cab outside.

They whirled away to Magersfontein Road, where Hallett gladly availed himself of an offer to eradicate most of the traces of the night's adventure. The chief inspector was waiting for him by the time he had finished a bath and a shave and made an energetic attack on his clothes with a brush. He also had changed. Flushed and cheerful, he looked more the churchwarden than ever by contrast with his late appearance.

"No need to hurry. Congreve won't have finished yet awhile and a bit of breakfast won't do any harm. Let me introduce Mrs. Menzies. And here's Bruin. Shake hands with Mr. Hallett, Bruin." He fondled the dog for a moment. "He's a rascal. Tried to spoil my garden yesterday, didn't you—you wicked old sinner. Come and have a look at my patch, Mr. Hallett. It's not big, but I do fairly well with my roses."

"I never talk business when I'm at home and never think of it if I can help it. I do all my worrying on duty. Some men let a case get on their nerves. It never does any good," he said when they were seated at the table.

The steady search of Mrs. Lyne's house was still progressing when they returned to Ludford Road. A number of fresh detectives had arrived to help Congreve, and they found Heldon Foyle stretched lazily out in one of the horsehair chairs in the sitting-room. He rose and shook hands with Jimmie.

"How are you, Mr. Hallett? . . . I got your report, Menzies. Nothing much doing, so I thought I'd drop down and have a look at things." He drew the chief inspector a little aside. "I didn't think *you* would have let Gwennie get one in on you. She complicates things. The Commissioner isn't pleased."

THE MAELSTROM

"It's against me, sir, and that's a fact," agreed the other ruefully. He made no attempt at excuse.

"It can't be helped, old man," said Foyle more sympathetically now that he had delivered his official reproof. "I'd have fallen into it just the same way. Come upstairs. Excuse us a moment, Mr. Hallett."

He led the way upstairs to a locked room and tapped softly at the door. It was opened very slowly, just wide enough to admit him. "Burnt paper," he explained laconically. "Come in slowly. Don't make a draught."

The chief inspector obeyed. There were a couple of men within the bedroom, which reeked of oil from a cheap stove on the washstand. The window was tight closed and the chimney was blocked up. In the grate were the blackened fragments of a mass of burnt papers. The big bed, too, was a chaos of burnt papers which had broken under the efforts of the two men to move them intact.

The superintendent and the chief inspector halted by the door. With infinite delicacy one of the constables lifted a sheet of burnt paper from the grate and placed it in a kitchen sieve. This he held over a steaming kettle on the oil stove while his companion with a transparent sheet of paper on which gum had been thinly spread in his hand, waited anxiously. The burnt paper softened rapidly and the gummed sheet was dropped upon it.

THE MAELSTROM

"That's the last, sir," commented one of the operators. "The rest is too broken up to be handled." He indicated the grate with a gesture.

The chief inspector moved to the bed and took a seat upon it. Heldon Foyle lit a cigar.

"There are two or three cheque-book counterfoils not quite destroyed," went on the man, and picking them off the coverlet handed them to Menzies.

"Very well," said Foyle. "Mr. Menzies and I will go through these things now. You can come to photograph them later on."

As the experts vanished, Menzies gingerly turned over the charred leaves of the cheque counterfoils. "Gwennie made the most of her time," he observed, "but she seems to have been too much rushed to make a complete job of it. These are on the same bank as Greye-Stratton's."

"Same cheques?" asked Foyle.

"Hallett may be able to tell us that. What are these other documents?"

It is a peculiarity of burnt paper that it often shows up quite clearly any writing that was upon it before it was consumed. Menzies wrinkled his brows as he studied the pasted-down portions that had been rescued. Some pieces were almost complete; some had broken and twisted under the process of restoration so that it was a matter of difficulty to follow the eccentricities of the writing which, in some cases, stood out dirty grey, in others brilliant black, and still again pale black.

"Listen to this," said Menzies. He read slowly: "'We are all right for the time being and if'—there's a piece missing there—'can be handled we shall be all hunky. Couldn't you square one of the bulls. You know some of them and it might be worth a shot, as it would simplify things. It's no good tackling M. But a couple of hundred with some of the others ought to go a long way. You can dig the money out and'— something else gone. 'Hallett is most dangerous just now. He absolutely must be settled if we are to pull off the game. That's up to you, as I'll have to keep below the water line.'

"'Better not write to me, but if you can get wind to Cincinnati pass me a word. Don't trust C. too much.' The rest of the letter's gone," finished Menzies.

The superintendent sucked his cigar thoughtfully. "That's Cincinnati Red," he commented. "You'll want to rope him in. He's been in London for three months or more."

"I'll have that seen to at once," said Menzies. "The rest of the letters can wait a little."

Foyle stretched out his hand for the blackened epistle. "Pity the rest of it's gone. The chap who wrote this thinks a lot of you, Menzies. He thinks you're above graft. I wonder if Gwennie has been trying to buy up any of our men."

THE MAELSTROM

"The letter's probably been written this last day or two. There's been no time yet. I'll pass the word that whoever is tackled is to bite."

"There might be a chance," said Foyle. "And I'll tell you what, Menzies. I'll bet you a thousand pounds to a penny that the gentleman who's so anxious to keep his head under the water line is Stewart Reader Ling."

"No takers, sir," said Menzies smilingly.

CHAPTER XIV

IN serene unconsciousness that he occupied any place in the thoughts of Scotland Yard men Cincinnati Red sat cross-legged, sipping a liqueur. Of late his lines had fallen in pleasant places. He had tasted sufficiently of the hardships of this world to appreciate comfort. The furnished flat which he held in Palace Avenue by grace of a trustful landlord was a luxury which more than pleased him.

Few there were who knew Cincinnati Red's real origin or real name. He was certainly a man of education and address. In the police archives he was registered as a " con " man—which in plain English means that he was a swindler. Moreover, he was a swindler of uncommon resource and daring who had a knowledge of every trick in the game. He had been bunco-steerer, gold-brick man, sawdust man long before these swindles became threadbare. He always managed to keep a little ahead of the ruck, and though he had had one or two bad falls in his time, he was probably, as he would have put it, " ahead of the game."

He might have been anything from forty to sixty. His luxuriant, once auburn, hair and moustache had greyed and his ingenuous frank hazel eyes were in themselves a guarantee of integrity. He wore evening dress as though he were accustomed to it and his manner was

THE MAELSTROM

that of an easy-going tolerant man of the world who had no enemies and thousands of friends.

Now, an American millionaire with a Bohemian taste for night clubs and a cosy flat where selected friends of wealth may be invited for no-limit games of chance, has small fear of the police. It is unlikely that a man that has dropped a hundred or two over baccarat or poker will squeal to the authorities, even though he suspects that something more than luck has favoured his charming host. Publicity does not appeal to him. And for any other than legal contingencies Cincinnati Red was prepared. It caused a bulge in the breast pocket of his otherwise well-fitting dress coat, but that could scarcely be avoided. There are few smaller reliable pistols than the pattern of derringer he carried.

So it was with thoughts far removed from the sordid commonplaces of crime that he pressed the bell and summoned his man to help him on with his overcoat. He made his way with dignity down into the street and stopped for a moment on the curb to light his cigarette.

A couple of men sauntered towards him. The taller of the two halted as they came opposite. "Isn't your name Tomkins?" he asked.

Cincinnati finished lighting his cigarette, dropped the match and ground the light out under his heel before replying. "No, my man," he drawled, "you've made a mistake. My name is Whiffen."

He calmly ignored his questioner and held up a slim

THE MAELSTROM

cane in his left hand for a taxi-cab. Someone gripped his right wrist and he wheeled in wrathful surprise. As he did so his other hand was caught. He made no resistance. His attitude was one of dignified and lofty indignation.

"What is the meaning of this? Leave me alone instantly or I will call the police."

"That's all right," observed one of his captors quietly. "We are police officers ourselves. Jump in, Alf. I've got him.   Now then. . . . . All right, driver. Scotland Yard."

It was as though they were handling a bale of goods, so neatly and impersonally was the whole thing effected. Cincinnati Red had been for once taken off his guard. He was more staggered than his manner showed. That the police should know of his presence in London was not astonishing. It was to be expected. That they should know exactly where to lay hands on him was a different thing. He thought he had covered his traces effectually—that no one could guess that Wilfred S. Whiffen, who lived unostentatiously and well at Palace Avenue was Cincinnati Red, whose record occupied a prominent place in the police registers of half a dozen countries. What puzzled him still more was the mere fact that even knowing him, the police should trouble to arrest him. Since his arrival in England there was nothing they could hold against him, as far as he knew. He was as dead certain as he cared to be about anything

THE MAELSTROM

that none of his victims had invoked the aid of the law.

The only reasonable supposition was that this was a sort of bluff that was intended to frighten him out of the country. He resolved to sit tight.

"If you people really are police officers," he declared acidly, "this foolishness will cost you your positions. I may tell you I am well known in the best circles both here and in New York."

His captors remained unimpressed. Cincinnati Red had been "rubbed down" before and he recognised the touch of efficient hands. One of the officers thrust a hand into his breast pocket and produced the derringer.

"Handy little thing, Alf," he commented.

"Will you answer me, my man?" said Cincinnati, accentuating every word slowly. "Am I under arrest, and if so, what for. I insist on being told. You will hear more of this." He was annoyed in reality and a vague alarm was growing in his breast.

"You keep quiet, old lad," said one of his captors with more familiarity than was consistent with the status of Wilfred S. Whiffen, whatever it might be with Cincinnati Red. "You'll learn all about it soon enough. Nobody's going to hurt you."

"That isn't the point. I insist upon knowing what all this is about. I have an appointment with Lord Windermere and——"

"He *will* talk," interrupted one of the officers

wearily. "Say, sonny, suppose you give it a rest for five minutes. Lord Windermere will have to wait. Oh! Here we are."

Very few criminals are taken to Scotland Yard on detention, whatever the reader of popular fiction is accustomed to suppose. And that fact gave Cincinnati Red something to surmise upon as he was ushered into the soft-carpeted room where Weir Menzies and Heldon Foyle awaited him.

They both rose with the welcoming smile of old acquaintances. His escort had vanished. "That you?" said Foyle, beaming. "Say, I'm glad to see you, Cincinnati. You're looking top hole, too."

"Sit right down," added Menzies. "Hope you've not been put to any inconvenience. We told our chaps not to alarm you."

Cincinnati Red looked from one to the other, suspicion working behind his bland countenance. He had in his time passed through the hands of both the detectives and it was useless keeping up the pose he had adopted with the younger men. Still this assumption of friendliness was beyond him.

"Well, you've got me here, gentlemen," he said suavely. "I didn't invite myself and I've got business to attend to." He pulled off his gloves and dangled them in one hand. "It's rather rough on a man when he has achieved a position for himself and is on the level again——"

THE MAELSTROM

"And you're on the level," said Menzies, rolling a pen between his thumb and finger. "Well, I think it is a shame to drag an honest workingman"—his eye wandered meditatively over Cincinnati's faultless evening dress—"away from his job—especially as the night clubs will soon be open. What line of commerce have you established yourself in?"

Cincinnati returned his glance more hurt than angry. Foyle struck in before he could reply.

"Let him alone, Menzies. What'll you have, Cincinnati? I've got some of the real rye here—or would you prefer anything else?"

It is unusual for an officer of the C. I. to work with his desk flanked with a decanter of rye whisky. It is still more unusual for him to profer hospitality to a crook in the very headquarters of police. Cincinnati became wary. He did not know what was going to happen, but he wanted to keep his head clear.

"Nothing, I thank you," he said.

"Just as you like. I thought you might like a drink while we had a talk over things."

Cincinnati knew as well as the men who faced him that the whole proceedings were totally irregular. They had no shadow of right to detain him while no charge was hanging over his head. He would have been justified in walking straight out of the building. Yet he knew Foyle and he knew Menzies, and he knew, in spite of their apparent friendliness, things might become unpleasant if he took a high line. He flicked a speck of dust off his boots with his glove.

"Don't be shy," he urged.

"Where's Ling?" questioned Menzies abruptly. His ruddy face had lost its good nature. He was leaning forward with hard, fierce eyes barely a couple of inches from the "con" man's face. The quickness of the question and harshness of his manner were all carefully calculated to make an impression that would throw the other off his balance.

Cincinnati seemed unperturbed. "So you're hunting up Ling. What's he been doing? On my soul I wish I could help you. I don't like Ling."

There was a moment's silence. Then Foyle twisted his swivel chair and lifted one of a row of speaking-tubes behind him. It was a simple, undramatic action, but somehow the "con" man's pulse beats quickened. The superintendent paused with the tube in his hand.

"You've got a clean sheet, of course?" he asked, and his voice, though quiet, was threatening. "Nothing we can hold you for? Or shall I put a wire through to Rome and Paris and New York?"

Now there had been incidents in Cincinnati Red's career as in those of every professional crook wherein the law had not claimed the penalty which was its due. It sometimes happens that only the most grave of a series of crimes is selected for definite legal punishment. There were cases that still might be proceeded with against the " con " man if the blue-eyed superintendent chose to induce his international colleagues to rake the cold ashes together.

"Don't rush a man," protested Cincinnati Red, a little less coolly. "I was saying that I'd help you if I could."

"Then get down to it," snapped Menzies. "We're in a hurry."

"The sweat box" is an institution unknown in English police circles. Nevertheless, the " con " man found certain similarities in the conduct of the swift and relentless examination of the two detectives. They gave him little time for invention even had he been disposed to mislead them. But like most of his type he put his own skin first, even if it came to betraying an acquaintance into the hands of justice.

"Guess I'll have a drink, after all," he said. He swallowed a draught Foyle handed him in a quick gulp. "I'll trust you not to let any of the boys know I have said anything," he declared. "I saw Ling about a week ago and I've known he had something big on for some months. You gentlemen know that I used to have considerable dealings with him. He'd shoot on sight if he guessed. . . ."

"You were one of the layers down in that forged circular note stunt of his," remarked Menzies. "Yes, we know all about that. Five years you got in Paris, wasn't it?"

THE MAELSTROM

"Three," corrected Cincinnati. "You'd have thought," he went on with more bitterness, "that he'd have let me in on the ground floor of any fresh job, seeing how I had the brunt of that. If it hadn't been for an accident we'd have made a pile. But no. He said they were full up."

The two detectives exchanged glances. Cincinnati Red, clever man though he was, had always been viewed with a certain amount of not altogether unjustified distrust by his associates in the underworld. The phrase in the letter warning Gwennie not to trust Cincinnati too much occurred to them.

"A lucky thing for you, too," observed Foyle. "Go on."

"Well, whatever the job is Gwennie Lyne is in it. Ling said he might have to lay close for a bit, but there might be a chance for me to sit in the game later on. That was to sweeten me, you bet. He wanted me to keep in touch with Gwennie—she lives down at Brixton now——"

"What address?" asked Menzies. There was nothing to be gained by giving Cincinnati Red any sort of a hint as to how far they were able to check his story. He gravely wrote down the address—the correct one—given by the "con" man.

"Well," went on Cincinnati, "it's no good asking me what the job is, because, honest injun, I don't know"— he shot a sideways glance at them—"you'll be more clear on that than I am. All I know is that it's a big thing."

"Do you know a Miss Olney—Miss Lucy Olney?"

Cincinnati shook his head. "Never heard the name before."

Two pairs of eyes were watching him closely. The chief inspector gave a slight cough into his moustache. So far the swindler had been convincingly plausible and if he were more deeply involved in the mystery than he appeared to be, he had taken a cunning line. "How did you come to take a flat in Palace Avenue?" demanded Foyle.

"Well," said Cincinnati slowly, "I don't know there was any special reason why I should take it there more than anywhere else——"

"Answer the question—quick," demanded Menzies; "don't talk round it."

"It was Ling who told me the place was to let."

"Ah. And I suppose you got your references from him?"

"That's so. But don't you run away with any delusions, Mr. Menzies. I've paid my rent regularly and honestly." Cincinnati was plainly grieved at the reflection on his integrity.

"We'll take your word. But I thought you weren't very friendly with Ling. Why should he go out of his way to do you a favour?"

Cincinnati shrugged his shoulders. "Oh, it didn't cost him anything, I suppose. He said he might want me to chip in sometime and it was handy for Gwennie and him to know where I was. He used to run up and see me sometimes. That's all there is to it."

"You haven't said how you were to communicate with Ling. Where is he?"

"I don't know where he is. Last I saw of him was when he used to take meals at the Petit Savoy—you know that little restaurant in Soho. He hasn't always been there lately. Sometimes a chap named Dago Sam used to come instead. If I got any urgent message I was to post it to T. S. Charters, Poste Restante, Aldgate."

"H'm." Menzies wrote out the address and looked questioningly at Foyle.

"That'll do for the present," said the superintendent. "The point is what are we going to do about you?" He shook his head at the "con" man. "You're an awkward problem, you know."

"You can trust me, Mr. Foyle," said Cincinnati. "I know when to keep my mouth shut. Why, I might be able to help you to get hold of Ling."

"That's decidedly an idea," said Menzies. "Wait a minute." He dashed outside and returned accompanied by the men who had captured Cincinnati Red. "If you'll go with these gentlemen, Mr.—er—Whiffen," he said politely, "Mr. Foyle and I will talk things over and see what is to be done."

CHAPTER XV

A HALF smile of triumph was on Menzies' face as he returned to his seat. "Ling is a judge of character," he said with a contemptuous jerk of the head in the direction of the door. "That chap would sell his father, and mother, and brothers, and sisters to save his own skin. Pah!"

"Handle him easy all the same," exhorted the superintendent. "He's a nasty man to get in a corner. He had a gun on me once in a saloon and if I hadn't been a quick shot with a beer bottle—well, I wouldn't be talking to you now. Hello! Good evening, Sir Hilary."

The gaunt figure of the assistant commissioner had entered the room, an open newspaper in his hand. "Good evening. They told me you were here, Menzies. Seen the *Evening Comet?* They've got a new clue for you. Seems that Greye-Stratton was a defaulting member of the Black Hand. It's true, because its special commissioner has found certain cabalistic marks chalked on the pavement which no one is able to decipher. Here's a photograph. Scotland Yard—that's one of you two, I suppose—is extremely reticent and would express no opinion when approached on the subject. Two columns."

"So that tom-fool published it," said Foyle, his eyes

THE MAELSTROM

twinkling behind his glasses. "He found some boy scout marks about a hundred yards away from the house and came up here full of it. He wasn't quite sure whether it was the Black Hand or the High Binders, but he's certain he's on the track and he left a photograph for you, Menzies."

"Obliged, I'm sure," said the chief inspector shortly.

"How are things shaping?" asked Thornton.

"Moderate, sir, moderate," answered Menzies. "We've just been talking to a gentleman who may be of some use—but I'm not dead certain yet." He fished in his pocket and produced some notes. "We've brushed away a lot of the fog at the beginning of the case and we've got something to concentrate on. I never like to be confident, but we've got heaps of suspicion to bring against one or two people and the evidence may come along. It makes it easier in a way that some of them are known crooks."

Thornton was standing in front of the fireplace, his hands behind his back. He jerked his coat-tails to and fro. "I don't follow that altogether. I used to understand that it was easier to run down an amateur than a professional. Surely their experience will help 'em to blind the trail."

"That's partly right," agreed Menzies, "but it cuts both ways. I can judge of my difficulties. Now I'm not clear about a lot of things, but I've got ideas on which I've not reported yet because they may turn out

THE MAELSTROM

all wrong. The point on which we are clear now is that robbery—at least straightforward robbery—was not the motive of the murder. Revenge is a possibility. Errol, Greye-Stratton's step-son, hated him like poison and it is clear that the old man dreaded some attempt on his life—though that may have been pure monomania with no foundation in fact at all. All the same Errol is the pivot on which we have to work. I, at one time, supposed him the actual murderer. I am not so certain now. Errol—by the way, we haven't found what name he passes under yet—and his sister are living in London apart from each other and apart from the old man. She is sole heiress. She is quietly married to Stewart Reader Ling—Errol's pal. Do you follow me, sir?"

" That's plain—and plausible as far as it goes," said Sir Hilary " It supplies a powerful motive. But, to be frank, it doesn't do much else."

" I don't pretend it does," said Menzies. " It would be mighty thin to put before a jury by itself, as you say. But now we come to Hallett. He hears a quarrel in the fog. A woman pursued by a man rushes up to him and puts a bundle of cheques into his hand. He goes to Greye-Stratton's house and is admitted about the time of the murder and knocked out by a man whose face he never saw. Twice he was brought into contact with a man—or possibly two men—who must know a great deal about the case. And yet he never saw them."

THE MAELSTROM

"I thought you were convinced of his honesty," said Thornton. "I myself believe he's perfectly clear."

"Wait a minute," said Foyle.

"I think so, too," went on Menzies. "But this is significant. Does the man who was in the fog, does the man who was in the house, know that Hallett never saw his features? We get the attempt to silence him first by threats, then by a pistol shot, then by abduction. This part, at any rate, links up some evidence. The Greye-Stratton girl's name is used to lure him to Gwennie Lyne's house. If she wrote the note herself—and, mind you, we've no proof she didn't—that connects her with Gwennie and the rest. I'm pretty positive in my own mind that she was the woman of the fog and that Hallett knows it—and she knows he knows. We carry the linking up closer by one of the burnt notes we found, which warns Gwennie Lyne that Hallett must be silenced at all costs. We guess that's Ling's writing and may be able to prove it. We've got collaboration in some plot—whether it's the murder of Greye-Stratton or not—partly established at any rate."

"But the cheques," said Thornton. "How do you explain the cheques?"

"I don't. I'll own they're beyond me at the moment. None of our enquiries have thrown any light on that, though we found some burnt stubs which may be the counterfoils in Gwennie's grate. However, that may be one of those things capable of a quite simple explanation at the right moment. Now there's the man we've just been talking to—Cincinnati Red. Of course, he's a crook and he wouldn't show up well under cross-examination if we should want to put him in the box. But what he says goes to help my ideas. He points out that Ling and Gwennie have had some big scheme on about which they've been very close. I'll not deny that I may have built up the wrong theory—time will show—but it's got a framework of facts and I can't see that they fit any other theory."

"How about Miss Greye-Stratton—Mrs. Ling?" asked Foyle.

Menzies scratched an eyebrow. "She's difficult," he admitted. "Whether's she's deliberately in the game or not it's hard to say. She's told Hallett something, too, but she seems to have hypnotised him. He's as tight as a nut when it comes to her. I've got hopes that I may make him see reason and then I shall have something to go on from the inside."

"You're going out with Cincinnati?" said the superintendent switching off the discussion. "I know you're prejudiced against guns, but if you are I think I'd put one in my pocket. You want to take care with the mob you're handling."

"I don't know," said Menzies casually. "I'd as likely as not hit the wrong person if I pulled a trigger. I'm taking Royal. He can have one if he likes. He's out looking after Hallett just now. The pair of them are eating somewhere. I daren't leave that young man alone or he'll be trying the amateur detective game again."

"Suit yourself then. Only don't blame me if Ling and his pals lay you out."

"I'll look after that," retorted Menzies.

He disappeared into his own room and changed the ink-stained alpaca jacket of office use for a tweed one. Then he sent a messenger out for Royal. The detective-sergeant and Jimmie Hallett shortly showed up. Menzies took them along to the subdued " con " man, who was smoking his twelfth cigarette and returning curt monosyllables to the attempts of one of his guardians to drag him into conversation.

"Here we are, Cincinnati," announced the chief inspector cheerily. "Think we were never coming? This is a fellow-countryman of yours. Mr. Hallett—Mr. Whiffle."

"Whiffen," corrected Cincinnati Red.

"Oh, yes. I beg your pardon. Whiffen it is. To us and to some of the Central Office folk he answers to the name of Cincinnati Red."

A flush mounted Cincinnati Red's handsome face. It was a curious thing that this man, known as a cunning felon in a dozen countries, should resent the tactlessness that introduced him to a fellow-American by a nickname. He bowed austerely.

"We thought of taking a walk down to the Petit

THE MAELSTROM

Savoy," went on Menzies. "We might see that pal of yours there."

"Oh, come, I say," remonstrated Cincinnati. "That's going a bit beyond it. If anyone saw me getting around with a couple of police officers where would I be?" He spread his hands in protest.

"It would get you into bad odour with the boys, wouldn't it?" said Menzies. "Kind of hurt your reputation?"

Cincinnati Red was plainly alarmed at the course events were taking. He was not a coward, but he never asked for trouble. To give Ling away was one thing—to seek him out barefaced in the company of detectives was quite another. Apart from any danger which Ling himself might threaten it would be advertising himself to the whole of the underworld as a man definitely unfit to be trusted. Although his present prospects were favourable enough there might at any moment arise an occasion for him to co-operate with acquaintances in some fresh nefarious scheme.

"It isn't that," he explained. "If I was seen walking with you it would give the game away."

The chief inspector twisted his fingers in his watch-chain. He was as well aware of the course of Cincinnati's thoughts as the " con " man himself. " Comfort yourself, laddie," he remarked. "We aren't quite so fresh as that. Mr. Hallett here will walk with you and Royal and I will look after ourselves. If you meet Ling or anyone else in his mob all you've got to do is to fiddle with the top button of your jacket. Savvy?"

"That's all right," said Cincinnati.

"And—just in case of accidents—Mr. Hallett's name is Mr. Green—Mr. Samuel Green."

"Samuel Green it is. I understand, Mr. Menzies."

Jimmie Hallett found the walk through the West End streets not without interest. Had not the circumstances of the introduction told him that Mr. Whiffen was a crook he would have had difficulty in arriving at that conclusion. Cincinnati Red could be a delightful companion when he chose. It was part of his profession. He had read widely and well, and his study of human nature had been vast. As a student of the newspapers he knew that Jimmie had been the first to raise an alarm after the murder, but not until now had he supposed that Ling had any connection with the crime. He laid himself out to pump Jimmie, but with little success. Hallett was willing enough to talk, but Cincinnati speedily found that he was expected to provide any loose information that might be floating around, instead of obtaining it. He dropped finesse and tried the point-blank method.

"This is a rotten business for anyone from across the water to walk into just when they are expecting to enjoy themselves. I'd just hate to be worried if I were in your place. How'd it come about, anyway? Did you know Greye-Stratton before?"

THE MAELSTROM

"It's a long story," parried Jimmie warily. "What about this Ling man? Known him long?"

"Some years," said Cincinnati. "You must not imagine, Mr. Hallett, that because of the circumstances in which we've met I am just a crook. I've had misfortunes. I made a mistake once and I've paid for it. You know what the police are—they're the same all over the world. They don't forgive men for rising from their dead selves. I've come to this country to start over again and my hands are clean. Yet here I am pulled into this because I once knew Ling. You saw the offensive manner of the ill-bred vulture Menzies just now. I daren't resent it."

Jimmie had heard the same story before. Police persecution is an unfailing text for the habitual criminal. He scrutinised Mr. Whiffen with smiling incredulity.

"Did you ever meet Ling's wife?" he asked.

"His wife?" ejaculated Cincinnati. "I didn't know he was married."

"I was wondering," said Jimmie. "That's all."

He followed Cincinnati through the swing doors of the Petit Savoy and a waiter glided forward to lead them to a table. Cincinnati brushed him aside and led the way through the throng of diners to a further room. Jimmie Hallett had to seek the support of a chair to steady himself. He heard Cincinnati Red speaking as one far off.

THE MAELSTROM

"Hullo, old man. How are you? Shake hands with my friend here—Mr. Samuel G. Green from Mobile."

The clean-shaven, keen-eyed man whom Cincinnati had omitted to name was shaking hands with him across the table. But Jimmie paid little attention to him. For by his side, half risen from her chair, **wide-eyed** and astonished, was **Peggy Greye**-Stratton.

CHAPTER XVI

"You!" she gasped. "You here?"

He, too, was taken aback. For a moment he was incapable of consecutive thought. He had fiercely combated, even to himself, Menzies' theory that she was a willing associate of the people who were being hunted down. But this encounter staggered his faith. If the Scotland Yard man's suspicions were right it was not at all a surprising thing that she should be dining quietly with Ling—Ling, her husband and the master brain of the conspiracy. Yet so assiduously had Jimmie accustomed himself to believe that she was rather a victim than an accomplice that her presence came upon him as a shock.

"You know my—this lady?" someone said as though mildly interested.

Jimmie pulled himself together. He threw a backward glance at the door. Menzies and Royal had not yet appeared.

"We have met before," he answered with a fine assumption of coolness. "Miss Olney, isn't it? Can I have a word with you?" He beckoned her aside, the eyes of the other two men following them with curiosity. "Is that man Ling?" he whispered.

"Yes," she answered. "What——"

He cut her short. "This is no time for questions.

THE MAELSTROM

The police are immediately behind us. They are going to arrest him, and maybe you, too. You must get away at once." He signalled to a waiter. " Is there another way out? Some people are coming in at the front whom we don't want to meet."

A gleam of gold between his fingers transformed the waiter into a quick ally. " If you will step this way, sir—this way, madam." He pushed forward half a dozen steps and flung open a door. They descended a couple of steps into a derelict side street, and Ling, who had watched them with a puzzled frown, turned to Cincinnati as they disappeared.

" What in thunder's the game? "

" Blest if I know," said Cincinnati. " Who's your lady friend? She seemed surprised to see my friend." He was fumbling with the buttons of his coat.

Suspicion sat black and lowering on Ling's face. His hand dropped to his jacket pocket and Cincinnati had a little apprehensive thrill as he heard a faint click and the bottom corner of the jacket pocket poked the edge of the table. He longed to look round to see if Menzies had entered the room, but he dared not turn his head. A waiter glided to his side and as he picked up the menu card, and with deliberation, gave his orders, he felt Ling's menacing gaze still upon him. The waiter moved away.

" There's some monkey trick on the board," said Ling in a low voice. " By God, I'll plug if you

THE MAELSTROM

don't tell me what's on. What are you doing with Hallett? Why did you bring him here? Answer. If you move or turn a hair I'll blow a hole through you, you dog!"

Cincinnati was between the devil and the deep sea—with the detectives behind and a desperate man in front. "Easy does it, Stewart," he said soothingly. "Easy does it. I couldn't help myself."

Between clenched teeth Ling spat a vicious oath at him. His eyes shot up and down the crowded aisles of the restaurant, always coming back to Cincinnati Red's face. There was a white scar an inch long above his left eye which now showed crimson, giving him an indescribably sinister appearance. He withdrew his right hand from his pocket, keeping it concealed with a serviette. The serviette lay at last carelessly crumpled in front of him and his hand was under it.

"See that?" he growled menacingly "There's two men just come in. Pals of yours, I guess. You'd better get your thinking apparatus started, for if those splits offer to come near me it's going to be an almighty bad time for you. You'd try to put it across *me*, you tin horn! I tell you, if I go out of this place with the cuffs on, you'll go out feet first. Think it out quick, you dirty squealer."

Cincinnati Red was frightened, badly frightened, though his face did not show it, save perhaps that it was whiter than usual. The waiter placed a plate of

THE MAELSTROM

soup before him and his hand was steady as he lifted the spoon. Ling himself, in spite of his passion, had lowered his tone and not a soul in the room beyond themselves knew that they were within measurable distance of tragedy.

"That back door those others used," he said quickly; "slip out. I'll hold the bulls back."

The serviette stirred impatiently. "Not on your tintype, my son. You don't pass on this hand. You'll stick closer to me than a brother. I'll trust you—while my finger's on a gun and the gun on you."

Menzies and Royal had seated themselves three or four tables away. Nothing seemingly was of less interest to them than the two crooks.

"I can't think of anything," protested Cincinnati sullenly.

"How much do they know?" asked Ling sharply.

"They raided Gwennie's shanty this morning. They're after her, but you mainly."

"You seem to know a hell of a lot," commented Ling crisply. "I suppose you've arranged to give 'em the office when they're to pull me. That would have been all right if Hallett hadn't gone off at half cock. Now the surprise packet is going to be mine. I'm going to drink this liqueur and my attention is going to seem to wander off you for a little minute—only *seem*, mind you. There's a menu card down by your hand. You've got a pencil. Now write on that that I suspect

[148]

nothing—that I'm going to take you round now to the spot where the rest of the boys are. Then give it to the waiter to pass to them."

The astuteness of the move appealed to Cincinnati. Ling was playing for time, to avoid immediate arrest. If the detectives thought they would make a bigger haul by postponing matters they would do so. The " con " man had no conscientious scruples about tricking them, but he was uneasy when he thought of the hints which Foyle had given him. If he could have safely betrayed Ling he would. Still, life was, after all, worth clinging to—even if a certain proportion of it had to be spent in prison. He followed Ling's instructions docilely and over his shoulder saw Menzies read the card and nod without looking up. Ling drank his liqueur slowly and there was a more complacent expression about his thin lips. Now that he had obtained a respite he seemed in no hurry to go. He regarded the " con " man with a sneer. "You're not fit for this sort of thing, Cincinnati," he said acidly. "You ought to stick to parlour games. A yellow streak doesn't matter there."

The other leaned back in his chair unmoved by the insult. " I'm not silly enough to butt my head against a brick wall," he answered equably. " One of these times we may meet on level terms." His eye dropped meaningly on the serviette.

" Not if I know it," retorted Ling. " I like you better as you are. You'll never be on level terms with

THE MAELSTROM

me. I wonder what I'll do to you," he went on reflectively "Did you ever hear how they used to treat witches in the old days in Massachusetts? They used to stick red-hot knitting needles through their tongues. It always seemed to me that wouldn't be a bad punishment for squealers." He pushed back his chair. "Get my coat, waiter. And this gentleman's."

They marched out of the restaurant side by side and a little walk brought them into Shaftesbury Avenue. Cincinnati had every nerve strained watching for an opportunity to escape. But Ling's vigilance never relaxed. "I've got very attached to you this last half hour," he explained in friendly tones. "I wouldn't lose you for anything. I want to hear you pitch a tale when we get time. It'll be a real pleasure to learn how you've been working yourself to help us and how I've been deceived by appearances into dealing with you harshly."

This tribute to his inventive faculties did not seem to afford Cincinnati Red any pronounced gratification. He grunted something unintelligible. Then· "If I were you, Stewart, I'd take a taxi. We'll never throw these splits off walking.

"Well, well," exclaimed Ling in well-assumed surprise. "It's you've got the brains. Fancy thinking of that. Never mind. The walk won't hurt us, and perhaps a little exercise'll do your chums good."

Cincinnati doubted it, but did not repeat his suggestion. He was very cloudy as to what his companion proposed to do. The trick in the restaurant he had supposed to be but a temporary expedient of Ling's in order to get away. Not to give the detectives the slip now they were in the open seemed like playing with fire. He knew Ling as a dare-devil, but for a man whose neck was in jeopardy he was carrying things jauntily.

It was in Bloomsbury that they swerved off the main road into one of those hideous streets of tall boarding-houses with iron-railed areas and forbidding front doors of mid-Victorian era.

"Nearly home, Cincinnati," encouraged Ling. "Now you'll be able to see things move. We'll see if there's any knitting needles in the house afterwards."

They ascended the steps of one of the most gloomy looking of the houses and Ling inserted a key. He carefully closed and bolted the door after him and ordered Cincinnati forward. There was a faint glimmer of light from a gas lamp in the hall.

"The back room will do for us," said Ling. "Get along."

A descent of a couple of steps led into a back sitting-room. Ling pointed with his pistol—he was carrying it openly in his hand now. "There's a chair. Sit down. I want you with your back to me. That's right. Now put your arms behind your back and keep still."

THE MAELSTROM

Cincinnati Red felt something encircle his wrists and a lashing was dextrously drawn tight. An involuntary cry escaped him. Ling finished the knot and, stepping in front, swung a smashing blow at the bound man's face.

"That's on account," he said fiercely. "If you don't keep still you'll get what's coming to you." He thrust his face, contorted with passion, close to that of the "con" man and Cincinnati shivered. "I can't do all I'd like to," he went on, "but I'll pay the bill in full some other time—you bet I will."

He stooped and tied Cincinnati's ankles to the chair-legs as effectively as he had bound his wrists. Then he lifted chair and all and staggered with it into the front room. He placed it by the curtained window and stood for a moment breathless. Cincinnati was no light weight.

"Now listen to me," he said incisively. "I'm going to turn up the lights and draw the curtains back so that your head and shoulders can be seen from the street. Your detective pals will be in sight somewhere and they'll be pleased to see you. I shall be behind the door and don't forget I'll plug you good if you play foxy. You've got to shake your head to them—see? Convey to them that everything isn't quite ready. You know how to do it. Lean a bit forward as though you were talking to somebody they can't see. It's up to you to keep 'em stalled off for a quarter of an hour."

THE MAELSTROM

He slipped the curtains back and retreated to the doorway, out of the direct line of sight of anyone in the street. Cincinnati cast a casual glance out on the pavement and made a motion with his head as Ling had directed.

He had a vision of Weir Menzies posed precariously on the iron railings four feet away. There was a smashing of glass as the detective leapt and the " con " man heard a vehement oath from Ling, followed by two sharp reports in quick succession.

Menzies tore furiously through one of the broken panes at the window fastenings. Presently he flung up the sash and half leapt, half tumbled within. Congreve stayed without long enough to put a whistle to his lips in swift summons and appeal and then followed his chief.

Cincinnati Red had fainted with a bullet wound in his shoulder.

CHAPTER XVII

THE chief inspector hurled himself blindly across the room. When a man is shooting at short range it is advisable to get at him as quickly as possible. But Ling had no intention of waiting. His plans had miscarried somehow—it was of no immediate importance how. The chief thing was to get away.

He took the stairs three steps at a time and flung up the landing window and cocked one leg through. The back of the house looked sheer on to a builder's yard twenty feet below. He poised himself, swore as he found that a portion of his clothing had become entangled in a nail in the window and turned momentarily. Menzies saw his silhouette outlined against the window for a second and the pistol flamed again.

"The back door, Royal," he roared as he apprehended the pursued man's purpose. "Get to the back door."

Then Ling leapt. It was a desperate feat in the darkness, but the crook's luck held. He fell heavily on his feet and hands, straightened himself and waved a hand lightly in the direction of the window. "Sorry I can't stop," he cried. "Give my love to Cincinnati," and disappeared at a dog trot behind piles of bricks and stacks of drain pipes.

Weir Menzies drew a long breath. There were pas-

THE MAELSTROM

sages in the comminatory service which occurred to him as doing justice to the occasion, but he maintained an eloquent silence. Words were too feeble. He could hear Royal striking matches and muttering softly to himself, and the sound made him feel better. He descended slowly.

"All right," he said as he met his breathless subordinate. "I know. There isn't any back way, of course. You can't think of these things when you're in a hurry. The tradesmen's entrance is in the basement in front. He wouldn't have risked his neck had there been any other way."

"He got away, then?" said the sergeant. Menzies remembered that he always had considered one of Congreve's shortcomings a lack of tact. He answered shortly:

"Jumped six or seven yards. Don't look at me like that. If I'd been a lightweight I might have followed him, but I'm getting too old for such foolishness. Who's that at the door?"

"I blew my whistle, sir; I expect it's the uniform men. He can't have got far. We might run a cordon round the neighbourhood."

"Oh, talk sense," retorted Menzies sharply. "He may be a couple of miles away before we can get the men. Hello, what's this?"

He held up his left hand. It was dripping with blood. He walked closer to the light and examined it with dispassionate curiosity. "That's funny," he commented. "I must have got a rap across the knuckles with a bullet." He wrapped his handkerchief around the injured hand. "Go and open the door or those fools'll have it down. I'm going to have a talk with Cincinnati."

The peril of capture in which Ling had been placed had not been due entirely to luck. His fertile resources had conceived a plan for a strategic retreat and was intended to combine business with pleasure—business in that Cincinnati was to keep the attention of the detectives, while allowing him comparatively ample time, to confound the active pursuit and pleasure so far that he had turned the tool of the police against themselves.

There was only one flaw in this scheme and that flaw had all but proved fatal—the supposition that the detectives would have implicit confidence in the good faith of the "con" man. To one unprejudiced or not tensely strung up by an emergency it might have seemed an unlikely hypothesis. Weir Menzies might use a crook, but he never made the mistake of trusting one.

A doubt had crept into Menzies' mind at the very moment he arrived at the Petit Savoy and observed that Hallett was no longer with the "con" man. How nearly he had been to acting then in spite of Cincinnati's dictated note no one but Royal knew. Against his instincts he had waited, but he had made up his mind to afford little rope to Ling. So it was that he had wasted no time when they had entered the house. The latter part of Ling's stage management had been entirely futile. For once in a while the chief inspector let intuition carry him on.

Able now for the first time to see Cincinnati's predicament, he gave a grave nod of comprehension. Some of the methods which Ling had employed became clear to him. He cut the cords and slit away the sodden dress coat at the shoulder. As deftly and gently as a woman he examined it.

"A clean flesh wound," he murmured. "Nothing much to hurt there. An inch or two lower and there would have been no need to hunt for evidence to hang Ling."

Royal had admitted a uniformed sergeant. "I haven't troubled about the cordon, sir. It seems that a builder's yard runs into a street backing on this. I have sent a couple of men round there."

"Right you are. It might as well be done as a matter of form. They'll not see anything of Ling, though. He'd got this all cut and dried and if we'd been a little later getting in we'd not have had a ghost of a notion which way he'd gone at all. If you've got a spare man out there, sergeant, you might send for a doctor. This chap's caught it."

Cincinnati Red opened his eyes and smiled uncer-

THE MAELSTROM

tainly. "Thought Ling was a better shot," he murmured.

"Hello, you've come round, have you?" asked Menzies. "Sorry for you, Cincinnati. How he came to miss me at that distance is more than I can fathom. I'm big enough."

The "con" man's smile broadened. "Say, you don't know Ling, do you? He wasn't shooting at you; he meant it for me, all right." He winced with pain as he moved slightly. "He always pays his scores, does Ling. I guess I'll have something to say next time we meet. If your people hadn't taken my gun away!—— He had me covered from the moment he saw me."

"I suspected that," said Menzies. "How'd you slip Mr. Hallett?"

"Me? Slip Hallett?" repeated Cincinnati.

"That's what I said."

"He slipped me, you mean," retorted the other querulously. "That's how it was that the whole thing started. There was a girl with Ling. Hallett knew her and carted her away through a side-door just before you came in. I thought it was part of the programme."

Menzies lifted his hat and scratched his hair with the brim the while he regarded Cincinnati with a steady stare. Jimmie Hallett had spoilt things again. There was some excuse for the bitterness with which his thoughts dwelt on that young man, who seemed to have the faculty of making himself a continual stumbling block to the investigation. Menzies had something of a taste for romance—in fiction. He even had no objection to it in real life as a general rule. But he hated it when it became entangled in his business, as it often did. One can as little be certain of what a woman will do as of what a man infatuated with a woman will do.

The expression of chagrin on the chief inspector's face faded as quickly as it had arisen. "Well, not exactly," he said with nonchalance. "He didn't do quite what I wanted him to. Still, never mind. Here's something else I wanted to ask you." He pulled a photograph from his pocket—the inevitable official full and side face. "Do you recognize this man?"

Cincinnati surveyed the photograph. "Sure," he answered. "That's 'Dago Sam' that I told you about—he's in Ling's lot."

"Thanks." The detective put the photograph back in his pocket. "I won't worry you any more now. I'll leave you to look after things here a bit, Royal. I've got several things I want to do and I mean to have a night's rest for once."

Yet, in spite of his intentions it was well after midnight before he sought the repose afforded by Magersfontein Road, Upper Tooting. His way lay first to the residence of a well-known coroner who lived in so inaccessible a portion of North London that even a taxi driver had difficulty in locating his residence. Mr. Fynne-Racton was a white haired, ruddy cheeked, little man whose calling in no way corresponded with his appearance. Although his name was well known to the general public his chief capacities were known most fully in a more select circle—the Microscopical Society.

He peered over his spectacles at the tiny fragment of cloth and the single thread which Weir Menzies took from an envelope. "Certainly, certainly, Mr. Menzies," he said. "I'll do my best and let you know. I wish you'd have come to me earlier. Of course I can guess that these things are concerned in the case we're all talking about. I won't ask questions, though—eh?"

"I might want you as an expert witness," explained the detective.

"And I might be asked if you gave me any suggestion," said Fynne-Racton. "Yes, yes, I understand. I'll do my best, Mr. Menzies. I hope it will be satisfactory. Good-night, good-night."

Menzies spent half an hour and a little longer at Scotland Yard and so home to bed and slumbers that did credit to his nerves. At breakfast the next morning one result of his labours stared him in the face as he opened his favourite morning paper. A double column portrait of "William Smith" appeared on the splash page and big letters in the heading propounded the query:

THE MAELSTROM

"DO YOU KNOW THIS MAN? IF SO, TELL THE POLICE.

"The above is a photograph of the mysterious prisoner now under arrest for a murderous attempt on the life of Mr. James Hallett, who, it will be remembered, is one of the chief witnesses in the case of the murder of Mr. Greye-Stratton. He refuses to give any account of himself and the police are anxious to trace his antecedents so that the full facts, whether for or against him, may be brought out when he is tried."

Menzies could be disingenuous when he liked. Though even the omniscient reporter did not know it, he had no longer much doubt on the subject of William Smith, or "Dago Sam," as he preferred to think of him. The hint given by the "con" man, even if later questions failed to amplify it, would probably prove sufficient to dig out all the personal history that was wanted. Nevertheless there was no reason for allowing either Gwennie Lyne or Ling to know how much he knew of their confederate. The apparently earnest search by newspaper might help to blind them as to how far the investigation had progressed.

He threw the paper aside and accompanied by Bruin walked reflectively round the garden with a sharp eye for caterpillars. Ten minutes before his usual time, he put on his hat and coat, flicked away an imaginary spot of dust from his boots, kissed his wife, and caught the city-bound car.

CHAPTER XVIII

HALLETT had not stopped to consider any complications that might arise when he had rushed Peggy Greye-Stratton from the restaurant. Even had he done so, his action would have been the same. In a flash he had realised how the black cloud of suspicion already formed against her by Menzies would be increased should she be found in amicable association with Ling. Even he himself held doubts,—doubts which no reasoning could have stifled but which he ignored until there should be more time to resolve them.

She obeyed him without question. He hustled her into a taxi-cab and gave an order to the driver. He sat by her side, his heart pumping hard. Outwardly, though, he showed little indication of emotion. "A close thing that," he commented coolly.

She was trembling violently. Her face was half turned towards him. "You said the police—the detectives were there; why? What are they going to do? How do they know?" A soft gloved hand lay on his knee where she had placed it unconsciously in her eagerness. He noticed that it was trembling. "I am quite calm," she insisted, although her bearing gave the lie to her words. "You must tell me."

"I am afraid," he spoke gently, though his heart was aflame, " that your friend will be arrested."

THE MAELSTROM

"Oh!" She dropped back against the soft cushions, her fists clenched, her face as hard as stone. Then suddenly she awoke to fierce life. "They mustn't. I must go back, Mr. Hallett. Stop the cab. Why didn't I think at first. I must warn him. Let me alone. If you are a gentleman you will do as I say."

She was striving to open the door and he had to use force to pull her back to her seat. "Sit still," he said. "You can do no good now. It is too late. You have got to think of yourself. If you go back you will be arrested. Will that improve matters?"

A fit of shivering shook her and she covered her face with her hands. Jimmie watched her sombrely. To him there was only one explanation of her agitation—fear for the man who was her husband. In a little while the fit passed.

"I suppose you are right," she said colourlessly. "But"—her voice grew tense again—"you don't know what it means to me. You *can't* know."

"That's all right," he said soothingly. "I can guess. We will talk over all that later. Nothing can be done until you are more yourself. If—if"—he suddenly became diffident—"if money can do anything to save him you must call on me. A loan, you know," he ended tamely.

He saw the blue eyes fixed keenly on him with a curious expression that was hard to analyse. "You think that that man Ling—is a murderer—that I want

THE MAELSTROM

to save him," she said breathlessly. And then, without warning, she broke into laughter—laughter that was akin to hysterics.

It was then that Jimmie Hallett did a thing which in the ordinary way he would have deemed impossible. He stood up, took her by the shoulders, and shook her roughly.

"Stop that. Stop it at once," he commanded harshly.

He had never had occasion to deal with a woman in hysterics before and the treatment was instinctive. He was relieved to find it effective. The girl quieted after one or two convulsive sobs. "I'm—sorry," she gasped. "I am better now. Where are we going?"

"I told the man to drive to the Monument. I didn't know where you might like to go and the important thing was to get away. One moment." He pushed his head out of the window. "Which is the nearest main-line depot to the Monument?" he asked.

The man slowed up to answer the question. "Depot, sir?" he repeated, puzzled. "Oh, you mean station. You'll want London Bridge."

"That will do." He dropped back to his seat. "It will be safer if we go a little way up the line and then return," he exclaimed. "They might try to trace you through the cabman."

She made a weary gesture of assent, and the rest of the journey was accomplished in silence. A few rapid

THE MAELSTROM

enquiries established that a train was about to start for Sevenoaks, and chancing the possibility of a return connection, Jimmie took two first-class singles. His suggestion of a train journey was not entirely prompted by the wish to blind the trail. That would have been as satisfactorily achieved merely by entering a station. He wanted to get at the bottom of the mystery surrounding the girl, and though he was no admirer of the compartment system of British railways, he recognised the advantages that an empty compartment would afford for a confidential interview.

The girl had rapidly regained her self-possession and her abstraction vanished as the train started. She flashed a half smile on him. "You will think me very foolish to have given way like this, Mr. Hallett. It's been good of you to take such trouble to serve a comparative stranger. I can't thank you properly."

"There's nothing to thank me for. I acted from purely selfish motives. I wanted to satisfy my curiosity—you remember I have only half your story."

She met his eyes steadily. There was still only the faintest touch of colour in her cheeks. She had taken off her gloves and was mechanically twisting them in her lap. He leaned forward and possessed himself of one of her hands. She tore it sharply away and a gush of crimson swept over her face.

THE MAELSTROM

"You mustn't do that," she said hastily.

"I beg your pardon," he muttered. "I forgot. You are married."

The crimson in her cheeks deepened and she took a long breath. Her blue eyes took on a new alertness. He had half expected, half hoped that she would deny it. Even the marriage certificate had not convinced him entirely, and her being with Ling that night had scarcely affected his hope. Yet he was a man of more than ordinary acuteness and common sense. He was ready to believe that there had been some incredible mistake.

"I am married," she repeated. "And you know. How did you learn?" He could hear her breath catch as she waited for his reply.

"I have seen the marriage certificate," he answered simply.

"And the police," her words came incisively, "they know?"

He nodded. "It was through them I learnt."

A revulsion of feeling was coming to him. Somehow her fresh manner had broken the spell. There was something of calculation about it—of the fencer standing with weapon poised for offence or defence. Hithertofore he had viewed her through a mist—content to accept what she had told him as the truth, and with faith that the inexplicable things would in time be made clear and her innocence apparent. He had brushed aside the suspicions of Menzies as the natural tendency of the police officer to put the worst construction on everything.

Now he began to wonder if after all Menzies had been right. Was she merely a cunning adventuress who had all along deluded him and laughed at his folly behind his back with her criminal confederates. Looking at it coolly, he told himself, he could see a score of reasons why it should be so. A couple of deep lines bit into his forehead. He had helped her escape and her first words had shown her solicitude for Ling. Afterwards she had tried to dismiss the impression she had created or erected by an assumption of the mysterious. Quite possibly her whole intention since they met in the police station had been to use him as a stalking-horse.

He had been gazing unseeingly straight in front of him. A light touch recalled his wandering thoughts. "What are the police doing?" she asked. "You have not told me how they knew that Ling and I would be there."

His face hardened. She was taking it for granted that she could pump him. "That is their secret," he answered bluntly, "as much theirs as your secrets are yours."

"I—I'm sorry," she stammered timidly. "You think I am taking advantage."

"I think, miss"—he corrected himself—"*Mrs.*

Ling, that there are several matters you should answer yourself before putting questions to me."

She winced at the stress he laid on the name and drew herself together. "I am to suppose that you distrust me," she said haughtily.

"That's a quaint way of putting it. Exactly what reason is there that I should trust you?" He spoke brutally. He felt the occasion was not one for delicacy of language. "You have told me a story that I then believed to be true—a story of devotion to a scalywag brother. You said nothing about a greater motive for loyalty to your gang—your marriage to one of the most notorious criminals in the world. I shall see something to laugh at in the way I've been strung—sometime."

Her lips were parted and her breast was heaving. Undeniably pretty she was with her flushed face and her eyes lighted till they looked like blue flame. There was neither shame nor contrition within their depths. "Why did you help me to-night, then?" she asked.

"Because——" He wavered. "Oh, because I was a fool, I suppose. I thought there might be some explanation. I see now"—he made a gesture with his hand—"there can't be. You vanished as soon as Scotland Yard got a hot scent. You were afraid I might get dangerous and you played on me with a note to get me into the hands of your pals. I fell for it all right, all right."

THE MAELSTROM

She stared at him dumbly. "You got my note, then?" she said after a pause.

He laughed shortly. "Yes, I got it all right. No mistake about that. And Gwennie Lyne got me."

She was leaning forward with her elbows on her knees, troubled thought in her face. "Gwennie Lyne? But you never came. And I don't know Gwennie Lyne. What address did you go to?"

"The address you gave—140 Ludford Road, Brixton."

"That wasn't it." She passed her hand over her brow. "There's been some trickery I don't understand. It was quite another place. I wanted a friend. You didn't come. . . . I thought—oh, I didn't blame you. There was no reason why you should run any risks to help me. . ."

He watched her with obvious disbelief.

"You think I'm lying," she said with another change of manner. "Very well. You shall see and learn for yourself. I will prove to you that I am not lying—that I have not tricked you. You can keep your own counsel. All I ask is that you will not betray mine."

"You may rely on me," he said icily.

The train ran into Sevenoaks and they alighted. There was a return train within a quarter of an hour and this they caught. Both were grimly silent on the return journey and for the most part Jimmie kept his eyes resolutely fixed on the blank blackness of the win-

THE MAELSTROM

dow. Once he surprised her watching him with an air of wistfulness. "A consummate actress," he thought and shifted his gaze again to the window. To question her would be only to invite another series of lies.

At London Bridge she took command, piloting him to the Bank and stopping a motor bus with an imperative wave of the hand. They ran through into the gloomy heart of the East End. "This is Shadwell," she said. "We get off here."

It was hard to reconcile the dainty figure in the neat grey costume with the slums and squalor into which they entered. Through narrow, desolate streets she led him, past here and there a drunken man or a riotous group racing from one public-house to another. At last she paused and tapped with her bare knuckles on the unpainted door of a tumble-down house. He was not without courage, but he hesitated.

"Are you going in there?"

"Yes. Are you afraid?" she taunted.

"I am," he admitted. "I may tell you I am armed."

Her lips curled. He got a vague glimpse of a slatternly old woman with curious eyes staring at them, and then the girl, without stopping to see whether he would follow, led the way within. He followed, mentally calling himself a fool. The old woman closed the door and they were left in darkness.

"Take my hand," she said, "I know the way. The fourth stair up is broken."

THE MAELSTROM

The hand he groped for and found was ice cold. He dragged his pistol out of his pocket and held it ready for instant use. There was going to be no repetition of the Gwennie Lyne trick if he could help it. At the first sign of treachery he was determined to shoot. He heard the creak of a door on rusty hinges as she pushed it back and released his hand from hers with a sudden jerk.

A thin light filtered out and he beheld a wretchedly furnished room with something lying on a mattress in the farther corner. He advanced cautiously, weapon ready. She pushed the door to and his pistol dropped as he saw the haggard, unshaven face of the sleeping man on the mattress. A man who turned restlessly at their entrance.

She pointed to the corner. "There you are, Mr. Hallett. That's my brother, James Errol. You have his life in your hands if you want to fetch the police."

CHAPTER XIX

SHE faced him by the thin light of the cheap oil lamp, her head defiantly tilted. He remained dumb, the pistol dangling by his side till he became conscious of the incongruity and replaced it in his pocket. The sudden spectacle of the sick man lying there in that miserable hovel had shorn him for the moment of the power of consecutive thought.

She lifted the lamp to examine the sleeping man and, replacing it on the table, readjusted a pillow with tender fingers. She rose and pushed forward a rickety chair. He complied with the unspoken invitation

"He is a fugitive from justice." She spoke softly lest the sleeper be disturbed. "Whatever he is, scoundrel though you think him, can I do less? But for me he would have been helpless. Would you have me desert him? Do you think"—she made a gesture of disgust—"that I like living in this place—these two sordid rooms which are the only place in London I could hide him in? Why, I daren't even have a doctor for fear of betrayal. And you thought that I was in league with the people who brought him to this. Well I am in league. They know where he is and a single word would bring the police down here."

The fire in her low tone challenged him to still condemn her. Once before he had reasoned out a theory of her attitude—a theory that had partly been broken down by the open scepticism of Menzies until the culminating point had been reached when he found her dining with Ling. At first the apparent significance of that had been lost, but it had been borne upon him with ever-increasing force that it was evidence that the letter luring him to Gwennie Lyne's house was no forgery but deliberately written by her. Now again he had to go back to the old line of reasoning. He wondered that he had permitted anything to throw him off it. Why, it was plain to the most dense intellect. Who so likely to pay off the old score of hatred of his father by a bullet than this mean, reckless waster, Errol.

"It was he—who killed Mr. Greye-Stratton?" he whispered hoarsely.

Her reply was inaudible. But the drawn face, the twitching hands left it in no doubt.

Without warning the man on the pallet raised himself on one elbow, his features ghastly in the dim light.

"Who says I killed him?" he gasped in a cracked voice "It's a lie—a lie, I tell you. Who's that you've got there, Peggy? Damn this light. I can't see. Tell him it's a lie—an infernal lie. I never laid a finger on the old man—old man—old man—old devil!" He gasped out the last word with shrill vindictiveness and fell back breathless.

She hurriedly lifted a small bottle from the mantelpiece, poured a little of the contents into a glass, and supported her brother's head while he drank, talking soothingly to him the while. In a little while his regular breathing told that he was asleep.

"I think you had better go now," she said brokenly. "I don't know why I should have brought you here— why it should matter to me what you think. You have seen and you are at liberty to believe what you like."

"Don't let us talk nonsense," he said briskly. "I begin to see that I have acted like a blackguard, but I can't leave you like this." He rose, crossed over to her, and laid a hand on her shoulder. "You have trusted me with the most important thing. Now you must trust me fully. You need a friend and whether you like it or not I am going to see this through. Where's the other room you spoke of? Let's go in there and talk."

With a glance at her brother she lit a candle and led him to the adjoining room, as poorly furnished as the other. "I can't offer you even a cup of tea, Mr. Hallett," she said with a feeble attempt at cheerfulness. "There is no gas and the fires are out."

"I don't mind defects in hospitality," he said. "They can be remedied some other time. Now tell me how it all came about and we'll see what's to be done."

She paused as though to put her thoughts into form. "You wondered why I never told you I was married," she said wearily. "It is true, all that you know. I

THE MAELSTROM

am married to that man"—a shudder swept her slim frame—"Ling. If there is any living thing that I detest, hate, and despise it is he. I want you to believe it, Mr. Hallett, when I say that I am his wife only in name. Never! Never!" he could see her face glow with her vehemence in the candle light—"shall I be anything more. He was a friend of my brother's—he had a hold on him, and to save him I consented to a marriage. It was a marriage of form and we separated at the registry office. Not even for my brother could I do more."

"This was before the death of your father?"

"Yes."

"Then it was Ling who knew he had committed forgery? It was he who held the threat of exposure over your head. The price you paid was—marriage?"

"That was part of the price. I thought it would silence him to have me bear the same name as himself. It was he who came to my flat the night of the murder with the forged cheques in his hand and demanded the full price of his silence—that I should take my place as his wife."

Jimmie bit his lip. He promised himself there should be a reckoning if ever he ran across Ling again.

"Then the murder took place. It was not difficult for me to guess what had happened when I read of it and I spent a terrible hour. I knew that the detectives

THE MAELSTROM

would soon learn enough to put them on the track and that at any moment they might seek me out. So I went to them, partly because I was anxious to see what they knew, partly because I knew suspicion might be aroused if I seemed to avoid them. You know more or less what happened. Then I was brought up for you to indentify me and I confess I had an anxious few minutes while you were walking up and down that line of women. I knew you had recognised me and when you denied it to the officers I could—I could have done anything for you.

"I hadn't a single friend in whom I could confide and then you appeared. I told you more—much more than I intended to and when you urged me to give the police full details I was half tempted to comply. But it seemed too great a risk to take. If there was any doubt —if there had seemed any doubt about my brother.—— How could I? To have told the police would have been to betray him.

"I realised how desperate things were when I knew I was being shadowed and you stopped the detectives. I hurried back to my flat and outside in the street I met Ling. I had neither the chance nor the desire to avoid him. 'I have been running great risks to see you,' he said. 'You must come with me at once. Your brother is hurt.'

"I distrusted him and my suspicion must have shown itself. He let me see plainly that he knew the truth,

THE MAELSTROM

and he added that my brother was lying injured at a house in the East End. 'He is nothing to me,' he added. 'He can die there like a dog in a kennel or the police can patch him up for another dog's death. There is the address.' He pushed a scrap of paper into my hand and went away without another word.

"If he had offered to accompany me I fear I should not have come. He must have known that. He was astute enough to understand that once I came here he could see me whenever he wanted. I found my brother as you have seen him. He was suffering from a knife thrust in the ribs which he told me was due to an accident. He was in great pain and I did not question him too much. Someone had bandaged it up, and the old woman below—the landlady of this house—was watching him. He had been brought here by two other men, she said. She did not know anything about him, how he had been injured nor who the people were who brought him. They had taken the two rooms and told her a lady would come to look after him. She wasn't one to ask questions or to pry into other folks' business as long as they paid their rent regularly. You know the kind of thing. It was then I wrote the note to you and gave it to her with some money to have sent to you."

"The old Jezebel," said Jimmie. "She must have made it over to Ling, or Gwennie Lyne, and they had the address altered."

THE MAELSTROM

"Well, you never came. I saw to my brother as well as I could, draining on my memory of some red cross classes I once attended. I think I was near going mad at night with my impotence, and the loneliness, and the thought of his peril. At about nine o'clock Ling came. He entered the room without knock or ceremony and smoking a cigar. He laughed when he saw how terrified I was. 'All right,' he said. 'I'm not going to hurt a hair of your head. You ought to be grateful to me, young lady, for all the trouble I've been taking. Still it's a family affair and I couldn't do less, could I?' He grinned at me hatefully and I don't know what I answered. 'You're a little bit off colour to-night,' he went on. 'I don't wonder. You haven't been used to this sort of thing. It would be wise to be civil, though.'

"He left me in no doubt as to the meaning of his hint and I constrained myself to a formal politeness. 'I'll not worry you any further to-night,' he said, 'but we've got to look our positions in the face. Now by to-morrow you'll probably be glad of a change. I'll come for you at seven o'clock and we'll go and have a dinner somewhere and talk things out sensibly. Mrs. Buttle here will look after your brother for an hour or two.'

"I was in his power, and of course there was no question of refusing. I had to make every sacrifice but the last one. To-night he called and we went to the place where you met us. I don't know how long we had been there, but we had practically finished dinner. He would talk of nothing but indifferent subjects, but there was something on his mind I felt sure 'Pleasure first,' he said when I tried to pin him down. 'We'll leave business till we have eaten.'

"Then when you came in I was bewildered. You rushed me off my feet, and not till we were in the cab did I realise what the arrest of Ling would mean. He wouldn't hesitate for a moment to betray my brother if he learned he is himself suspected. If Mr. Menzies has arrested Ling he will probably know all by this time." She glanced apprehensively towards the door, as though she feared the immediate entrance of the police. "Now I have told you everything, Mr. Hallett. Can I ask you now what—what——"

He understood her hesitation to frame the question as he understood now her eagerness to extract information from him in the train. But there was still something inexplicable on the face of her story. No reason, no motive other than that of a sort of blackmail had been given for Ling's actions. The personality of Ling as he understood it was entirely alien to any unselfish action. So far as her story had gone the man had committed no crime—no legal crime—that would bring him within the law. Why then the attempt on his life by William Smith, why the attempt to make him a prisoner by Gwennie Lyne, why the apparent importance which Menzies attached to the arrest of Ling?

He explained what had happened so far as he knew it, and little puzzled wrinkles appeared in her white forehead. "Now Ling isn't an altruist," he ended, "any more than Menzies is a fool. The gang has not been butting into this game merely to save your brother. And Menzies isn't red hot after them for no reason at all. If the case were as you think it would be simple enough. The hue and cry would be all after him." He made a motion of his hand towards the other room.

"Ah!" She looked at him thoughtfully and then walked slowly up and down the narrow confines of the apartment. "It's no good," she exclaimed at last.

"It may be as you say, but it's all too complex for me. Even if someone else is bound up with this crime, my brother's danger remains the same. That is all that concerns me."

Hallett found something to admire in the singleness of purpose that actuated the girl, even though it was to shield a man who was certainly a scoundrel and, in all probability, a murderer. "There is yourself to be considered," he remonstrated. "You are in deep waters."

"I shall find a way out." Her tone belied the confidence of her words.

THE MAELSTROM

He scratched his chin. "The first thing to do is to get your brother away from here—somewhere where these crooks cannot get at him."

She shook her head. "That is out of the question. It might kill him to be moved. Besides, there is Mrs. Buttle. She would tell Ling and he would find me somehow."

"Then there is only one other thing. This is no place for you. You had better get decent lodgings somewhere and I will stay here. You can rely I will do everything possible for your brother."

Again she shook her head. "That is quite out of the question, though I am grateful for the offer. The only chance of safety is for me to remain here."

He lost patience "Hang it all," he cried. "You can't. This house—this neighbourhood—why how can a child like you stay here alone? If you won't allow me to take your place I must get rooms in the neighbourhood."

"I thank you very much, Mr. Hallett," she said, "but you will see it is impossible. Anything you did would only attract attention to the house. You can see that. I promise you, if you like, that should ever I need you I will send for you. It will be a comfort to know that I have at least one honest friend on whom I can rely."

He was still uncertain. "I don't like it," he grumbled. "Anything might happen suddenly. It would take an hour to fetch me even if you had a reliable messenger." Then, as she showed no signs of relenting, "Very well, it shall be as you say. Here"—he took his automatic from his pocket and passed it to her—"you might feel safer if you have this. Do you understand how it works?"

He explained the mechanism to her. She held the weapon rigidly at arm's length. "Like this?" she asked.

"Great Jehosophat, no! That is how they do it on the stage. Take your finger off the trigger. Never put it there till you mean it to go off. And use the second finger, not the first. Point your first finger along the barrel. If you haven't time to take aim, all you have got to do is to point your finger and you will hit whatever you are pointing at. Hold your arm more loosely. That's the idea. Now put it away. I feel better to think you've got it."

She held out her hand to him. "Thank you. And now good-night, Mr. Hallett. I will write you—sometime."

He took her hand and held it. "Do you know that I was just going without asking you the name of this place? I *might* have something to tell you, you know."

She released herself with some confusion. "I will write it down." She scribbled for a second and then passed him the address.

THE MAELSTROM

"A very interesting picture," sneered a voice. "Mr. Hallett, I presume—or Mr. Green, from Mobile?"

The girl gasped. Red-eyed and flushed, with a rent in his jacket, Ling was regarding them from the doorway.

CHAPTER XX

HALLETT's fists clenched. He was poised for a rush when restraining fingers on his sleeve recalled to him that he had not only himself to consider. There might be a satisfaction in thrashing Ling, but it would be too dearly paid for. Moreover, for all they knew, he might not be alone. He was leaning against the doorpost with one hand in his jacket pocket. There was a cigar between his teeth and his lower jaw jutted out. His green eyes, alert and menacing, took in the little by-play that restrained Jimmie. He had evidently expected and been prepared for violence.

Jimmie dropped his hands with a boyish laugh. "My name's Hallett," he said. "We have met before. Mr. Ling, isn't it? This is rather unexpected. I thought some friends of yours had arranged an invitation for you?"

Ling grinned. "They sure did, sonny boy. They held four aces but I scooped the pot with a straight flush. I wondered what your little game was. Now I know." He continued to inflect a meaning into his words that made the blood surge in Jimmie's veins. " I thought you'd be the kind of fool that'd come right on here. You see, Peggy was hardly likely to desert her darling brother and you wouldn't leave her, eh? How's that for Sherlock Holmes? It won't do, though, it **won't** do. I'll have to be seeing a lawyer about this. Lucky I'm an indulgent husband, eh, Peggy?" His voice changed. "You stand right where you are, Hallett. It won't be healthy for you if you take another step like that. I hate violence—especially before ladies."

The other man remained stock-still. He knew what the hand in Ling's pocket was gripping. His mind was actively seeking for a solution of the immediate problem. Ling held the doorway, the only exit from the room, and he recognised perfectly well that this man, whose friends had twice before made attempts to secure his silence, was little likely to let him go again. If he had not made over the gun to Peggy he could have felt on more level terms.

"Sherlock Holmes would have carried it a bit further," he said. "Has it flashed across that limpid intellect of yours that I'd take care not to put my head into the lion's jaws if I'd not taken precautions to keep them propped open. If this place isn't surrounded now it will be in five minutes. Those friends you missed won't be put off a second time."

Ling started. Then his features relaxed and he laughed.

"Good bluff," he said. "You nearly had me stampeded that time. But it's no go. You've sent out no message since you came in and if you'd given it before the splits would have been here by now." He spat on the boarded floor. "Say, Mr. Hallett," he went on with

THE MAELSTROM

the air of a man laying down a tentative business proposal. "I've got you now cold. Suppose we come to terms. I'm willing to overlook the compromising circumstances of your little jaunt with my wife tonight——"

"That's enough," ordered Hallett coldly. "If you insult this lady again, gun or no gun I'll smash your lying tongue down your throat."

"Tut, tut!" The green eyes gleamed amusedly on the young man. "I must be careful. I didn't mean to get your goat. We'll call it off then. What I'm aiming at is this. There's no sense in making things more uncomfortable than we've got to. If you put me to it I've got to see that you keep out of mischief. Give me your word that you'll take the first boat back to New York and never say anything about what you may know and I'll take it. That's fair, and it isn't everyone who would do it."

"You want to get me out of the way?"

"That's so. Stay out of England for a year and keep your mouth shut."

Jimmie stroked his upper lip. "That's very obliging of you, Ling. I feel flattered at your supposition that I should keep my word. I seem to be an embarrassment—though I don't know why."

"You *are* an embarrassment."

"Why?" repeated Jimmie artlessly.

He had one hand behind his back and was signalling

to Peggy. He hoped fervently that she would understand what it meant and pass the pistol. Once he regained that he could close the conversation when he liked.

"Cut it out," retorted Ling. "You don't need telling. I'm making you a fair offer. Will you take it or leave it?"

Hallett's concealed hand waved frantically. Would she never understand? "My dear friend," he said airily. "Can't you see I'm trying to make up my mind. I haven't your faculty of quick decision. My wits move slowly. If you'd only tell me why. You'll forgive me, but I don't quite see where you come in. I could understand why some people should wish me— er—disposed of, but although I dislike your appearance and your ways, there's nothing I could do would hurt you. Why can't you live and let live?"

Ling eyed him doubtfully. "This is funny, isn't it? I'm not going to stay here all night. I've sent for some people who won't be disposed to argue with you. You'd better hurry and make up your mind."

It was evident that the girl would never understand the meaning of that signalling hand. Jimmie shrugged his shoulders and remained in an attitude of thought. A querulous voice came from the outer room.

"Peggy! . . . Gone away again." The voice was like that of a plaintive child except that an unchildlike oath slipped out. "And she calls herself a sister .

leaving me here like this . . . alone with the old man all alone . with the old man. I tell you I didn't—I couldn't. . . . He's a liar. . . . Peggy, come and take him off. . . . Those long fingers— long, lean scraggy fingers. . . He'll strangle me. . . . Blast it, why don't you come and take him off."

The high-pitched voice rang out in shrill alarm. Ling had taken a pace back into the other room, but he was too cautious to take his eyes off Hallett. "It's Errol," he laughed. "Gave me a start for a minute. Make's you feel as if someone's walking over your grave."

"He's delirious," cried Peggy. "I must go to him." She raised her voice. "All right. I'm coming."

"Not by a jugful you don't," said Ling. "He won't hurt for five minutes. I don't allow anyone to get behind me till Mr. Hallett here's made up his mind—not even you, Peggy."

The voice inside moaned and then burst into a series of insane chuckles. "He's going now. . . . He thinks he's going to get away but he won't. It's no good your hiding. . . . I can see you. I'll get you this time."

Through the open door Jimmie could now see him. He had pulled himself off the pallet and, lamp in hand, was advancing stealthily towards Ling, crouching as he moved and still chuckling. Jimmie's hand fell calmly

THE MAELSTROM

on the back of the chair nearest him. Things were coming his way.

The changing shadows caused by the lamp-light told Ling something of what was happening. His head shifted to look over his shoulder for the fraction of a second—just long enough for Jimmie to lift the chair and bring it down with crushing force. Ling crumpled limply and went down.

"Ha, ha!" shrieked Errol. "That's got the old devil. . . . Now we'll burn him we'll make sure this time."

Before either of them could anticipate his purpose he had flung the lamp on the stunned man. There was a smashing of glass and a bolt of flame shot upwards. Peggy Greye-Stratton sprang forward with a horrified cry, but already Jimmie had his coat off and spread over the flames which had begun to lick at Ling's body. Luckily the reservoir of the lamp was of metal and little of the oil had escaped. In a few minutes he had the flames under.

He stood up, breathing hard. The girl was coaxing her brother back to bed and he was still weakly shouting in his delirium. Hallett went to her aid, but he found his help unnecessary. Errol was as weak as a kitten. He lay on his mattress panting.

"I can manage now," she said. "You had better go, Mr. Hallett. He said he had sent for help. Go—go quick."

"I don't know about that. It's impossible to leave you here alone now."

Errol, exhausted, had fallen asleep once more. She came over to Jimmie "It's no worse for me now than it was before. Besides, what can you do. You will be sacrificing yourself for no reason at all." She literally pushed him towards the door. "Please, please," she entreated.

A little thrill of delight passed through him as he recognised that all her alarm was for him. There was reason in her persuasions, too. Any danger that she was in was not likely to be either increased by what had happened or diminished by his further presence. He would only be exposing himself to the needless risk of being cut off by Ling's friends.

"I suppose I'd better," he said reluctantly, "but first I'll have a look at Ling. I didn't hit him as hard as I might, but it would be as well to make sure."

She permitted him to return to examine Ling, and as soon as he had reassured himself that the man was only stunned he contemplated his work with some satisfaction. Here and there the blazing oil had scorched his clothes, but had done no further damage.

"Hurry," said the girl " Oh, do hurry."

"Just one moment." He hastily ran his hands through the unconscious man's pockets. A few papers from the breast pocket he stuffed into his own. In the

THE MAELSTROM

right-hand jacket pocket he found a pistol, which he also took possession of. He stood up.

"There, that's done."

"You are going now?'

"Yes, I'm going." He caught both her hands in his impulsively "If things had been different, Peggy—if—if——"

She released herself, flushing hotly. "You mustn't—you mustn't!" she cried. "Oh, why don't you go."

"Good-bye," he said abruptly and swung out on to the dark stairs. As he fumbled for the latch of the front door it was pushed open from without. He came face to face with a woman on the step. He recognised the slattern who had admitted Peggy and himself. She gave a short ejaculation of surprise and then brushed by him.

He moved thoughtfully out into the open street. Something there was about her that seemed familiar—it might have been the eyes, the walk, or her voice. He had gone a hundred yards when he came to a sudden halt.

"I'd bet a thousand dollars to a cent that that woman's Gwennie Lyne."

The discovery half inclined him to return. The dark figures of two men brushed by him and he walked quickly on, turning as the sound of their feet died away. He moved back till he was opposite the house and watched, irresolute. No sound came from it and he turned away again. It seemed hours before he had got clear of those desolate streets into a main road and encountered the comforting blue uniform of a constable. To him he addressed a question.

"Taxi," repeated the man, studying him with speenlation. "Lord bless your heart. You won't get a taxi here at this time of the night. Where do you want to go?"

His eyes opened wider as Jimmie named his hotel. But he made no comment. "Keep straight on till you get into the city," he said. "Then you might get a cab."

It was three o'clock in the morning, before, wearied in body and mind, he dropped thankfully into bed.

He was still in bed when the detective arrived at his hotel and he sat up to receive him. His chin was jutted out doggedly and there was a wary look in his eye. He regarded the chief inspector, ominous that events which concerned him were afoot but uncertain how much was known.

"Come in, Menzies," he said heartily. "I couldn't stop to see the fun out last night because I met a friend and wanted to get her out of the way of any trouble. How did it go?"

Menzies dropped to rest at the foot of the bed. "I didn't come up here last night," he said solemnly, "because I couldn't trust myself not to break your jaw."

Jimmie's eyebrows shot up in ingenuous astonishment. "So! I didn't know you allowed personal feelings to interfere with your duty. You're a pugnacious brute, Menzies. There's some cigarettes on the table behind you. Help yourself and pass me one. Now"—he sent out a blue ring of smoke—"tell me why you want to smash me."

His attitude was different from what Menzies had expected. There might have been defiance, a blank wall of obstinacy, but this touch of badinage, even though the defiance and obstinacy might still be behind it, was a little more difficult. Menzies' opinion of Hallett went up. He exhibited his bandaged hand.

"This is one reason. Cincinnati Red got another and worse one. I don't know how he is this morning, but if he dies it's you who'll have to be thanked." He had no fear of the "con" man's wound proving fatal, but Jimmie's chaff needed a little quenching.

Hallett's face grew more serious. "Gun-play, eh? I'm sorry to hear that. Still, you bagged your man."

"Bagged hell," said Menzies. "I beg your pardon but even my vicar could forgive me in the circumstances. Of course we didn't. However, I didn't come here to satisfy your curiosity but my own. Where did you leave that woman? Where is she now?"

Hallett lay back in bed and laughed. "I see now," he gasped. "That's quite a natural mistake. You've heard that I took a girl away and you think it was Peggy—Miss Greye-Stratton."

THE MAELSTROM

"Mrs. Ling," corrected the inspector. "I don't think—I know." He menaced the other with his forefinger. "I'm not going to fence with you. Out with it."

Jimmie frowned. "Don't take that tone with me," he warned. "I'm about sick of being bullied. I tell you for your own satisfaction that it was not that lady. It was someone quite different, a friend of mine, who happened to be dining in the restaurant. I took her out because I didn't want her to be there when the trouble arose. Now take that or leave it. I don't care a tinker's curse whether you believe it or not." His hand sought the bell over his head.

"I should leave that bell alone," ordered Menzies curtly. "It won't do to push me too far." Hallett dropped his hand. "You can tell the lady's name, of course, and bring her to prove it?"

"I have said so," said Jimmie coldly.

Something flashed for an instant in Menzies' hand. "Then you're a liar," he cried and his weight crushed the other back on the bed. The detective's left hand was not so badly injured as to be totally useless, and Jimmie, taken by surprise and at a disadvantage, was unable to put up any sort of a fight. In three minutes his arms were round a bedpost and a pair of patent self-adjusting handcuffs encircled his wrists.

It needed the physical tussle to make his equanimity give way. He was angry—very angry, and the crowning indignity of the handcuffs chafed his spirit even more than his wrists. The detective calmly extinguished a smouldering spark that threatened the bedclothes and tossed Jimmie's cigarette away. He might have been a block of wood for all the notice he took of his passion and his protests. He resumed his seat and went on quietly smoking his cigarette with an air of placid satisfaction.

Jimmie realised quickly that his most barbed epithets were passing over the detective's head. The first spasm of wrath passed. He gulped something in his throat. "If you haven't gone mad," he said, his voice vibrating with the effort he made to control himself, "perhaps you'll be gracious enough to explain."

"That's better—much better," said Menzies encouragingly. "You'll soon be polite if you persevere."

"Well"—Hallett choked again. "Tell me, what are you arresting me for?"

"I'm not arresting you, sonnie. Oh, yes, I know. I'm going to act in an even more flagrantly illegal manner. I'll take the risk of being broke. You can't tell me anything about that. You'll have plenty of chance to appeal to your ambassador. Or if you like you can bring me before a police court for assault."

He spoke with a certain bitterness that was not lost upon his hearer. Weir Menzies had spent a lifetime in the service of Scotland Yard and knew exactly what he was risking. He was behaving, as he had said, with

THE MAELSTROM

flagrant illegality that could scarcely be justified even on the suspicions he harboured. He had faced Ling's bullets more cheerfully than this, which, if anything went wrong, would lead to inevitable dismissal from the service.

Jimmie wriggled himself out of bed to a sitting position. "This is a fool's game to play," he protested more mildly. "What do you expect to gain by it, anyway?"

"I don't mind telling you now you're more or less in your senses. By the way, I apologise for calling you a liar. It slipped out. But "—he brought his clenched fist heavily down on the bedclothes—" I warned you what would happen if you stood in my way. You spoilt things last night—I'll do you the credit to suppose that it was without deliberation. Still you were tacitly on your honour and it was treachery to me when you did what you did."

Hallett flushed "Easy, Mr. Menzies. You'd have done the same in my place."

"I wouldn't," denied the other. "I've been fair to you all through and you've done your best to thwart every scheme of mine because——" He checked himself suddenly as he saw the change on Jimmie's face. "Then you insult my common sense now by telling me that this girl was at the Petit Savoy—that it was someone else."

"You don't know all the circumstances," said Hallett.

"No, but I'm going to. I formally ask your permission now to search your clothes. I warn you I intend to do it whether you give me your permission or not."

Hallett hesitated for a moment. "Oh, very well, then," he said at last. "Go on."

CHAPTER XXI

IT is easy to see a mistake after it has been made. Jimmie recognised his with the first chill touch of the handcuffs. He had merely dropped out of his clothes the night before, not troubling to remove or inspect anything. The least he should have done was to have placed the address Peggy had given him in safety.

He raved helplessly. Weir Menzies sat on the end of the bed and waited imperturbably. Jimmie did not pick and choose his words.

"Bad language won't help," said Menzies, once again the stern moralist. "Make up your mind quick; I can't wait here all day."

Hallett suppressed the vitriolic retort that rose to his lips. He was in no position to justify violent language. "Say, this is a joke, isn't it?" he asked.

"I don't joke," retorted the inspector grimly.

"Look here," said Jimmie with inspiration, "you own that you're doing an illegal thing. Now I'll tell you what I'll do. Unfasten these things and run away for five minutes and when you come back you can search all you want to. There'll be ten thousand dollars in it for you too." Ten thousand dollars, he reflected, was a small price to pay for the preservation of the secret he held.

Menzies' ruddy face had taken on a deeper tinge of

crimson. "You're wanting to bribe me," he said thickly.

"That's a nasty word," said Jimmie. "Illegal searchings are not your duty—and how can it be bribery if all I ask you to do is to keep within the limits of your right. Come. I'm a fairly rich man and I'll make it fifteen thousand."

A brawny fist was shaken within an inch or two of his eyes. Menzies had for the moment let himself go and was shaken with anger. "You dirty reptile," he blazed and then suddenly checked himself. "The C. I. D. aren't grafters," he went on more mildly. "If you'd been in London longer you'd have known that. It isn't fair, Mr. Hallett"—he shook his head reprovingly—"it isn't fair."

Jimmie observed him with some astonishment. He did not know the scale of pay of English detectives, but he imagined that fifteen thousand dollars would have removed most scruples. "Don't get in a tear about it," he said. "For a man who plays the game like this"—he glanced at the handcuffs—"I don't see what you've got to complain of if you get insulted. You're not a police officer now, remember. You're a common or garden burglar."

Menzies had resumed his placid equanimity. It was difficult to reconcile the placidity with which he was now enveloped to the resentment that had shaken him a moment before. "I suppose I am," he remarked.

"That is if you won't give me the permission I asked for a while ago."

"I'll see you burn first," retorted Jimmie.

"Then I must go on with it," said Menzies, and quietly began to possess himself of the scattered articles of attire that littered the floor.

He went through the pockets methodically, laying the articles in an orderly heap on a chair one by one as he examined them. Jimmie saw him pause over a scrap of paper on which Peggy had scribbled her address. "Does your friend—the lady who isn't Mrs. Ling—live at Shadwell?" he asked. "That's a bit of a change from Palace Avenue, isn't it? I'll use your telephone a second, if you don't mind."

"Make yourself at home," said Hallett. "Don't mind me."

The detective lifted the receiver. "Give me a line. . . . City 400. Is that the Yard? . . . I want Royal or Congreve if they're there. Yes, Mr. Menzies speaking. Hello, is that you, Congreve? . . . Oh, gone out, is he? Anything fresh, Royal?"

The man at the other end of the wire seemed to Jimmie to be intolerably loquacious. A grin slowly stole over Menzies' set features. "That's darned funny," he commented at last. "So you've got it from two ends. Curiously enough I've just run across the same address here—that's what I rang up about. I'm in Mr. Hallett's rooms at the Palatial. He's very annoyed with me, Royal. . . . Eh? . . . No, they'd better not do anything unless they spot Ling. Keep close observation on anyone in or out. You'd better come on here."

He turned to Hallett and tapped the paper in his hand. "If this is all you're upset about, Mr. Hallett, you needn't blame yourself or me. This address has cropped up at the Yard from two other sources. Some of our men are breathing the salubrious air of Shadwell at this minute. If I hadn't been in a hurry to see you I'd have known it half an hour or more ago. Promise me you'll sit quiet and wait without interference while I finish off and I'll unhook you."

"I don't take back anything I've said," declared Jimmie, "but I'll promise that. I'd like to admire your methods in something more solid than pyjamas and that's a fact. Do you mind if I order breakfast?"

Menzies smiled as he shook his head. You'll not starve if you wait ten minutes till Royal comes. I'm not going to take any chances of you sending a warning, directly or indirectly. Not that it would do any good if you managed to slip anything through. A mouse couldn't get in or out of Levoine Street now."

It was a palpable hit. Hallett had hoped that the entrance of a servant might give him an opportunity to convey something to Peggy. His face fell as the other exploded the plan. He stretched himself as Menzies unlocked the handcuffs.

THE MAELSTROM

"Yes, I guess I can hold out that long. I wish you'd forget your profession sometimes, Menzies. I'd hate to have to suspect a man of evil because he wants his breakfast. Say, if it's not giving away secrets, how did Scotland Yard get on to the address?"

Menzies postponed his rummaging for the moment. "There's no secret about it," he said. "It was only a question of how long a well-dressed girl, obviously of the superior classes, could live in a slum without attracting notice—especially when she's being looked for by the police. A report that she had been located by our Shadwell people was received this morning. Then again—you remember that note she sent calling you over to Brixton?"

"Well!" said Jimmie.

"That was handed over to an expert for more detailed examination than we were able to give it ourselves. Royal hasn't told me anything but the result, though I can guess how it was done. Very few inks are chemically alike. The expert must have applied tests which brought out the fact that certain words in that note had been written in a different ink from the others. You follow me? The inference would be irresistible and a properly skilled photographer would be able to bring out the underlying words. All automatic, Mr. Hallett—we were just bound to find her."

"I suppose you were," said Hallett, absently enveloping himself in a big dressing-gown.

THE MAELSTROM

The chief inspector picked the revolver from a heap of belongings he had abstracted from the young man's pockets and weighed it carelessly in his hand while he scrutinised the young man from under his half-shut eyelids. "I may have been doing you both an injustice," he confessed. "I'll own I can't make out why she wanted you at Shadwell and how it came about that the note got altered by someone—apparently without her knowledge."

"Can't you," said Jimmie indifferently. He began to appreciate the point which was being led up to.

"Now," went on Menzies mildly, "I know you've your own notions as to which side of the fence you'd prefer to be, but it's certain you've got some inside knowledge. You're wise enough to know what will most likely be happening in a few hours. Why not give me the right end of the thing? No one need ever know it came from you and I'll do my best to keep things pleasant. I only want to get at the truth. Nothing can stop that. But you can make it come a bit quicker if you like. Of course I don't believe she's the sort of girl who'd be in it bad."

An involuntary laugh broke from Jimmie, though he was feeling very far from merriment. "Trying a new tack," he said. "Why, I thought you'd loaded the lady up with all the crimes in the calendar. Still, I'm glad to see some glimmerings of common sense and I'll reward you. She's perfectly innocent of anything—

rather the other way about. Now if you go running yourself into trouble don't say I didn't warn you. Because if you do involve her I'll get the biggest lawyer that money can buy to raise particular hell for your benefit."

"Ah?" Menzies caught his breath. "So you fixed the thing last night. She's told you the whole story or you wouldn't be so cocksure. Do you know what the penalty is for an accessory after the fact in a case of murder?"

Watching acutely he caught the slightest change of countenance in the young man. It was gone instantly. "I've half a mind to take you in on that charge and let you try that lawyer for yourself," he pursued.

"And make yourself the laughing-stock of the country," countered the other. "Why, you haven't a shred of evidence that could justify it and you forget I'm an American citizen. You wouldn't hear the eagle scream —nunno."

"You're quite sure about there being no evidence— quite sure?" Jimmie felt an uneasy thrill run down his spine. "I could justify your arrest a whole lot if I wanted to. This, for example, would almost do by itself." He held up the revolver. "You were carrying an automatic yesterday. Now it's a revolver—and a revolver, moreover, with the initials J. E. G.-S. engraved on it—the revolver that used to belong to Mr. Greve-Stratton." He swung it carelessly to and fro by the muzzle.

THE MAELSTROM

Jimmie started. "You don't say?" he exclaimed. "Why, I got it——" He paused.

"You got it from Ling," filled in the detective. "Quite so." He broke it apart and squinted through it. "There's three chambers been recently fired." He looked up enquiringly. "Go on."

There was just the right touch of expectation in his voice and manner as though he took it for granted that Hallett intended to continue his explanation. But Jimmie had no intention of doing so. He had been surprised into half an admission, but he was to be drawn no further. It might be that nothing he could reveal could affect the course of events, but having given his word to Peggy he intended to remain silent. He was scarcely prepared to admit even what the lawyers call common ground.

"You're doing very well by yourself," he commented. "You don't need my help."

There had been little serious intention behind Weir Menzies' threat of arrest. On the face of things, as he had explained, he could have justified the action. Nor would he have hesitated had he believed that any real good would come of it. He would have been as ruthless of Jimmie Hallett's feelings as he was of his own energies if thereby he could have gained a step. Of course Hallett's infatuation—that was Menzies' private word for it—had been a stumbling-block and it would be still advisable to look after him. But to put him under lock and key would be to seal his lips utterly—Menzies had judged his character aright in that—and if treated in another fashion he might yet be useful. Nevertheless, the threat was a bludgeon to be used if necessary.

He put the revolver aside and went on with his inspection. He hesitated over the letters and then, with a muttered apology, opened one. There were four all told and he steadily ploughed through them. "Ling must be very fond of you," he observed with heavy irony. "Not only have you the pistol, but some of his personal letters. Lord!" he burst out, "what game were you playing last night? I'd give a lot to know. You certainly have the knack of dropping into the thick of things."

"Yes, there were some letters," agreed Jimmie coolly. "I haven't had time to read them. Anything of importance in them?"

"There are no addresses," evaded Menzies, "and he doesn't seem to have saved the envelopes, so we can't tell where he received them."

A knock at the door heralded the appearance of Royal, who nodded a genial good morning to Hallett and then glided unobtrusively to a seat. Menzies twisted the letters in his hand with an air of uncertainty.

"I've got two courses open to me," he explained to Hallett. "One, as I said just now, to arrest you. The other is to take your word that you won't attempt to leave your rooms here nor to send any message to anyone until I see you again. In that case I should leave Royal here with you."

"You've got an everlastingly cool nerve," observed Jimmie.

"Hang it, man, what do you expect?" said the other impatiently "The alternative is more than ninety-nine men out of a hundred would offer you."

Jimmie shrugged his shoulders resignedly. He saw Menzies' difficulty—saw also that the chief inspector was determined at any cost to keep him out of the game. Inwardly he writhed at his own impotence. If he could only have got one word to Peggy Greye-Stratton. . . .

Outwardly he was philosophic. "No cell for mine," he said cheerfully. "You've got the drop on me and I've got to do what you say. I will pass my word, though I'd take it kindly if you'd send on what news you can. Do you play piquet, Mr. Royal?"

CHAPTER XXII

UNLESS circumstances dictated haste Weir Menzies was never in a hurry. In essentials he was a business man. He was always ready to seize a fleeting opportunity—but for choice he preferred method and exactitude rather than gambling on luck. There was nothing he could do at Shadwell for the time being that could not be done equally well by the men already on duty there.

The tactics of the moment were quite clear in his mind. Peggy Greye-Stratton, by herself, was of minor importance compared with the possibility of laying Gwennie Lyne and Ling by the heels. The direct route to that objective seemed to lay through her. Moreover —though he would not admit it, even to himself—he felt a certain personal animosity. Both Ling and the woman had contrived to humiliate him professionally. He wanted to locate them—and then

He was perched on a high stool before his tall desk in the chief inspector's room. The dossier of the case lay in front of him—reports, statements, photographs, everything that had been gathered together by the elaborate machinery of the C. I. D.—neatly typed and carefully indexed. Also he had his own Greek notes and several facts not yet incorporated in the dossier.

He rubbed his hand through his scanty hair and chewed at the end of a quill pen. For five minutes he

THE MAELSTROM

allowed his thoughts uninterrupted flow and then there came to him Foyle, spruce and alert with twinkling blue eyes.

"Quite a dust up last night, I hear," he observed.

"Some," agreed Menzies. He got down off his stool, reached for a tobacco jar and filled his pipe. "I was coming in to see you, sir. I'd like to arrange to have fifty men on tap. It's likely I'll want 'em to-night."

Foyle polished his pince-nez. "As close up as that. I heard that you'd got an address. But fifty men! That means a raid. You'll have the newspaper men there."

The superintendent hated unnecessary limelight on the operations of the C. I. D. and he was not blind to the effects of human nature. Among fifty men, however carefully picked, there was sure to be some who had been carefully cultivated by journalists and he knew that a friendly hint would be passed on to Fleet Street before many hours were over.

"I only want them available," explained Menzies. "I don't know that I'll use 'em. We may be able to do things quietly, but if a house-to-house search is necessary and there should be any more gun-play——"

"Right you are. I'll see they're at hand for a call. Now about things in general?"

"I was just thinking it out," said Menzies. "I can't just place things, though I've got more than enough to act on."

THE MAELSTROM

The other removed his glasses. "What you mean," he smiled, "is that you don't want to commit yourself to anything till you're sure."

"That's so," agreed Menzies. "You'll remember when we went over Linstone Terrace Gardens we couldn't find Greye-Stratton's pistol. I came across it this morning. In fact I have it here."

"Hallett?" ejaculated Foyle with a lift of his eyebrows.

"Hallett it is. I've just come from him. I did think he was safe last night. He was out of my sight for less than three minutes—and I'm blest if he wasn't on the warpath on his own again—or rather with the girl. She's got that young man absolutely dazzled. It seems that they met Ling after he dodged me. Now where she's concerned you couldn't make him talk, not if you used a—a "—he wrestled for an illustration—" a can-opener. And he now knows a deuce of a lot, too. If I could draw it out of him I'd have the case pretty complete or I'm a fool. Look here." He ran through the papers on his desk and picked out two. "I picked these papers off him just now." He read:

"'Dear Stewart—I was right pleased to get your letter and shall be glad when you come over again. Teddy is just fine and says he would like to see his dad again. It would be fine if only we could settle down and you didn't have to be sent on those long business journeys any more. As I wrote you last time, the show has gone bust and I am resting. So if you can spare a little money I would be glad of a little cheque, though I hate worrying you, specially when you are so full of business. I wish sometimes you had a regular berth here. Of course, the money would not be so big, but it would be certain and we could all be together. But I won't worry you, old boy. Much love from Teddy and from CHRIS.'"

"A woman," commented Foyle. "You'd better burn up the wires, Menzies."

"That's seen to. This is the other letter: 'The bulls have tumbled to me. Have just dropped one in the cellar along with J. H. and am clearing in case his pals turn up. Am coming straight you know where and am sending this by messenger in case you are out. Come along and see me.'

"There's no signature to that. It doesn't need one. I'm wondering how Hallett got these things and the pistol."

"And I'm wondering," said Foyle, "how you got them from Hallett. Have you arrested him?"

Menzies met his chief's gaze steadily. "No, sir," he said.

A ready smile broke over Foyle's face. It was not always advisable that he, as head of the department, should know exactly the methods by which a result had been obtained. Men with the experience and sagacity of Weir Menzies could be trusted not to endanger the reputation of the C. I. D. He ignored the chief inspector's lack of candour.

"Well, I suppose he'll keep. If the evidence doesn't crop up elsewhere we'll have to see what can be squeezed out of him in the witness box. Don't you wish this was France, Menzies?"

"I never held with French methods, sir. I call a man down and take my chance sometimes, but the third degree isn't what it's cracked up to be. I believe in judicious firmness and mildness."

"I expect that's how you treated Hallett. Never mind that, though. Ling wouldn't have parted with those things willingly. Your young friend must have been fairly successful in handling him. How do you figure it all out generally?"

"Well," Menzies rubbed his chin meditatively. "There's money somewhere, though that's to be expected. They're not folk who'd set out for a coup without a stocking to draw on. They've been spending money pretty freely for boltholes. There was Gwennie Lyne's house at Brixton. Then there's this Bloomsbury place into which Ling carried us last night. I've just been reading the report of some enquiries Royal made. Ling took the whole place furnished a month ago under the name of Ryder. He's never actually stayed there."

He glanced under his heavy eyebrows at the superintendent, who jingled some keys in his pocket, and returned a look of interrogation.

"It's solid, unpretentious, and central," prompted Menzies.

The superintendent gave his keys a final irritable shake. "When it's a jar," he murmured.

"Just the place for a newly married couple to settle down till all the legal formalities in connection with Greye-Stratton's property were settled," went on Menzies.

"Oh! I thought it was a riddle. That's just like Ling. He'd have things cut and dried. Well, why didn't he—or they?"

"That's what I want to ask the lady. Hallett's got a glimmering of the reason, too. Personally I can think of a hundred answers to the question. The only thing is to know which is right."

"Ling," observed the superintendent with apparent irrelevance, "hasn't the record of a man who'll handle tar without gloves. He's always up to now found his tools to do the actual work. Gwennie Lyne's the same breed. That leaves two people to pick from—Errol and Dago Sam. If it came to the choice I'd go nap on Errol."

Menzies smiled sardonically. He had a great deal of

admiration for and loyalty to his chief, but he was human enough to be pleased when he could register a score.

"Then you'd be wrong, sir," he said.

"You think that because Ling had Greye-Stratton's pistol he——"

"Not altogether. There's another little point, though I only came across it yesterday. Did you notice the fireguard in Greye-Stratton's place—I mean in the room where he was found dead?"

"A heavy brass thing, wasn't it?"

"Yes. I was having another look over the place yesterday when I found a thread had been caught in one of the sharp edges. I didn't speak about it because I wasn't sure it had anything to do with the case. It so happened that, in his hurry to get away last night, Ling tore a bit of his coat. I took 'em both along to Fynne-Racton to have a look at under the microscope. He now says definitely that they're exactly similar."

"That's useful, laddie," observed the superintendent. "A nice little bit of evidence to justify his arrest for murder—but you'll have to go further than that for conviction. There's going to be a big fight when this comes on for trial. The pistol doesn't count. You haven't even got Hallett's word that it came from Ling and if you had you can see the line of the defence. It's word against word and you can see what counsel would do with Hallett." He made a gesture as though ad-

THE MAELSTROM

dressing an imaginary jury. "And this man, gentlemen—this American, Hallett. He has sworn that the pistol produced was taken from the prisoner Ling. Ling has denied on oath that he ever saw the weapon before. You'll not need reminding, gentlemen, of the peculiar and extraordinary circumstances under which this man Hallett became associated with the case. He is found in a locked room with the murdered man and he tells a confiding police officer—mark you I am not saying a word against the police—an honest enough detective whose intelligence perhaps runs in narrow channels . . ."

Menzies eyed his chief ruefully. "Thank you, sir," he said drily.

Foyle's eyes twinkled genially. "Well. You know that's what they'll say. It's the obvious line of defence. As for the cloth"—he snapped his fingers—"a common cloth sworn to by a dozen experts as being worn by ninety-nine out of a hundred men. There's heaps of evidence of motive and no doubt you'll be able to get it in, but there's gaps in your other evidence, Menzies, and don't you go forgetting it."

Menzies tapped his pipe on the heel of his boot and grinned. Foyle was indulging in no mere captious criticism. It was not unusual for the weak links in an important investigation to be thus examined when it was on the point of closing up, for the C. I. D. likes to be prepared. The work of the department does not finish with the catching of a criminal. Every shred of relevant evidence has to be drawn up in lucid detail from which the Treasury solicitors prepare a brief for counsel. It does not do to take anything for granted. Menzies could picture, too, the cross-examination of an unwilling Jimmie and the conclusions that might be drawn from it.

"There's the girl, of course," he muttered thoughtfully. "She'd be even better than Hallett in a way. If we didn't have to put her in the dock she might be persuaded to tell what she knows."

"Aren't you forgetting she's Mrs. Ling?" said Foyle. "You can't compel a woman to give evidence against her husband."

"Against her husband—no," said Menzies.

CHAPTER XXIII

THERE was no outward evidence that Levoine Street was under any extraordinary police surveillance. Now and again a blue-coated constable picked his way at the regulation two-and-a-half miles an hour down its sordid length. In the taproom of a dingy public-house a couple of shabby loafers were playing dominoes with a not infrequent casual glance through the open door into the rain-sodden road. There was no public-house at the farther end of the street, but two waterside labourers had secured a " kip " in one of the few lodging-houses in the street and through the dirty windows their gaze also commanded the street.

These were, so to speak, Menzies' advanced posts. Not one of them had ever been stationed in that division of the East End. A divisional detective, of necessity, gets well known to the criminal fraternity of his neighbourhood and as facial disguise is more common in novels than in the ordinary routine of a detective's work, it is easier and safer to employ strangers in a locality where the presence of a local police officer might arouse undesirable speculation or comment.

Not that the divisional detectives were idle. Half-a-dozen or more were wandering with apparent aimlessness about the vicinity, though never by any chance showing in Levoine Street itself. Yet it was scarcely likely that anyone leaving that thoroughfare would escape the notice of this outer fringe of watchers. That was what they were there for.

Twice that day had Mrs. Buttle journeyed into the main street—once to the butcher's, once to a post-office. And each time, curiously enough, one of the waterside labourers or one of the saloon loafers had lounged indifferently in the same direction, dropping back after three or four hundred yards, while the hard-bitten detectives of the H division took up the unobtrusive escort. It was monotonous work. All those taking part in it knew that their vigil might go on for weeks, perhaps for months, and then end without any result.

Meanwhile, Detective-Sergeant Congreve had routed out a colleague in the division and was more actively engaged. Together they walked along the Commercial Road until they reached a corner shop. The lower half of the big plate glass windows had been blackened and staring white letters announced

DR. KARL STEINGURT.
Dispensary. Hours 8 till 10 A.M. 7 till 9 P.M.

The pair pushed their way into the room—bare save for a cupboard and table and a series of hard wooden forms. Women crowded the latter, some with children, some without, and a shrill clatter of tongues died away for the instant as they took stock of the newcomers.

THE MAELSTROM

An anæmic young man busy juggling with bottles and pill boxes nodded abruptly to the vacant end of a bench.

" Y' want the doctor? Sit down there and take your turn." He returned to his dispensing. " That'll be thruppence, Mrs. Isaacs—to be taken as before. Eh? No, you know very well what the rules are. If you ain't got the money you shouldn't have come. Now who's next? Don't you hear the doctor calling? "

Indeed, a querulous guttural voice from the top of the stairs which led out of the dispensary was shouting fiercely and two or three women pushed forward. The anæmic dispenser shrilly demanded quiet—an order of which not the slightest notice was taken. The argument as to precedence threatened to develop to physical violence and Congreve's colleague stepped forward and took hold on the dispenser's thin arm.

" That Dr. Steingurt upstairs? " he demanded.

" Why the blazes don't you go and sit down? " demanded the assistant, feebly wrathful. " He can't see y' all at once, now can he? 'Ere, let go my arm."

" It's Mr. Hugh—a rozzer," said someone, and the tumult stilled. The assistant lost his air of authority as a pricked toy balloon collapses. " Say, you can see the boss is busy. Won't I do? What do you want? "

" You won't do, son," said Hugh. " We're going right up to the doctor now and you'll have to get these ladies to excuse him five minutes."

Congreve meanwhile had pushed himself to the stairs.

THE MAELSTROM

Hugh followed. A dozen steps brought them to the consulting-room and face to face with a swarthy little man in a frock coat and dirty linen. Heavy circular spectacles gave him the appearance of an owl.

"Doctor Steingurt?" asked Congreve. Hugh had softly closed the door behind them.

The doctor glanced at them through his gold-rimmed spectacles. "Vot's the matter with you, eh?" he demanded briskly. "Speak up, now. You see I haf a lot of people waiting and as I only charge sixpence——"

Hugh muttered something below his breath. Congreve cut in. "We're not patients. You'll have to give us a little of your attention without any fee this time, doctor. We're police officers."

"Id is most ungonvenient that you come at this time," protested Steingurt. "I told the goroner"—he waved flabby hands at them—"that I should not gome again. I was legal—oh, I know the law. I am not a jarity. The child would have died anyway and the man which called me didn't haf my fee. Why should I gif up a night's rest for nothing? Dere is the hospital for paupers." He grew more excited. "I tell you I vill not gome to that goroner's court any more. I will see my solicitor. I will not gome."

Both detectives remembered the standing feud between the coroner of the district and Steingurt.

"It is most highly ingonvenient," he repeated, "to

[221]

come in my gonsultation hours and drag me down to that nasty court youst to talk nonsense."

"Steady, doctor," remonstrated Congreve "We've nothing to do with that. You were called out last night—or rather this morning. That's what we want to talk about."

Steingurt blinked behind his spectacles. "I am always being galled out. I will look at my book if you like. Dere iss nothing wrong?"

"We'll know that when you've told us," said Congreve sharply. "You went to Levoine Street. Who did you see? Why were you called?"

"That's so," agreed Steingurt. "It was a little girl—a bad case of diphtheria."

"Really!" The detective's voice was silky. "And how much were you paid to keep your mouth shut?"

The doctor glared at him and suddenly advancing a step shook a fist in his face. Congreve delicately extended the tips of his fingers and touching the other's chest pushed him backwards.

"This is a gonspiracy to insult me," protested Steingurt "I don't believe you are police officers. You had bedder go or I will have you thrown out."

"Was it ten pounds or twenty?" persisted Congreve steadily. "It looks to me as if you knew there was something fishy on or you wouldn't be so unwilling to talk."

"I gannot talk about my patients. It is profes-

THE MAELSTROM

sional eddiquet—you know very well." Steingurt seemed to have lost a little of his confidence. "You've got no right to question me."

"Just you listen to me, doctor" Hugh, big, overbearing, threatening, pushed his way into the dialogue. "We know all about professional etiquette, but we know a lot more about crooks—and those who get mixed up with them. Savvy? We ain't here for lip-trap so don't you try us too far. Suppose we take him along on suspicion—eh, Congreve?"

Hugh was admirably suited for his work in the East End—big, absolutely fearless, direct. He knew exactly when to adopt the customs and language of his surroundings and his peremptory air had its effect.

Steingurt became civil. "If you will sit down, gentlemen, I will tell my assistant we mustn't be disturbed."

"That's sensible," said Congreve.

The doctor gave his orders and returned thoughtfully. "You know this neighbourhood," he said. "I am a busy man—very busy. I gan't enquire into the moral character of everybody who gomes for me, can I? It's a big bractice, gentlemen—one of the biggest in the world. And every night I get waked up. Last night it was an old woman—and she rings and knocks. I was afraid she would have the place down. I told her to go away. 'You're wanted,' she says. 'I'll keep on ringing till I bring you down. I want to talk to you. It will be worth your while.' So I went down and opened the door on the chain.

"'You must gome along with me at once,' she says. 'Don't stand there gibbering like a monkey, but get some clothes on and gome.' She pushed a folded banknote through the door and when I opened id, id was for five pounds. 'There's four more of those flimsies waiting for you,' she says, 'if you hurry up and come and keep your jaw shut.' 'Where to?' I asked. 'Never mind,' she says. 'Are you goming or must I get someone else?'

"So, of gorse, gentlemen, twenty-five pounds is twenty-five pounds. So I went. The woman she said nothing of where we were going, bud I knew the district. She took me along to Levoine Street and let me in to one of the houses with a latch key. 'There's a man fell downstairs and hurt himself,' she says. 'I'm afraid it's concussion.' I wondered what she knew of concussion, but I says nothing and she dakes me upstairs. There was a man there. He'd hurt himself pretty much, but it wasn't concussion, and when I'd bandaged him up I told her he'd be all right if he was allowed to lie still for an hour or two. She says sharply, 'Very well, then, that's all right,' and counts out the other five-pound notes and gives them to me. 'You'll forget you've been here?' she says and I told her I would. 'Not that anyone's likely to ask,' she goes on.

"And then, when she was bringing me down, she says,

THE MAELSTROM

'While you're here there's someone else you might look at,' and she knocked at a door and called out. A young lady answered it—a real young lady—not a girl like you mostly see around here. The old woman says something to her that I couldn't catch and I went in. There was a young man lying on a pallet in a corner. 'What's the madder with him?' I asked. 'God fooling round with a knife or something and hurt himself,' said the old woman. The girl didn't say anything and I could understand I wasn't expected to ask questions. The man was pretty done up with a knife wound and it looked like touch and go with him. There was a fever on him. So I did what I could for him and the old woman volunteered to come and fetch some medicine. There, now, you've got the honest truth, gentlemen."

"Didn't it strike you," said Hugh slowly, "that when you find a man with a knife thrust and another with something like concussion—both *accidents*—that you ought to have told the police? How do you know one of 'em ain't died?"

"It was none of my business," protested Steingurt. "I was paid as a medical attendant, nod as a detective."

"Are you likely to be going back there again?" asked Congreve.

Steingurt shook his head. "Not unless they send for me."

"It was dark when you were called out. Do you

think any of those people would recognise you again?"

The doctor was doubtful.

"Would you recognise any of them? Give us a description."

Although the officers painstakingly took down the descriptions it was plainly useless. The ordinary person is always at a loss in attempting a portrait.

"Well, good-bye, doctor," said Congreve. "We may call again later on."

Outside Congreve hustled his companion along the wet pavement. "Come along," he said, "I want to telephone to Mr. Menzies. I've got an idea."

CHAPTER XXIV

ALTHOUGH his right arm hung limp and the set of his well-cut morning coat was somewhat spoilt by the bulge of the bandages on his shoulder Cincinnati Red looked almost as spruce and debonair as ever. He listened with immobile face to Menzies' expression of sympathy.

"I'm right sorry," the detective was saying. "It was hard luck on you. You didn't guess he was wise to the gag or it might have been different. I'd back you against Ling every time."

A whimsical, humourous smile lighted Cincinnati's features. "I get you," he drawled. "You're handing out a soothing syrup dope. I'm on to those curves. What you giving me?"

"Would you like to have another cut at Ling?"

The "con" man drew his shaggy brows together and observed Menzies narrowly. "Will a duck swim? Wait till my shoulder gets well. If you're driving at some more stool-pigeon business I'm not hankering after it, but I might be tempted—if it sounded good."

"Well," Menzies crossed his knees and passed the cigar box, "we've got Ling located to an extent. You'll be pleased to learn that he found a rough house after he gave us his little show. He got manhandled at a place in Shadwell and they had to have a doctor."

Cincinnati rubbed his hands. "That's all to the

good, chief. Say, I'd like to buy the guy who did it something."

"It was only a knockout," explained Menzies, "and we unluckily did not get on to it till this morning. We believe he got away in the night, but we're not dead sure. Anyway he can't be far from the house we've located and we know there are some other toughs in it. Would you care to call on the house and see who's there? There'll probably be someone who knows you and you'll be all right."

"Yep," said the other crisply. "Likely thing. What chance would I stand walking into a wasps' nest like that? It's no bet. Call it off."

"Why I didn't think there was a yellow streak in you, Cincinnati," said Menzies. "I wouldn't ask you to do it if I thought there was any danger. There'll be plenty of my people on hand, and you're not likely to get into any trouble. Didn't I tell you that Ling had slipped out. I'd go myself or get one of my chaps only it would be better if it wasn't a stranger. I'm asking it as a favour."

The "con" man stroked his moustache in irresolution. He was really bitter about Ling and would cheerfully have contributed any effort that would add to the discomfort or peril of his erstwhile colleague—so long as he ran no avoidable hazard himself. He was under no illusions in regard to Menzies' efforts to persuade him. He knew that the chief inspector had little bias towards

THE MAELSTROM

him—that he regarded him merely as a crook—a crook who happened to be useful and who might be coaxed into helping the law by fulfilling an instinct of revenge. Not that he had any compunction as to paying off old scores that way. It was just the question of risk.

"You'll let me have a gun, of course?" he asked.

Menzies shook his head. To use Cincinnati to achieve a purpose was all very well. But a gun in the hands of a revengeful man backed by the semi-authority of the police was quite a different thing.

"There won't be any need for a gun," he said. "We'll be at hand if there is any trouble—but there won't be any if you handle the job tactfully. Not that I wouldn't let you have a gun if I had my own way, but you know how I'm tied down. Well, shall we consider it settled? I won't forget you acted like a white man, laddie—some other time."

After all, reflected Cincinnati, there was no reason why he shouldn't chance it. It would put him right with the police and very likely, as Menzies said, there would be no fuss. Until his shoulder healed there would be little card-playing at his flat and if he refused the police would probably become unduly attentive to any other enterprise in which he might embark.

"I'm with you," he said.

"Good for you, Cincinnati," exclaimed Menzies. "I guessed you would. I have taken the liberty of having some clothes got ready for you. You can't trail the

THE MAELSTROM

East End in glad rags, you know. If they're not your usual fit so much the better."

He glanced at his watch. It was half-past five. "I'll have those things sent in to you," he went on. "I'll be back in a minute."

He was whistling softly as he passed along the corridor. He paused to tap at Foyle's door and to poke his head inside. "All fixed up, sir," he said. "I'm going to rout out those men you promised me."

As he closed the door a man touched him on the sleeve. He raised his eyebrows in question as he saw a brown-faced, silk-hatted man of medium size in a much worn frock coat. Then recognition came to him. "Why, it's you, Congreve. They've done you well. How's the likeness?"

"It's fair, sir," said Congreve complacently. "In a bad light with anyone who doesn't know Steingurt well I'm likely to pass. Of course, I'm a bigger man, and as I hadn't a photograph I had to explain to Clarkson's people what to do as they went along."

"Makes you feel like a detective hero in a novel, doesn't it?"

"More like amateur theatricals," grinned the other. "I feel like the late lamented Guy Fawkes, and I'm in deadly fear lest my moustache should fall off."

The chief inspector became business-like. "I don't need to tell you, Congreve, that it isn't any private

THE MAELSTROM

theatricals. Start the boys off for me, will you. They can report at Shadwell till they're wanted."

"Very good, sir," said Congreve.

Night had long fallen when Menzies and Cincinnati Red emerged from the underground station at Shadwell and, with coat collars well turned up, struck off briskly through the driving rain in the direction of Levoine Street. They spoke little. The chief inspector paused at last and nodded towards a shambling figure that was hurrying a dozen paces in front of them.

"Keep your eye on that chap," he said. "He'll give you the office when you get to the house. Remember not to make any trouble if you can help it. We just want to know what's doing."

"I get you," muttered Cincinnati—and found that he was addressing nothingness. For a substantial churchwarden Weir Menzies had an astonishing faculty on occasions of obliterating himself.

Yet he was nevertheless keeping a keen vigil on the "con" man. It was as well to be sure and Cincinnati's heart might yet fail him.

He emerged into visibility again under the light of the corner public-house in Levoine Street. The two loafers were still at their everlasting game of dominoes and one turned an incautious look upon him. Menzies was fumbling with his shoelace. He saw the "con" man's guide trip and lurch heavily opposite one of the houses. A moment later Cincinnati was rapping at the door. It opened at last and he stood in colloquy with someone unseen for a while. Then he stepped inside and the door closed.

The chief inspector walked to the private bar and ordered a Scotch and soda, which he drank slowly. Once he looked at his watch and answered absently the barman's comment on the weather. In Magersfontein Road, Upper Tooting, the apathy of one of its prominent horticulturists to weather conditions might have been set down as an affected eccentricity. Something worse might have been thought of a churchwarden who, with bowler hat tilted at the back of his head, stood sipping whisky and soda at the bar of the low class East End public-house. But Menzies had forgotten that he was either a churchwarden or a gardener.

Twice more he looked at his watch and a slight frown bit into his forehead. Never too ready to put implicit confidence in a crook, he was wondering if Cincinnati had put the double cross on him.

There was in point of fact no justification for these doubts. Cincinnati Red was feeling too sore with Ling to dream of playing false with the police. The door had been opened to him by no other than Mrs. Buttle herself, who stood determinedly in the doorway and scrutinised him with a stare in which there was no recognition.

"Well?" she demanded with some asperity and an unnecessary loudness. "What do you want?"

THE MAELSTROM

Cincinnati smiled pleasantly upon her and leaning forward spoke in a low voice. " Is Mr. Ling in? No, no "—he raised a deprecating hand as he saw a denial forming on her lips. " I'm a pal of his. You tell him that Cincinnati Red is here and wants to pass him a word. Say the little trouble last night was all a misunderstanding and I've come to clear it up and put him wise to one or two things."

She appraised him grudgingly for a while. " I don't know nothin' of any Ling," she grumbled loudly. " I'm a honest, 'ard-workin' woman and I ain't no use for blokes what comes talking riddles to me."

She made as if to close the door and for the fraction of a second her face was under the full rays of the street lamp. His foot strayed absently over the lintel. It was part of his profession to be a shrewd judge of faces and in that respect there were few men, even at the Yard itself, who could have taught him anything.

" So it's you, Gwennie," he said quietly. " I might have guessed it. You'd better let me come in."

She dropped her cockney accent instantly and a wry smile showed on her face " Yes, sonny, it's me," she said. " How did you get on to it? "

" Your eyes," he said succinctly. " Can I come in now? "

She laughed. " Say, don't you think you've got a gall? Ling is gunning for you."

Cincinnati went a shade paler. The recollection of

the detective cordon around the neighbourhood, however, gave him confidence. He returned her laugh. "I'm not a piker, Gwennie. A little heart-to-heart talk with Ling or you'll put that all right. I was run right on to it, Gwennie. I couldn't help myself."

"Come right in," she said genially.

He followed her without hesitation and she took him up the creaking stairs into a little unused room bare of furniture. "How did you know where we were?" she demanded. "Did Ling tell you?"

"Sure!" he agreed nonchalantly and instantly he saw the trap into which he had fallen. It was wildly improbable that in the circumstances of their last meeting Ling would have told him anything of this retreat. It was a mistake unpardonable in a man who made his living by his wits, but to try to retrieve it would be even worse.

"I'll go and tell Stewart you're here," she said swiftly. "You won't mind waiting a minute."

He did mind. He minded very much. Gwennie Lyne was altogether too complacent in accepting his visit. He knew that she was certain that he was playing the game of their antagonists and the thought of the police cordon was not quite so comforting. He had learned part of what he had set out to know. She was in the house and the probability was that Ling was also. He was unlikely to get any further chances of making sure and he wished fervently that he could see an opportunity of carrying his information back to Menzies. Did Gwennie know or guess that the place was surrounded? Did she think that this was merely a reconnoitring expedition or a reconnaissance in force? He had been a fool, he reflected, to so weakly fall in with Weir Menzies' suggestion. Of course, the police wouldn't care what happened to him. They were using him as a cat's-paw to test the hot chestnuts before drawing them out of the fire.

He had calculated on the readiness of his wits to extricate himself from any dilemma in which he might find himself placed and now his blunder had exposed him. He could only wait on events. He assented quietly and she left the room.

There ensued a nerve-racking period of waiting. His ears were strained to catch the slightest sound and he could hear movements below. In that room where he could meet anyone who entered face to face he felt comparatively safe. But his imagination played tricks when he contemplated the possibility of creeping downstairs and so into the open street. On the dark staircase or in the gloomy passage Ling might be waiting. His nerve was going and he dared not risk it. The window looked out, as far as he could see in the blackness, on a bleak prospect of tiny back yards, and after a sombre inspection he decided that there was no escape that way.

The house grew unnaturally quiet and his waning

courage began to return to him. There was a possibility, after all, that his former friends had been as badly scared by his arrival as a spy as he was by the knowledge that they had penetrated his purpose. Very likely Gwennie Lyne had left him there while she and her confederate quietly slipped away. If so, they must have already fallen into the hands of the police, and Menzies and his detectives would be in the house at any moment.

He picked a candle off the mantelpiece and opened the door. At once he became aware of a determined and incessant rapping below. Somewhere near him he heard someone stir, and promptly blew out the light and waited with the door an inch or two open. There was a swish of skirts on the landing and he heard light footsteps descend the creaky stairs. Apparently the front door had been very securely fastened since he had arrived, for he heard the withdrawing of many bolts and the rattle of a chain. Then a soft, guttural voice.

"Goot evening, miss. I yoost thought I would come along to see how my patient was brogressing."

CHAPTER XXV

It was not exactly what Cincinnati Red had expected. Nor did he anticipate the low, musical voice that answered. He had assumed that Gwennie Lyne was the only woman in the house and somewhat impatiently he waited for developments.

"Oh, yes. I wasn't expecting you, doctor, but I am glad you called," he heard someone saying. "Will you come up? He is asleep."

He wedged himself against the crack of the door. Who was asleep? Was it Ling? Why should he need a doctor, anyway?

Apart from these problems he had a sense of relief. Even if any designs were contemplated against him they would scarcely be carried out with the doctor in the house. What was to prevent him walking boldly out behind the visitor when he went. He heard the woman and the man pass by him on the landing. Then a splash of light showed that they had entered the room opposite.

He crept gently out and stooped to the keyhole of the room into which they had vanished. Within his line of sight there came a vision of the back of a frock-coated man stooping over someone laying beneath a clutter of bedclothes in the corner. A girl was holding a lamp to light the doctor's examination. Cincinnati

THE MAELSTROM

caught his breath as he saw her features and he remembered her as the girl Hallett had rushed from the Petit Savoy the previous evening.

The doctor stood up. " I will not disturb him now," he said. " He seems fairly comfortable. I will send you some different medicine presently with directions. Remember he is not to be moved on any aggount or I will nod answer for his life. And now for my other patient."

She put down the lamp. Cincinnati raised his head and sniffed gently, suspiciously. " There is no other patient, doctor," she said. " The gentleman you saw last night is gone."

" Gone " The doctor's voice held unmistakable evidence of disappointment. " He is gone? Where is he gone? "

She shook her head. " I don't know. I am only a lodger here. Perhaps Mrs. Buttle—the landlady—could tell you."

A vivid bolt of flame leapt with appalling suddenness up the stairway, illumining the whole place in a blaze of light, and a hoarse cry came from Cincinnati. He pushed the door open and flung himself in on them.

" Petrol! " he cried. " The murdering devils! For God's sake get out of this."

The girl shrank back before the pallet as though to protect the man lying there. Her eyes were fixed in a kind of fascinated terror on the " con " man's face. It was not the fire that terrified her so much as his appearance there. When last they met he had been in association with the police.

"Go away," she shrieked. "You shan't touch him."

"They have set the place ablaze," he repeated. "We are trapped."

The doctor was the only one who seemed unmoved either by the fire or by the "con" man's dramatic appearance. "Don't be a mad fool, Cincinnati," he said quite quietly. "Here, stand aside and let's have a look."

He pushed Cincinnati away and glanced through the open doorway. The smell of burning petrol was wafted upwards and the first burst of flame had given way to clouds of dense smoke through which he could dimly perceive many coloured flames devouring the woodwork of the stairs. The incendiaries had done their work well. The whole bottom floor had been set alight as if by magic and the dry, rotten flooring was blazing like tinder. Although it had only been a matter of a few seconds since Cincinnati Red had raised the first alarm it was already plainly impossible to reach the street by the stairs.

The doctor closed the door quickly and stepped back, removing his spectacles as he did so. "The gov'ner will be annoyed about this," he commented. "It's a good move. They'll have a fine chance to get away in the confusion."

The terror in Peggy Greye-Stratton's eyes deepened.

THE MAELSTROM

"You are not the doctor!" she cried. "Are you—detectives?"

"I am a police officer," admitted the frock-coated man. "My name's Congreve. My friend here is not. But don't you worry, miss. We're not going to hurt you. Here, you, Cincinnati. Come along into the front room. We'll have to get down through the window. Someone in the street will surely have had the gumption to get a ladder. Now don't you go getting frightened, miss. We'll have you out of this in two shakes."

The "con" man and he passed into the front room. Peggy sank into a chair and buried her face in her arms. Realisation of the peril she was in from the fire was sunk in the more insistent dread for her brother which the unexpected advent of Cincinnati Red and the calm confession of identity made by the disguised detective had aroused. Their presence had only one meaning for her.

The sick man raised himself on one elbow. "Peggy," he whispered. "Peggy." His eyes were shining with an unnatural light, but his voice was quite normal.

"Yes?" she said.

"It's all up, old girl; I've been awake for the last five minutes. That was a detective, wasn't it. And the house is afire. Well, I'll take my medicine. I've been a rotter and it's up to me now to do the first decent thing by you I've ever done. You get along. I'll look after myself."

THE MAELSTROM

She laid a hand soothingly on his shoulder and held herself under stern control. "You've been dreaming, boy," she said with a smile. "Lay down. Everything's all right."

He resisted the soft pressure and pointed to the wreaths of smoke now curling lazily under the door. "That isn't much of a dream, Peggy. Better go. I know what I've got to do and you'll only be in the way."

Congreve poked his head into the room. "Now then, miss, here's a ladder. You first and then we'll see to your brother."

She held back. "I'll not go," she declared. "I'll not let you arrest him."

"We'll see about that after we've got you both out," said Congreve gently. "Now come along like a good lass and don't argue."

"No."

It was mere madness, but she was past logical reasoning. Even the genial Congreve almost lost his temper. He started forward, but before he could reach her Errol had risen from the bed. His face was grey and drawn with pain, and those unnaturally bright eyes shone fiercely out of their sunken pits.

"Do as the man tells you," he said, and added an oath. Excitement seemed to have lent him strength. With a quick movement he lifted her bodily and staggered with her towards Congreve. "Take her," he said curtly.

In her brother's hands she had been almost passive but as she passed to the detective she struggled like a wild thing. It was all that he, who was a man of no mean physical strength, could do to hold her. He had to call Cincinnati Red to his aid before he could get her across the outside room to the window.

"Steady, miss," he said soothingly. "You don't want to be burnt alive, do you?"

She paid no heed. All her efforts were concentrated on the one purpose—to free herself and stand between her brother and the danger of arrest. She saw nothing except that all she had done and suffered during the last few days had been for nothing.

A low cry went up from the crowd that had already assembled outside the burning house as they appeared at the window. The fire engines were dashing up. The two men placed her down for an instant and she made one final effort to break away.

"Of all the silly women," muttered Cincinnati irritably.

The window was open and a head now appeared at it. Peggy felt herself abruptly swung off her feet again and almost before she was aware of it she was in the street and half a dozen men were moving her swiftly away. Cincinnati had followed her down the ladder and he gave a great breath of relief as he found himself once more in the open air.

Congreve had returned to the door of the inner room, which had swung to. He tried to push it open with his foot, but to his surprise it resisted the pressure. "Now then, Errol," he shouted. "Come on. It's your turn. Open the door. It's caught."

The voice that replied was muffled, but it had a note of determination. "It's not caught. Look after yourself, Mr. Policeman. I'm going to take my chance. You don't lay your hooks on me."

The burly figure of Menzies squirmed its way through the window and a couple of helmeted firemen followed. "Hullo, Congreve," he said casually. "Here's a fine old mess. What's wrong?"

His subordinate jerked a thumb towards the door. "Errol in there," he said shortly. "Door locked. He won't come out."

The chief inspector raised his boot and smashed with the heel against the panels. A mocking laugh came from the interior. "Don't do that again," said Errol. "I've an eight-shot automatic here. Don't you run away with the delusion that you're going to take me."

"The deuce you have, laddie," muttered Menzies. "Here," he wheeled on one of the firemen, "lend me your axe. Pass the word to your people to send up a length of hose. Congreve, you get out of this."

THE MAELSTROM

He struck with the axe at one of the panels, and as the wood smashed and splintered the thudding report of an automatic answered and an irregular hole showed a few inches from where he had hit. He moved quickly back out of the line of fire.

"He means business, sir," said Congreve, who, for once, had disobeyed an order. "You'll never be able to make a hole to turn the hose on him. We can't save him if he won't be saved."

Menzies made a helpless gesture. "Hang it all, man, we've *got* to get him. He's part of my evidence." He turned to one of the firemen "What are the chances of getting the fire under?"

The man shrugged his shoulders. "The chief might be able to tell you. I don't reckon we'll do much myself. There's gallons of petrol been used and you can't put that out with water."

The brow of the chief inspector furrowed. On a larger scale he was faced with a similar problem to that which is dealt with almost every day by the huge policeman with a small but obstreperous drunken prisoner. The policeman gets the aid of other constables as large as himself, not because he cannot manage by himself but because he might harm the man in custody did he exert his full strength.

Only by violence could Errol be saved, but the probabilities were that in making the attempt several other lives would be sacrificed. Menzies had no doubt

THE MAELSTROM

that any of his men would risk that eight-shot automatic, if need be, purely as a matter of course. He, himself, for that matter, was willing to take his chance, but his sober common sense told him it wouldn't do.

He climbed down into the street and engaged the divisional officer of the fire-brigade—a heavy-jawed young man in sea boots, his face begrimed and bloodshot.

"Suffering snakes!" ejaculated that individual when the position had been made clear to him. "I don't see what we can do. If there's a madman with a shooter locked in the first room it's for you police to deal with him. Our job's putting out the fire and I don't see that we can save the place anyway. All we can do is to prevent it spreading. I've been in there "—he nodded towards the door out of which a thick volume of smoke was emerging—" and I tell you they haven't spared the petrol. The house is doomed, Mr. Menzies, and if your pal is going to shoot anybody who tries to get at him he can roast for me."

The detective concealed his annoyance. In the fireman's place he would have felt the same. He would have to count Errol out of the game. He dismissed him from his mind for a moment and put another enquiry. The divisional officer nodded his head energetically.

"That's so. That's so. Who ever set it alight knew

what they were doing. It could have all been done in three minutes or less. As far as I could see this is what happened. It's partly a guess, mind. Some old clothes were soaked with petrol and thrown or placed on the stairs and at the bottom. A washbowl full of petrol was placed at the bottom and others with petrol in some of the rooms. Some tape was soaked in paraffine and laid from one to the other. A length carried to one of the windows and a match applied to it from outside would have set the whole place ablaze in ten seconds." He broke off to shout a curt order and Menzies, with a word of thanks, moved away.

The fire had interfered with some of his arrangements but he had by no means given up hope of laying his hands on Gwennie Lyne and Ling and their confederates that night. He was playing against astute antagonists who were bound by no rules and who had the advantage of working on the defensive. He appreciated the significance of their move and lost not a moment in attempting to counter it.

Orders were given that no man was to approach the fire and, getting on to the telephone, he sent a hurried explanation of the new development to the headquarters station of the division. To the subdivisional inspector of the uniformed branch who had been lurking quietly in the vicinity and now came at a run with his whistle between his teeth, he had outlined certain ideas, and at each end of Levoine Street detachments of constables had

THE MAELSTROM

sprung up as if by magic and were lined across the street.

All thoroughfares that entered Levoine Street were similarly guarded and no one except police officials and firemen were to be allowed to approach nearer than several hundred yards. Above all, no one was to leave the street. Menzies had determined that he would not allow his purpose to be rendered impossible by the collection of a big crowd. It was inevitable that there should be some sort of gathering, for within the cleared area there were two hundred or more houses, nearly all of which were human ant-heaps. But that could not be helped. In any case he had determined to sift the collection individual by individual if necessary.

Within half an hour he had been promised reinforcements of two hundred constables—more than sufficient to maintain clear the area in which search was to take place. More than that, every detective in London who could be spared at short notice was hurrying to the spot.

He told himself that all that was possible had been done, yet he could not disguise from himself that in spite of all the resources of intricate organisation the odds were against him.

The double row of police at the end of the street opened and a motor-car pushed through and ran silently to a standstill. He recognised Helden Foyle and one or two of the high administrative officials at Scotland

Yard. To them he briefly outlined what had occurred.

"There were plenty of men who'd have volunteered to fetch Errol out," he added, "but I didn't feel justified in letting 'em take the risk."

"You were right, Menzies," agreed the superintendent. "There'd have been the deuce of a howl if any lives had been thrown away like that. Nothing can be done but let the fire burn out. You've lost Errol, anyway. I guess you did right in having the streets blocked."

"No need for secrecy now so far as Ling is concerned," commented Menzies. "Instead of making a quiet house-to-house search it will have to be done pretty publicly. That's why I wanted more men. As soon as the fire's over and the excitement died down a bit I'm going through this district with a fine-tooth comb."

"Miss Greye-Stratton?" said Foyle interrogatively.

"Yes, I've thought of her. She's in the 'Three Kings' at the corner there"—he indicated the public-house—"for the time being. Half off her head. We may surprise something out of her presently or she may talk of her own accord. Errol being out of it may make a difference, but I've sent to Royal to bring up Jimmie Hallett."

Foyle blinked. "Can't seem to keep him out of it," he laughed. He dug one forefinger into the chief inspector's rotund waist "You infernal old matchmaker," he said.

THE MAELSTROM

A sharp cry and a confusion of orders came from the firemen. Brass helmets clanked and dodged ludicrously away from the burning house. The roof collapsed like cardboard and a shower of sparks flew upwards.

"Exit Errol," said Helden Foyle calmly.

CHAPTER XXVI

LIKE most detectives of experience Weir Menzies had a certain cynical outlook on life. Yet at heart he had most of the domestic virtues. Still it was part of his professional code to use every possible means—which included every possible person—to achieve his ends.

He slipped his arm in friendly fashion through that of Jimmie Hallett, when that young man turned up in a taxi-cab, accompanied by the watchful Royal.

"We're on the same side of the game at last, my boy," he said genially. "I knew you'd hate to be out of this show and so I sent for you. Errol's done for."

"So Royal told me," said Jimmie coldly. "You've got a knack of mucking things up, Menzies."

The chief inspector accepted the gibe. "I'm not one of those omniscient amateur detectives," he said placidly. "Don't bear malice, Hallett. You'll own you played me up a bit before I started to get my own back. But that isn't what I wanted to talk about. Tell me now, Errol was in this bad somewhere. Was it only to protect him that Miss Greye-Stratton was keeping her mouth—and yours—shut?"

Jimmie lifted his shoulders. "You remind me of a newspaper man I used to know. He once went to interview a jeweller who, after heavily insuring his stock, was found bound and gagged beside an empty safe. The

THE MAELSTROM

newspaper man being a tactful person anxious for a story, opened his interview with ' tell me now, mister—did it really 'appen? ' "

Menzies laughed in delighted appreciation. " I've no tact," he said. " I'll own it freely. Honestly though now, aren't I right? "

Jimmie frowned thoughtfully and withdrew his arm. " Yes," he said in a burst of confidence. " I don't see any harm in saying that's how I figure it."

" She doesn't much care what happens to Ling? "

A flush mounted to Jimmie's temples, but the darkness of the night hid it from the detective " I won't say that. I don't know. I've no right to speak for her."

They were opposite the " Three Kings." Menzies dropped a hand on his companion's shoulder and gently piloted him to a private door. " We'll get in and see the poor girl," he said. " Should I be wrong in thinking that it was Ling who brought Errol into this affair? If that is so she won't have much love for him—eh? "

The young man came to an abrupt halt. " See here, Menzies. How much do you know—or rather how much *don't* you know? If, as you say, we're both on the same side of the game now, you've got to cough up."

" I'll trust you," said Menzies with lowered voice and a confidential air. " Gwennie Lyne and Ling, with some of their confederates, are, I believe, within half a mile of where we stand. The round-up will begin

presently and we'll probably get them. I don't want—
I'll admit it—to have to rope this girl in as well, because I believe if she's done anything to bring her within the law at all it was under a sort of compulsion. If she still keeps silence she'll force my hand. I don't only want to get Ling, I want more direct evidence against him."

He had told Jimmie Hallett nothing that he did not know, but he had adroitly side-tracked the demand for information. They passed into the house. Peggy was reclining in an armchair by the fire in a sort of shop-parlour parted from the saloon bar by a glass partition shrouded by lace curtains. The landlady of the public-house was sitting with her. With a muttered excuse, she rose and departed.

The girl was pale and an infinite weariness was in her face. A flicker of interest was in her eyes as she nodded to Jimmie. "You know? It was good of you to come."

Jimmie crossed over to her and took her hand. "You are all right?" he asked anxiously. "Not hurt?"

"Only tired," she said.

"We have had a doctor," explained Menzies, who had taken another armchair and was extending his feet to the cheerful blaze. "She's perfectly normal, but the shock has been rather trying. We shall soon have you as bright as ever, Miss Greye-Stratton. There's one or two things I'm going to tell you now that may cheer you up."

THE MAELSTROM

"I thought you were going to round up Ling?" interrupted Jimmie.

From the dissenting gesture which Weir Menzies made one would have imagined that the capture of Ling was a matter of trivial importance. His eyes twinkled. "In a hurry to turn me out—eh? There's plenty of time for that. We don't want a big audience for that sort of thing. We'll let the crowd get to bed. Now"—he became serious, and placing his elbows on his knees, leaned forward towards the girl—"I've talked to Mr. Hallett here and I've come to a conclusion."

Jimmie again interrupted. "Hadn't you better leave that," he said.

Menzies' ruddy face glowed benevolently. "Don't you chip in for a moment, Mr. Hallett. I know exactly how Miss Greye-Stratton feels. If you only knew it I'm her fairy godfather. Now listen, I'm going right through this case with you and will see where we all stand. I'm going to show you my hand."

He paused for a moment, waiting as if for Hallett to say something. Jimmie remained silent. He was half suspicious of this new move, for he had learned that Menzies' candour was usually in the nature of bait. In that he was right. A detective has often to employ the weapons of the confidence man.

"We'll begin at the beginning," said the chief inspector, laying the stubby forefinger of his right hand into the palm of his left. "Let's make it supposition,

THE MAELSTROM

shall we? Suppose now, Miss Greye-Stratton, you were to come into a big fortune on the death of your father. There's the starting-point of the whole thing. Suppose your brother to have fallen into the hands of a gang of American crooks. Now I want to say nothing against your brother, Miss Greye-Stratton—whatever he was he has paid the penalty, but he was a weak man. We can agree on that.

"Very well. Still supposing, we will agree that he bragged a bit about his rich relatives. It is the kind of thing he would do. The whole story would have been twisted out of him in five minutes. Then the thing became absurdly simple. There was little risk about it. All that had to be done was to seek you out, marry you to one of the gang, and wait for nature to take its course with the old gentleman."

Peggy, who had been listening apathetically, roused herself to life. Her eyes were like stars.

"You, my girl"—he spoke with a kind of paternal patronage—" can have little idea of the infinite pains which really great criminals go to in organising their projects—how they plan point by point, slowly, carefully, sometimes for months. Their first business was to get Errol irrevocably into their clutches. That was easy enough. He is wanted by the American police for uttering forged Treasury bonds——"

"That is a lie," broke in the girl impulsively. "He assured me——" She cut off the sentence shortly.

THE MAELSTROM

"He assured you," finished the chief inspector placidly, "that he had not committed any crime before he forged your father's name to the cheques which you passed to Mr. Hallett in the fog."

Hallett jumped to his feet. Peggy's gaze had deserted Menzies and, reproachful and accusing, was fixed on him. "You——" she choked.

Menzies waited with the resigned air of a man who has been interrupted in a story. He gave no sign that he had deliberately seized the opportunity to surprise one or both of them into an admission.

"I never told you," denied Jimmie vehemently. The protestation was meant for the girl. "How did you know?"

"It's of small importance," said Menzies. "You've only confirmed that of which I am certain. I knew because it was an irresistible inference—an inference you couldn't get away from in a court of law. I'll come to that in a minute. I knew about Errol in America without any magic. I asked Pinkerton's to rake him up for me, that's all. He had used another name but they got on to one or two episodes. He came to England a year ago, near enough—and curiously enough Ling, Gwennie Lyne, and Dago Sam, and probably some others, arrived about the same time by separate boats."

"How do you know that?" asked Hallett.

"How do you get at ancient history?" retorted

THE MAELSTROM

Menzies scornfully. " By research. I didn't find Ling's collar stud nor Gwennie Lyne's shoe buckle in a state-room. They were over here and they had been in New York. The Central Office in New York lost sight of them at a certain date. I got from Miss Greye-Stratton—she will remember that I went into the matter closely—the approximate date of her brother's reappearance in England, and then it was only a question of patience."

He had abandoned the hypothetical method of stating his case and went on like a patient school-teacher demonstrating a subject to a class of school children.

" Now at various times we picked up our facts and corroborative details. Mainly they were the cheques passed over to Mr. Hallett, the visit of Stewart Reader Ling to Miss Greye-Stratton's flat and particularly the one he paid the night the murder was committed. Ling dropped a wedding ring, which was found by the lift attendant. Miss Greye-Stratton followed him out hatless and in a hurry a few minutes later.

" Don't imagine that I jumped to an irrevocable conclusion then. I found—it was merely a matter of having marriage registers at Somerset House searched—that she had gone through a form of marriage with Stewart Reader Ling. Then I had more than a suspicion of Errol. You were certainly uneasy when you came to see me, Miss Greye-Stratton, though I'll do you the justice to say you controlled your feelings well.

THE MAELSTROM

But the biggest fool that ever stepped could see that you were holding something back.

"I confronted the pair of you by as near surprise as I could work it, but you did me down. But the main thing began to stick out as plain as a pike-staff. Ling an adventurer, Dago Sam—whom I then only knew as William Smith—a tough from Toughville, Errol a wastrel, and you an heiress. The combination worked itself out. Why should you deny that you had passed the cheques over? Why should you have held back anything when we had a chat? You were either in the game yourself or you were doing it for someone else. Clearly you were afraid of Ling and you had quarrelled in the flat. It was clear too that you were not in love with him. Why had you married? There had been compulsion of some kind and the cheques were concerned or you wouldn't have been so eager to get them away. They were proof of someone's guilt. I should say that when we searched Greye-Stratton's house we did not come across a single thing that had reference to even the smallest banking transaction. Clearly all bank-books, pocket-books, and so on had been taken away or destroyed.

"I thought I saw the outlines of the scheme. Errol had forged his father's name and that had been used as a lever to induce you to consent to the marriage. The part not according to the programme was that Ling wanted you to live with him, either because he had fallen

THE MAELSTROM

in love with you or because he thought that it would be easier to lift the fortune if he was your acknowledged husband."

"The murder?" she said eagerly. "You have not spoken of that?"

"Do you mind if I smoke?" he asked. "I can think better with a pipe. Thank you. No, I haven't dealt with the murder yet. I was just coming to that. Here's a point I haven't spoken about. Perhaps you can help me though I don't attach much importance to it. A woman had visited him twice during the last year. Was that you?"

"It was I," she admitted.

He remained silent.

"I did not like asking him to see me," she went on. "It wasn't pleasant. I asked him to do something for my brother. It was after I had made my final appeal to him that he promised to think over it. It was a week or two before his death that he sent, under cover to me, a packet addressed to my brother. It contained the forged cheques and a curt note that that was all he might ever expect."

"I thought so," said Menzies. "That explains how Ling got those dead cheques. There was an abusive letter written by Errol to your father of which we found the charred remains in the grate. Whether through that letter or some other letter or threats made in person the old man went in fear of his life."

Peggy shivered.

"By all the laws of probability Errol was the murderer. Even on the line of reasoning I have indicated he was the most likely man. Mind you, even yet I am not sure. The motive of the crime is clear enough and any one of the gang may have tired of waiting. It is possible—and a likely thing considering the characters of the persons concerned—that his sense of grievance was deliberately worked upon to fan into flame the fierce hatred he nourished against his father. I'll own I held that theory strongly for a while. Later I abandoned it. He may have been an accessory, he may even have been in the house at the time that the murder took place; he certainly knew who was the murderer."

The tense look on Peggy's features was relaxed. She drew a long breath of relief.

"That is my opinion," resumed the detective, "and I'll tell you why. Mr. Hallett's call at Linstone Terrace Gardens could not have been foreseen. He was admitted and knocked out. Likely enough, if the man who had hit him had had all his wits about him he would have finished the job. Anyway, subsequent events showed that the gang believed that he had caught a glimpse of the murderer's features and that as an awkward witness he must be intimidated or kept out of the way.

"Remember that Errol was only a tool in this conspiracy—a stool-pigeon. The rest of the gang would have been pleased to see him out of the way so long as they were safe themselves. If I know anything of Gwennie Lyne and Ling they would easily have arranged that if he had killed Greye-Stratton he should have been the scapegoat."

" That is to say," put in Hallett, who had been listening with an eagerness no less intense than that of the girl, " that if it had been Errol who opened the door to me they would not have worried whether I should recognise him again or not. They would have let him take his own risk? "

" You get it," said Menzies. " One of the master brains was concerned. It certainly wasn't Gwennie Lyne—the person you saw was a man. Of the known folk mixed up in this business that leaves Ling and Dago Sam. Sam we'll put aside for the moment. Who was the person who was most concerned in the successful carrying out of the original coup—whose safety or danger affected the pockets of the rest? " He half closed his eyes as though he were weary of laying down the course of the case and went on drowsily. " That singles out the man who had married Miss Greye-Stratton—Stewart Reader Ling. If he was arrested for the killing where do the rest of 'em stand? " He answered his own question. " The show was busted."

" I'm not saying that Treasury counsel would follow the line I'm laying down if we ever get Ling in the dock. There's more than one thing that bears me out,

THE MAELSTROM

however. A thread of cloth was found near the dead man which corresponds to a suit that Ling was wearing on at least one occasion. You, Mr. Hallett, took off him one or two things of importance, among them Mr. Greye-Stratton's missing pistol—the pistol with which probably the murder was committed."

He roused himself and tapped his pipe on the fender. " Now I promised you I'd lay down my hand—a thing I've not done to outsiders before a case was completed for twenty years. I have done it because I believe it will remove any scruples you may have in clearing up some matters. Miss Greye-Stratton—I may be wrong but I don't think so—has probably been actuated by an idea that her brother had committed a big crime and a desire to save him from the consequences."

She looked up gravely. " I thought," she murmured in a low voice—so low that she was scarcely audible— " that he might have shot my father in a fit of passion."

" I guessed there was something of that sort in your mind." He sat suddenly upright and slapped his thigh. "What a maundering old fool I am. Here I've been talking my head off and I've clean forgot to say what I really meant to. Do you know, Miss Greye-Stratton, you're not married at all. Ling was married before he met you."

Jimmie Hallett's face surged a vivid scarlet with emotion and he felt his heart pumping like a steam piston. He stole a look at the girl as she scrutinised the detective in wide-eyed amazement. Her eyes became detached for a moment and met his. Then the flush of colour into her cheeks rivalled his.

"Not married," she repeated.

"I told you I was your fairy godfather," chuckled Menzies.

CHAPTER XXVII

"THAT's perfectly true," he said. "He was tied up tight to an actress in New York five years since. I gather the little woman doesn't quite know what sort of a crook he is. There was a letter from her in your pocket this morning, Mr. Hallett. I guess you either hadn't the time or curiosity to read it. I sent a cable to New York and the answer was brought out from the Yard to me here. He's a married man, O. K., and if we didn't have this other thing up against him we could pull him for bigamy. The move smells of Gwennie Lyne. She wasn't going to put her pal's hooks into the money bags unless she'd got a collar and chain on him. If the part of the bridegroom had been played by a single man she might have had to whistle for her share of the plunder. But a man who was already married couldn't put the double cross on her."

Jimmie's spirits had unaccountably risen to the wildest exuberance. He clasped a hand down on Menzies' shoulder with a force that caused the other to wince.

"You garrulous old sinner," he exclaimed. "I take it all back. Consider yourself staked to the best dinner that this little old village can produce the minute you say you've got an evening."

"You take what back?" demanded Peggy, more for the sake of covering a certain confusion than from any

THE MAELSTROM

curiosity. Jimmie's face grew hot as he remembered the handcuffs.

"There was a little academic discussion this morning on a point of professional ethics," said Menzies.

"Hardly academic," laughed Jimmie. "I should call it a practical demonstration."

"We differed, anyhow. But I'm being switched off my line. I'm just making clear Miss Greye-Stratton that you've got no family ties now to prevent you speaking out. I want you to tell me everything you know. Will you be as frank with me as I with you?"

The brief wave of happiness that had come to her with the knowledge that she was not tied to Ling was followed by a return of depression. "I am willing enough to tell you anything I can now," she said slowly. "But won't it do when all this horrible business is over. I am tired, so tired."

"Come, Menzies. You can see how it is. Another day won't hurt. You don't think Miss Greye-Stratton's made of iron."

Menzies took out his watch. "If it hadn't been for me young fellow, my lad," he said, "you'd still be playing piquet with Royal at the hotel. In half an hour I've got to be digging Mr. Ling out and I guess this young lady can stand a quiet talk meanwhile. Now, Miss Greye-Stratton, please. Tell me everything your own way, and if any question occurs to me I'll ask it."

His manner, suave though his voice was, admitted of no further dispute.

"I'm unreasonable, Mr. Menzies," she said. "I can see you're quite right."

"Go on," he said, and lit a fresh pipe.

He smoked quietly while she told him her story, occasionally interjecting a question as some point became obscure. An ejaculation of appreciation escaped him as she told how she had refused to be a wife in anything but name to Ling.

"Good for you, Miss Greye-Stratton."

Her vivid face ebbed and flowed with colour as she went on. When she had concluded he scribbled a few Greek notes on the back of an envelope. "That bears out things as I placed them," he commented "There's a point that's puzzling me, however. Your brother had a knife wound which he said was due to an accident. Do you believe that?"

The peremptory question took her unawares as Menzies had meant it to. She reflected for a second before replying. "No," she said slowly. "I do not."

"Did he say anything more—no hint or explanation of any kind?"

"He never said a word and I never questioned him. He was never in a condition to be questioned."

The chief inspector gnawed absently at his moustache. "I'll own it puzzles me a bit," he said. "If it was Ling who did it, why didn't he make a clean job of it? Anyway, why should he get Errol up there and send for Miss Greye-Stratton to nurse him? People don't do things like that."

"Remorse," suggested Jimmie.

Menzies smiled. "Try again. You don't know Ling."

"It's too far-fetched, I suppose," said Jimmie thoughtfully, "to think that it was done with the idea of bagging me. Besides, how should he judge that Pe—Miss Greye-Stratton would write to me?"

"Much too far-fetched," agreed the other man drily "But you've given me some sort of an idea. You were not the only person they wanted out of the way. If Miss Greye-Stratton took the bit between her teeth they realised that she could make things pretty hot for them. They would want to keep an eye on her. I suppose you are sure"—he addressed the girl—"that Errol really was wounded? It wasn't just a frame-up?"

"I'll answer that he was a very sick man when I saw him," said Jimmie.

"Yes. Of course. I forgot your little scrimmage. Still, I think we've got a motive, and I'd sooner have a motive to build an assumption on any day than a heap of cigarette ash or scratches on a watch."

"I don't see that it matters," exclaimed Jimmie, who secretly nursed a little contempt for what he considered the detective's over-subtlety. "Isn't it a by-point, however you look at it? You know that Ling did the killing. You can get him for that. All you've got to do is to catch him."

Menzies' smile broadened. "Now that is nice of you," he said suavely. "There's only one little objection to it. I don't *know* that he's guilty. I don't *believe* that he is. There never has been a case except when a murderer has been taken red-handed, of conclusive proof. It is only when you feel that a man is guilty that the worst difficulties begin to crop up. A detective has to examine every side-path. We'll take it that so far as the wound is concerned it was no frame-up. No sane person would believe that an injury like that was an accident. Now if Errol had got it in a row apart from this case he'd have no reason not to tell his sister. If Ling had done it, or had it done purposely, Errol probably would have been mad enough to give the gang away."

"Unless he was scared," said Hallett.

"Precisely. Unless he was scared. But I don't think he was scared. What I believe happened was that someone got out of hand and tried to do Errol. Who it was we'll very likely find out when we know who's standing in with Ling. The gang probably had something else mapped out to keep Miss Greye-Stratton under their wing, but they jumped to this racket." He pointed his pipe towards her "It meant that if you had a sick brother you'd be as anxious to keep out of the way of the police as any other of them. Oh, they're a wise mob. I'd bet any money if I was a betting man that you never had any suspicion of Mrs. Buttle being anything but what she was made up to be?"

Peggy stared at him.

"She was Gwennie Lyne. There isn't an ounce of the Cockney about her."

"I'd have sworn it was she when I came out last night," said Jimmie.

"I wish to blazes you'd said so then," said Menzies. He glanced at his watch again. "Well, if anything more occurs to either of you people perhaps you'll let me know. I've got to get to work again. I've sent for a police matron and a nurse, Mr. Hallett, so perhaps you'll stay with Miss Greye-Stratton till they come. They'll be able to make arrangements."

Jimmie's eyebrows jumped up, but the girl was before him "A police matron?" she repeated.

"I could understand a nurse," said Hallett. "But, as Miss Greye-Stratton says, why a police matron? You're not proposing to put her under—under any restraint?"

A little flash of temper showed in the chief inspector's face. It was gone instantly. He placed his hands on the sides of his chair and heaved himself up ponderously. "Not in the least," he said urbanely. "I'm only remembering that a little while ago some people pre-

THE MAELSTROM

ferred to try to burn her to death rather than run a risk of her telling what she has told. I don't believe she's in any danger now, but I should deserve to be broke if I didn't see that she was protected. That's why I sent for the matron, and what's more "—he thrust his hands into his trousers pockets and jingled some coins—" she won't be left alone night or day now till this case is over."

Peggy's eyes met Hallett's and in their blue depths there lurked an appeal. Torn as she had been by the travail of the last few days she instinctively shrank from contact with strangers. It was not that she did not see and understand the reasonableness of Menzies' proposition. It was just one of those psychological phenomena of which there is no explanation. She had a latent impression conjured up by the use of the word police matron of a hard-featured, strident-voiced disciplinarian and she still retained enough of her old independent spirit to resent even the suggestion that she should be placed under any control.

Hallett answered the appeal.

"You're going a little beyond your rights, Menzies. If Miss Greye-Stratton doesn't object I haven't another word to say. But she's a free agent and you can't force protection on her against her will. So far as that goes I should consider it a privilege if she'd allow me——

Her face gleamed with gratitude. " I could go back

to my flat," she cried, " and I could get a friend to come in to stay with me."

Their failure to see his point of view exasperated Menzies, the more especially as he had been at some trouble to send for a matron of his acquaintance, the antithesis of Peggy's imaginings—a little grey-eyed person whose sympathetic tact and good-nature had more than once tamed even the fiercest of suffragettes who came under her influence.

" You're a pair of young fools," he said bluntly.

Jimmie bowed.

" You'd better get it out of your heads that I'm going to stand for any of this nonsense," he went on. " A fine thing to have you blundering round London on your own if Ling or any of the others slipped us now. I tell you, any danger you were in before wouldn't be a circumstance to what it would be now. We've stirred up this hornet's nest and they're ready to sting. They won't stand on ceremony if they can put anyone who can testify against them down and out, believe me."

" That's a bluff," said Hallett coolly. " You're trying to frighten Miss Greye-Stratton. I guess she'll take the risk as I will."

" I guess she won't," said Menzies, a little flushed about the temples. He was thoroughly honest in his belief that she might find herself in peril if she were allowed to go without surveillance at this stage. At the

THE MAELSTROM

back of his mind, too, there lurked a suspicion that he had perhaps exposed his hand too openly and until matters had matured he didn't want to take any chances.

"She's been shaken up a bit," he went on, "or she'd see that it would be sheer stupidity to get out of touch with us—sheer fatuous stupidity."

"Well, what are you going to do about it?" demanded Jimmie. "She naturally prefers her own friends, and I will say I agree with her. Going to threaten to arrest her as you did me?"

The detective cocked a moody eye at him. "Something of the kind. Don't you forget I've got power to detain a person on suspicion without making any actual charge. What's to hinder me doing that to both of you if you persist in this attitude?"

"Surely," persisted Jimmie, "considering what Miss Greye-Stratton has passed through——"

"That's just what I am considering. I hate to use the appearance of force, but if you won't be reasonable I've got to see that precautions are taken for her own sake. Now wait a minute. Forget I'm a police officer for a minute. Miss Greye-Stratton, I'm sure I'm speaking for my wife when I ask you to be our guest for a few days. We'll do our best to make you comfortable."

She almost laughed in her relief. "Thank you very much," she said. "It's silly of me, I know, but I just

THE MAELSTROM

hate the idea of a police matron. It would make me feel as if I really were a criminal."

"That's all right, then," he said, and smiled across at Hallett. "Any objections?" he asked.

"You're a sport—sometimes," said the young man and held out his hand.

CHAPTER XXVIII

THE minute search of the enclosed area on which Weir Menzies had set his heart he knew to be no trifling business. The crowds, both inside and outside, the still unbroken cordons had thinned as the fire burnt out and no promise of further spectacular action presented itself.

So far as was humanly possible the detectives and uniformed police had seen that no authorised person had entered or left the cordon. If Ling had ever been inside they were confident he could not have broken out.

Menzies had a high respect for the brains and audacity of both Gwennie Lyne and Ling and though he believed he had managed to isolate them, as it were, in an island of some hundreds of houses, he was not altogether confident of the result.

The whole district was a human rabbit-warren.

The sifting of the ruins was going to take time. Enquiries which in a better class district might have resulted in something tangible were not to be thought of. The breed of liar who inhabited those slums would talk —oh, yes, he would talk. A flood of information or misinformation would be let loose at a second's notice.

Moreover the difficulty of the search was going to be increased by a number of people who had their own reasons for avoiding association with the police.

Menzies bit his lip as Foyle, the collar of his waterproof well turned up to protect his face from the driving rain, approached.

"Nasty weather for a job like this," he commented. "How did you get on?" He jerked his head towards the public-house.

"Oh, her." Menzies shrugged his shoulders. "That was as easy as pie. She coughed up everything. She's a good girl and I've invited her to meet Mrs. Menzies."

The superintendent wiped the raindrops off his pince-nez. "I sometimes think you're more human than you give yourself out to be," he observed drily. "You've been the dickens and all of a time in there. Have you forgotten Ling? You've stopped this rats' hole. When are you going to begin to dig him out?"

"Might as well begin, I suppose," agreed Menzies, a little doubtfully. "We'll have the streets cleared absolutely first, I think."

No one of the scores of detectives took any part in this opening move. A dozen uniformed men began to steadily sweep away the few remaining groups of spectators. There was nothing unusual to be noticed about this process except by those individuals who had no retreat within the surrounded area and so were driven by ones and twos on to the detachments still lined across the roadway.

They were dealt with with swift precision. There were few questions and no argument—at least upon the side of the police. The senior officer at each barrier had a formula. " You will have to accompany a constable to the station until you have given an account of yourself and enquiries have been made." From that edict there was no appeal. Menzies' net was a wide one and he was willing to accept the risk of some estimable citizen being caught in it and raising a storm about his head.

Not that that was likely, for Heldon Foyle had volunteered for the task of sifting those who were brought into the police-station and he had an inimitable faculty for smoothing the creases out of the most irate citizen's temper. Menzies was left to conduct operations on the spot.

It was an advantage that both Gwennie Lyne and Ling were known crooks. Their photographs had been circulated and among the assembled detectives were at least a dozen who had been on occasion in personal contact with one or the other. This simplified matters, enabling Menzies to split up four parties to start at different points.

None of them were novices at the game, and weapons, official and unofficial, bulged in many pockets. They had been warned there might be gun-play and though in London a crook is allowed first shot that is no reason for allowing him a second or a third. Nevertheless it was nervy work.

The bulk of the army of detectives merely hung about the street with their eyes open, in case they were wanted. Comparatively small parties entered the houses to view the inmates, by now mostly asleep. Now and again the light from a lantern or an electric torch would rest longer than usual on the face of one of the sleepers, or someone would pull back the blanket which by accident or design had been shifted so as to conceal features.

Those who were aroused for the most part took this domiciliary visit with apathetic curiosity. Sometimes a growling curse would be thrown at the officers, sometimes an attempt at rough chaff, which the detectives answered in kind. Only when they were met with oppositiou did the stern purpose beneath their good humour show itself.

A short, stocky Cockney Irishman, red-haired and obstinate, barred the passage at one house. " An' it's meself that wants to know what for ye are troublin' dacent folk at this hour at all, at all," he demanded.

" That's all right, Mike," said the burly Hugh good-humouredly. " We're police officers. We're just taking a look round. Look out of the way."

The Irishman's jaw jutted out and his face became bellicose. " It's not me house that ye'll be turning upside down," he announced. " Ye've no right at all, at all, an' by the Splindour of Hiven I'll paste the fir-r-st blagguard o' ye that tries to come it." He shook a beefy fist at them. " I'm a respectable man and I know the law."

THE MAELSTROM

One of the detectives brought up from the river police peered forward. He was an Irishman himself. "That you, Tim Donovan?" he said. "Sure the last toime we met you had a lot of ship junk that some omadhaun had stuck in your cellar. An' you in the marine dealers' trade, too. We've lost sight of ye since then. Do ye want to meet that magistrate again or is your cellar full now?"

The reminiscence—an episode in which he had figured as the receiver of stolen ships' stores—appeared to infuriate him. "It's meself ye forsworn Judas," he snarled, "an' if ye'll just kindly step up it's meself that'll measure the length of me fut on your carcase. Not a hair o' any of ye comes into my house."

"That's enough," commanded Hugh curtly. "Stand aside if you don't want to be taken for obstructing the police."

"Come and make me, ye big oaf," challenged the little man, and swung a blow. Hugh, who held the heavy-weight police championship, swayed his body and the Irishman swung half round. Hugh's hand descended on his collar and he was jerked forward into half a dozen willing hands and held securely while a little rumble of laughter went round.

The house, like most of the others, was packed with humanity, and as the river man had suspected, a store at the back full of rope and metal explained Tim's unwillingness to allow unimpeded access to the premises.

THE MAELSTROM

That, however, was a minor matter in the circumstances. Of far more importance was the fact that among Tim's coterie of lodgers was only one who had not been awakened. He was sleeping in the remote corner of one room with his face turned to the wall.

Congreve it was who walked over and casually lifted the blanket. One glimpse he took and the next moment he had his arms round the kicking, cursing occupant and had lifted him bodily to his feet. An automatic pistol dropped on the floor and a couple of men hurried to Congreve's assistance. The struggle was brief.

They dragged their prisoner—he was fully dressed—towards the door and two or three lights fell on a face that was distorted with rage—a sallow, thin face with a hawk-like nose, and high cheek-bones surmounted by a shock of thick, curly black hair. He wore a reddish brown suit of American cut, the skirts of the coat sagging low over his hips and the wide peg-top trousers with a well-defined crease. Glaring from his necktie was an enormous pearl pin—too big to be genuine.

He ceased his struggles as soon as he realised their futility, and stood scowling round on the police. "Tell dem gazebos to take de spotlight off me," he complained. "I ain't no stage prima-donna."

"Get him outside," ordered Congreve. "The guv'nor'll want to see him."

He walked meekly out into the street with his escort and Congreve sought out Menzies. "We've pulled one

THE MAELSTROM

thug who looks a possible, sir," he reported. "Big Rufe Isaacs shamming asleep in his clothes with a gun by his side. I grabbed him quick and he didn't get a chance to use it."

Menzies removed his pipe from his lips and a look of interest came into his face. "Big Rufe, eh? Good business. Has he got shiny elbows or do you think—— This isn't the kind of place he'd hang out in while he's got dough."

"That's what I thought when I spotted him. He's no bum. Looks as if he could afford the Carlton if he wanted it rather than Tim Donovan's doss-house."

"Fetch him along. No. Wait a bit. Ask the 'Three Kings' to let us have a room and cart him in there. I'll come and talk to him."

Big Rufe, as the manner in which he had been taken showed, was one of those crooks who are not averse from running desperate chances and probably if Congreve had not acted as quickly as he did murder would have been set alight in Tim Donovan's boarding-house. Had he had brains he would have been as formidable an international criminal as Ling himself. But he had no brains—only an immeasurable audacity and a degree of cunning that had carried him through until both New York and London had got to know him. For him to embark on an enterprise unaided was to court immediate disaster, and after tripping several times he had wit enough to recognise the fact and to attach himself when possible to the banner of some more masterful crook who could plan as well as execute. He was an admirable tool when working under directions and away from liquor—a skilled mechanician with a brute courage that had, more than once, got him into trouble. Like most crooks he was a free spender.

Menzies had a little doubt that one of the unknown factors in Ling's gang had at last been run down. Big Rufe, out of luck and without a penny in his pocket, might have been found in an East End doss-house without any deduction being necessarily drawn from it; but Big Rufe, flush and well dressed, in Levoine Street and with a gun in his hand could have only one explanation.

The man was palpably uneasy when Menzies walked in upon him. The chief inspector greeted him affably. "Bad job this of yours, sonny. You look to be in it bad."

Rufe had all the philosophy of the captured crook. He would cheerfully have shot Menzies or anyone else if by doing so he could have secured a chance of escape. But once taken he held no futile animosity. Violence, either of speech or action, he knew would be merely silly. His mouth glistened with gold filling as he smiled cheerfully.

"Not," he ejaculated. "No pen for mine. If you'se de wise guy you'd take these mittens off." He shook his wrists, on which the thoughtful Congreve had taken the precaution to encircle handcuffs. "Say, this will be funny stuff for the Sunday supplements wit' you Scotland Yard bulls, I don't think! What do you reckon you're holdin' me for, huh?"

"Persecuting a poor down-trodden American citizen again, Rufe, eh?" commented Menzies. "We can't help it. It's the way we're built. Let us down light with your journalistic pals."

"G'wan," commented Rufe shortly. "Cut it out." He was grinning, but there was an uneasy look in his eye. The usual gambit of the crook—and it does not matter what grade in the criminal hierarchy he adorns—is bluff when he is run to earth. It is an easy weapon to handle and can do little harm if it fails.

"Just as you say," agreed Menzies amicably. "What are you doing up in this quarter, Rufe? I thought Piccadilly was more your mark."

The other was ready. "There's a kiddo, chief—y' know I wandered down to——"

"What's her name?"

"Enid Samuels. She——"

"Where does she live?"

"Her boss, he's got a little cigar factory down Commercial Road. She's a cigar-maker. Say, chief, you ought to see her—she's a peacherino——"

"Aren't you wasting time?" said Menzies acidly. "Look here, Rufe, you know you'll get a square deal from me. You didn't come to meet your kiddo, your

Enid, your peacherino, with a gun. You didn't expect to find her in Tim Donovan's kip, did you? What kind of suckers do you take us for to swallow that? You know what we want. Where's Ling and the others laying up?"

Rufe blinked several times in succession. "Come again," he murmured. "I don't get you."

The chief inspector crossed his knees and eyed the prisoner placidly. From his breast pocket he took an official blue-coloured document. "This is your dull night, isn't it?" he asked. "You know all about English law, I reckon. I can't put you in the sweat-box. A police officer mustn't ask incriminating questions of a man he intends to arrest. I can't make you give yourself away, Rufe, can I?" He shook a menacing forefinger.

The prisoner shuffled his feet uneasily and his insolent eyes lost something of their boldness. He was shaken and he showed it. "There ain't nothing against me, anyway," he agreed.

"No." There was an intonation of polite surprise in Menzies' voice. "Nothing at all. Just a few little things like arson and conspiracy to murder don't count in this game. I reckon Gwennie has been playing you for a Rube."

The beady black eyes caught fire. "I ain't nobody's fool," he cried. "Gwennie can't put it over on me."

THE MAELSTROM

"I'm glad you feel like that, Rufe." From Menzies' air he might have been chatting confidentially with an intimate friend in whose troubles he took a sympathetic interest. "Shows a trusting nature." Rufe glowered at him suspiciously. "Funny, though, isn't it? Here's the mob of you go out for a hatful and when you miss your jump who gets left behind? Why, Dago Sam, and Errol, and you. Gwennie isn't in the basket, I bet you. No, nor Ling, either. That's what I mean when I say they played you for a Rube."

Two deep vertical lines etched themselves in Rufe's forehead and his lower jaw dangled. It was part of the soundness of the detective's position that the other did not know how much he knew. He had instilled into Rufe a profound distrust of his confederates. The crook was being deftly provided with a new point of view calculated to stir the idea of reprisal in his mind. His hands opened and clenched.

"If I thought that," he said, and suddenly paused and raked the detective with his gaze. "How do I know you ain't stringin' me?" he demanded.

Menzies flung his hand out in a listless gesture. "It doesn't matter to me," he said. "I just hate to see folk double crossed, though." He leaned forward. "D'ye see, Rufe, you were due to get left anyhow. They were using you to pull the chestnuts out of the fire, but do you reckon you'd have been in at the share-out? I don't."

"That's your word," persisted the other doubtingly. "You want me to squeal on 'em. You're some sleut'. Where do I come in if I put you wise?"

"I get 'em anyway," answered Menzies indifferently. "You'd maybe save some time and trouble." He spread his hands out wide. "You're no chicken, Rufe. You know what you're in for. I can't help that, can I? I guess you'll take whatever's coming to you like a white man. But after the dirty way they've treated you you ought to get a come-back on them. Hadn't you now?"

In point of fact Menzies had no knowledge as to whether Rufe was being treated fairly or not by his confederates. He was working on the line of least resistance. It is never at any time difficult to arouse in the mind of a crook a surmise that he is being double-crossed by his associates. Rufe had neither the skill nor the wit to conceal in his features the fact that the seed Menzies had sown had fallen on fertile ground.

"I guess dem gazebos ain't worrying about me any," he admitted. "But they're in it as bad as me, ain't they, chief?" He shot a cunning glance at Menzies.

"Worse," agreed that individual. "Of course, there's that little job of Errol's, but I know you, Rufe. You wouldn't go for to do a thing like that without he properly asked for it."

It was a long shot, but by no means a shot at random. The very character of Big Rufe had been sufficient to convince Menzies that here he held the most likely author of the knife thrust which had laid up Errol. He spoke casually, as though the fact was what lawyers call common ground, and he had his reward.

"You're on to it," said Rufe eagerly. "Dat guy was too fresh. He took liberties, you understand, and when he pulled a gun on me he got what was coming to him."

The chief inspector's face was immobile. He gave no sign of having scored another peg in his investigation. Leaning over against the door, Congreve, apparently more interested in his finger nails than in the conversation, jerked his head without looking up and Menzies knew that he had heard and appreciated the importance of the confession.

"You know what you're saying, Rufe?" Menzies warned. "Of course, it isn't news to me, but I'll have to say you owned up. If you didn't mean it I'll forget it. Not that it will make much odds."

"Sure I know," said Rufe with a definiteness that showed he had made up his mind. "I ain't blind. You guys have got it all fixed up for me an' I don't make any trouble—see." He squared his shoulders. "Why should I be denying it? If it's me for it you bet I want Ling for company."

There was no need to correct the crook's impression that his admission was a work of supererogation. It made things promise to go easier. So long as Big Rufe believed that things were utterly hopeless for him so long would he do his best to see that he wasn't lonely in the dock.

"We'll pull him presently," said Menzies confidentially. "If he's inside our lines he can't get away."

The gold fillings in Rufe's mouth flashed again. He was amused and made no attempt to conceal it. "You're off your bearings there," he said. "You don't really think you get Ling as easy as that, do you? He ain't inside no cordons. No, sir."

For half a second Menzies wondered if he had underestimated Big Rufe. Was the man as simple as he seemed or was he trying to deftly confuse the trail? The reflection was swept away as swiftly as it had arisen. Rufe was not the person to get such a notion or to carry it out if he did. He would not so willingly have committed himself to save his dearest friend.

"He had a private aeroplane waiting, I suppose?" he said with heavy irony.

Rufe's wide-mouthed grin extended still further. "En she quay?" he said with deliberate mystery.

"En she quay?" Menzies frowned. "Now what the blazes do you mean by that? You aren't trying to come the funny boy on me, are you, Rufe?"

"Huh" Rufe was plainly disgusted. "You're a right smart Alick, ain't you, not to know what that means?"

THE MAELSTROM

"My education's been neglected. Tell me."

Rufe squinted cunningly sideways at his interlocutor. "I'm telling you nothing—see? If any mutt says I squealed, I didn't—see?"

Menzies began to see daylight. "Of course, you didn't, Rufe. You wouldn't do such a thing. I get you."

"Why," went on Rufe reminiscently but with an air of intense seriousness, "I got left for a sucker as you said just now, chief. I been hanging round a joint back o' this street with Ling lately. We could see Gwennie's place from the back window. There's a room there she didn't use and Ling framed it up wit' her only this morning. And if she wanted us around she was to put a handkerchief across one of the panes in daylight or light up a candle after dark."

The chief inspector bit his lip. The possibility of a system of signalling had been so obvious that he had overlooked it.

"Well, when that tin horn Cincinnati came nosing around Gwennie begins to smell something an' she tipped us the office. You better bet we came round and Ling and Gwennie fixed the show for fireworks. I didn't have any hand in that. I swear I didn't."

"Get along," ordered Menzies sharply. "How'd they get away?"

"Gwennie took her chance and beat it out the back in the yards before we put a light to the place. She's

THE MAELSTROM

an active old lady for her age and she seems to have a sort of ruspect for you, chief—kind as if she knew you'd block all bolt-holes from the front. She had a bit of an argument with Ling about it. He holds that there'd be time for a getaway from the front because we came that way and calls her down for a mutt giving the game away by climbing backyard walls. She wouldn't argue. 'If you've any sense, Stewart,' says she, 'you'll do what I'm going to. The bulls'll be waitin' outside for Cincinnati.' Dat woman's got some sense, chief; but Ling, he didn't see it. And I didn't reckon there was much to it till we got lit up. Ling, he stays behind. 'You go see if the old lady's got it straight,' he says. 'Day'se not looking for you anyway.' So I beat it and sees the cops holding everybody up just as the fire-engines come. I lights back, but I didn't get the chance to get at Ling. But he must have tumbled to the racket because the next I see of him he came out and walked straight down the street and through your lines, boss, and not one of your guys was wise to him. He's some nervy is Ling."

"You mean that Ling walked right through our men without being held up?"

"Sure. If I'd have thought of the gag I'd have done it, too." His eyes twinkled. "Can you figure it out."

Menzies bit hard at a mouthful of moustache. Even Congreve had lost all interest in his finger-nails. Suddenly the senior detective's face lightened. "Congreve,"

THE MAELSTROM

he said, "slip out and find what fire crews have gone away. If the divisional fire superintendent is still there ask him to have a roll-call taken."

"You'se got it, boss—at last," said Big Rufe.

CHAPTER XXIX

THERE was wailing and gnashing of teeth among the men of the C. I. D. as knowledge of Ling's escape spread. Yet the simplicity and audacity with which it had been carried out earned for it a chagrined admiration. Luck had attended the crook better than he knew. The district fire call had brought steamers from many stations and some of the firemen were strangers to each other—a fact which had made the risk of detection infinitely small.

Nevertheless, it must have needed an iron nerve to have waited as Ling had done in a back room of the blazing building till the moment was ripe for his expedient. He had reckoned astutely enough that the firemen would have their hands full at the front of the house at the commencement of operations and that at the most only one or two would penetrate through by the blazing staircase to the back to have a look at things. On that hypothesis he had acted and the first fireman to get through had never known what hit him as Ling dropped a sandbag across the nape of his neck.

It had taken little enough time to change the man's outer garments—the brass helmet, the heavy jacket, the trousers and big sea-boots—but even so, he had to fight his way, choking and gasping, through the smothering mixture of flame and smoke to the open air.

THE MAELSTROM

The uniformed police at the lower end of the street remembered a fireman with grimed face and bloodshot eyes—one keen-eyed officer had even noticed what he took to be a bandage under the helmet—come towards them at a lumbering trot. As Ling had calculated, there had not been the shadow of suspicion in their minds as breathlessly he had ordered them to make way, muttering "We want to see if we can get at it from the back." And so he had vanished, leaving one more victim to be buried in the ruins of the burning house.

Mortifying as it was, no one could justly be blamed. The uniformed police had acted hastily in cutting off access to and from Levoine Street, though one end of the street which backed on to it—Paradise Street—had been included in the cordon, the other had been left open.

The mistake had been an easy one to make. Levoine Street itself ran straight as a pencil its entire length; Paradise Street, on the other hand, ran parallel back to back with Levoine Street for perhaps a quarter of its length and then swerved widely away at an obtuse angle which brought its bottom end out something more than half a mile from Levoine Street. If Gwennie Lyne had scaled the back walls safely she could have reached the house in Paradise Street from the back and escaped through the front without anyone being a whit the wiser. Ling, too, would have made for Paradise Street if only to effect a change back into normal clothing.

THE MAELSTROM

All this had now become apparent to Weir Menzies and blackened his brow and soured his temper as he reflected how easily it might have been avoided. His cordon of detectives had been wider and had included Paradise Street until he had weakened it by calling in some of the men. However, there was little to be gained by repining. The back yards of the houses in Levoine Street had already been scoured and now a second party of searchers was at work among them, though hope of picking up any trace of Gwennie was feeble. The only chance was that if she tried to get away from Paradise Street she might be brought up by one of the outlying detective patrols.

Although the search of the cut off area seemed now a waste of time, Menzies gave no instructions for it to cease. There was always a possibility, however faint it might be. His main hopes were centred on Big Rufe.

"What's the number of that shanty in Paradise Street where you and Ling were hanging out?" he asked.

Rufe gave it readily enough. "You don't reckon they'll be waiting there for you, do you?" he asked. "I guess you'll find the curb scorched, they got away so fast."

The same idea was in Menzies' mind. He would cheerfully have given odds of a million to one on it, but nevertheless the place had to be gone through. He drew his chair a little closer to the prisoner.

THE MAELSTROM

"What did you mean just now by 'en she quay'?" he asked.

Rufe shook his head doggedly. "No guy ain't goin' to sav I gave Ling away," he persisted. He was apparently obsessed with something of that curious trick of mind which will induce a dishonest witness with some shreds of conscience to kiss a thumb instead of the testament in court under the impression that perjury is thereby avoided.

Menzies recognised the attitude. Rufe had had no objections to betraying Ling, but he would not definitely give away his fresh hiding place. He wanted to feel that he could deny having done so if occasion warranted and he was giving a hint capable of only one construction. A less self-controlled, less experienced man than Menzies might have been exasperated. The crook had been plain enough except on this one point. To argument and expostulation alike he blandly shook his head.

There was, it seemed to Menzies, a chance of it being a piece of recondite American slang. If that was so it was new to him.

He sent Rufe away to the police-station under escort and strolled out himself to see how things were progressing. It was getting on to one o'clock and the house-to-house search was on the point of finishing. Congreve loomed up through the drizzle.

"No go, sir," he reported. "House as bare as

THE MAELSTROM

Mother Hubbard's cupboard except for some tinned stuff, some stale bread and half-a-dozen travelling rugs. Front door and the yard door were both open."

"I was afraid so," said Menzies. "We don't seem to have any luck, do we?"

"I don't know." Congreve smiled behind his hand at his chief's impatience. "If you don't mind my saying so, sir, it seems to me we haven't much to grumble about. A week ago we were right in the cart. Now we do know the story and we know the murderer."

"Yep. And you've been long enough in the service, Congreve, to know that troubles only begin when a man is spotted. Tell me what 'en she quay' means and you'll be talking sense."

"Give it up," said Congreve decisively.

"Well, I'm going to knock off now and go up and see Mr. Foyle. We've about cleared up here. You might ask some of the boys about that. Perhaps some of 'em may know. Where's Royal?"

"Dry nursing Hallett in the 'Three Kings'."

"On my soul I nearly forgot about him," declared Menzies and hurried away.

He found Hallett and Royal, who appeared to have become fairly intimate, swopping tall stories in the public-house with Cincinnati Red as an interested onlooker. Peggy Greye-Stratton had long ago been sent away to Menzies' house. Royal stopped in the middle

THE MAELSTROM

of a creditable imitation of the peculiarities of a certain famous judge. The chief inspector stood regarding them for a minute. "Well, boys," he said cheerfully, "I suppose you know the show is over for to-night. We've been diddled again."

"Some gink," murmured Hallett softly.

"You don't get my goat, my lad," smiled Menzies.

"Ling seemed to manage fairly well," smiled Jimmie. "You're finding out you've got a man's size job, aren't you? All right"—as Menzies moved threateningly towards him—"I take it all back. You're it. The real Sherlock. You could eat a dozen Lings before breakfast, just to get an appetite. Keep off. I apologise. I beg pardon. I eat dirt. I"—he gurgled.

"Seriously, though," said Menzies, "I'm shutting up shop for to-night. It's after closing hours, but we'll see if we can get one drink if we talk kindly to the landlord—all except Hallett."

"Me?" said Jimmie "You think I'm drunk?"

"Well," Menzies drawled, "I've known men go up in the air with less reason. Say, I'll let you have that drink and own up you're sober if you'll answer one question."

"Shoot," said Hallett.

"What does 'en she quay' mean?"

Jimmie bent his brows in painful thought. At last he shook his head. "That's one on me. I'll bite." He waited expectant.

THE MAELSTROM

"It isn't a catch," explained Menzies. "I want to know."

Cincinnati Red looked up. "I've got an idea what you're driving at," he said. "I ought to have caught on before, only I didn't think of it. I've heard that Ling hits the pipe. I don't know for sure. He's never let on."

"An opium smoker?"

"Sure. That's what 'en she quay' means. They say that he's been a dope fiend for years. That explains why he goes all to pieces sometimes. He can't keep away from it for long."

There was dead silence for a moment. Both Menzies and Hallett had forgotten their duel of badinage. The chief inspector's face was very thoughtful. There could be no over-estimating the value of the knowledge— knowledge which was likely to shorten the pursuit by no one knew how long. Like many important clues it had come out, as it were, by accident—an accident nevertheless that would not have happened but for the search of Levoine Street.

Instead of having to begin again the hunt for Ling— anywhere, everywhere—there was a fixed point on which to focus. Menzies knew something of the craving which men will take terrible risks to satisfy. Even in flight no man ridden by the habit would put himself out of reach of the drug. Reasoning as he imagined Ling would reason, it would be perfect policy to lay up in

THE MAELSTROM

one of those illicit dens which in spite of police vigilance exist near the docks of every great port. For his own sake the versatile Chinese takes ample precautions against a raid. In ordinary circumstances such a place would be the last in which Ling would be looked for.

"That looks good to me," he said. "I don't think I'll be able to stop for that drink, after all. You ever smoked opium?" He addressed Cincinnati.

"I've tried the dope," admitted the "con" man. "I keep off it now. Bad for the nerves."

"Then you're the man I want. You'll know the gags and'll be able to prompt me. Come along." He seized the other's coat-sleeve. Cincinatti sat' tight, passively resisting the pressure.

"What are you going to do?" he asked.

"Find if there's any opium joint round about here and run through it with you."

Cincinnati did not seem to find the programme enticing. He was too close to the bad quarter of an hour spent recently on the same quest. "Nix," he said emphatically. "It's your business, Mr. Menzies, and maybe you'd like to see it through. But it isn't mine by a long chalk. I've had all the excitement I want to-night and the quaint little yellow man won't be disturbed by me."

"Afraid?" sneered Menzies.

"I am," admitted the "con" man bluntly. "I've done all you asked me to, but I'm no sleuth and there won't be any pension for my widows and orphans if somebody hands me one. Why don't you take one of your staff?"

"Because they've mostly cleared away home and I don't want to spend an hour or two hunting for the right man. I want to get after Ling right now."

"Say," drawled Jimmie. "Aren't you getting on too fast. You don't even know that Ling is in an opium joint, and if you did you don't know where the joint is."

Menzies' brow corrugated. "I'll find it," he answered grimly. "It isn't the finding of it that worries me."

"Then, Sherlock," said Jimmie, "since our friend Whiffen has waived the honour why not let me be M. C. I'll own that I didn't know, or have forgotten, the meaning of 'en she quay,' but I'm no tenderfoot when it comes to opium joints. I think I might bluff any Chinaman you're likely to run across. I have had some experience in San Francisco."

"You think you can get us in if I find the joint? I don't want any trouble so that he can slip out a back way while we're arguing at the front. It's got to be done quietly. Remember, he's killed one man in order to get away to-night and he won't stand on ceremony with us."

"I'll be discreet," promised Jimmie. "I shan't make any trouble unless it comes. You bank on little Willie."

Menzies gave a curt nod. "Very well. That's a

bet. You wait here and I'll be back in an hour or less. You needn't stop unless you want to, Cincinnati. I'll not forget you did your best for us to-night." He moved swiftly away.

"Queer chap, your chief," commented Jimmie to Royal. "How can he expect to find the place in an hour? If the police had any information about one I suppose they'd have raided it long ago."

"If he says he'll locate one in an hour you bet he'll do it," declared Royal. "He's that kind of man. There's very few people who can walk over Weir Menzies and get away with it, and Ling isn't one. The guv'nor's always got something up his sleeve. Once he gets his teeth into a case like this one you can break his jaw but you won't make him let go."

"I owe him something," said Jimmie, "though I like getting at that everlasting dignity of his. He doesn't seem willing to admit that he can make a mistake. Here's a bad blunder to-night, for the instance. Surely on a job like this it would have been simpler to take the house with a rush instead of messing around and letting everybody of any importance slip through his fingers."

"I wish I was an amateur detective," said Royal solemnly. "It looks easy, don't it. Just chew on this, though. All Mr. Menzies knew about that house was that Ling had been there last night. That was no proof that he was there to-night. If we'd raided that place and found neither Gwennie nor Ling there where would we have been now?"

"Just where you are," argued Hallett doggedly. "You haven't got 'em now, have you?"

"Oh, deliver us," ejaculated Royal wearily. "Can't you see that he *had* to make certain before running a raid? The news would have been all over the shop in two ticks and if our birds had been laying up elsewhere they'd have flown and we wouldn't have stood the ghost of a chance of catching up with 'em. Got that? Very well. The guvnor arranges to see if they're at home before jumping. If they hadn't been we'd have waited for 'em to walk into the trap. You turn that endways and upside down and inside out and see if there's any flaw in it. As it is we've bagged one of the small fry of the gang, filled up practically all our evidence and got the tip where to look for Ling."

"Luck," persisted Jimmie. "I never said he had no luck."

"It's the sort of luck that's got a way of following Weir Menzies. Of course, he goes off the line sometimes, but he's only human. It's only in books that detectives never go wrong. If Weir Menzies was that sort of detective—why, he wouldn't be in the C. I. D.; he'd have Rockefeller and Vanderbilt and Rothschild in his vest pocket. The C. I. D.," he concluded gloomily, "never gets justice done to 'em in print—except perhaps in 'Judicial Statistics'"

THE MAELSTROM

Jimmie grinned at the heat of Menzies' defender. "I never said he was a dub," he declared.

"You never *said* so. That's what you meant all the same," replied Royal with warmth. "You've just seen some of the surface parts of his operations and you don't know either the resources or the limitations of the machine he is driving. No detective that was ever built could stand for a day alone against organised crime. You let a marked grasshopper down in a ten-acre field and set somebody else the business of catching him. That's about as easy as some of the jobs that come our way. Luck! Huh!"

"You've convinced me," said Jimmie solemnly. "You've got Vidocq, Sherlock Holmes, Dupin, Cleek, Sexton Blake and all the rest of 'em beaten to a frazzle."

"You ready?" said the voice of Menzies from the doorway.

CHAPTER XXX

IT is no reflection upon the activity of the divisional police that there should be an undiscovered opium joint in Shadwell. There is all the difference in the world between a deliberate search with a definite object and a preventive vigilance much spread out. Menzies had special reason to believe that an opium den existed somewhere in the district and it became a question merely of locating it.

That problem was not so formidable as it looked. It all turned on a question of advertisement.

Even illicit trades must advertise. A gambling-house, a whisky still or an opium joint do it in different ways from the proprietors of a breakfast food, but in essence it is the same. They must have their public—a definite circle of patrons to keep trade humming. Sooner or later some hint inevitably reaches the ear of authority, and the cleverest keepers of such places time their flittings accordingly.

Although Menzies did not analyse the mental process that had made him so confidently assert that he would find the opium den in an hour it is probable that he relied on these facts rather than on any hope of melodramatic deductions. It is a pity to spoil a popular illusion, but it is true that the greatest detective suc-

THE MAELSTROM

cesses in real life are achieved simply by asking questions in the right way of the right person.

His starting point was the landlord of "The Three Kings" public-house.

That gentleman, an elderly, hatchet-faced individual with a temper much soured by dyspepsia, was in his shirt sleeves, leaning on the counter of the public bar. Formally the place was closed in accordance with the licensing regulations and he was simply waiting until it pleased Menzies and his companions to turn out. Had they been other than police officials they would have been shunted into the cold street at the stroke of half-past twelve.

"Hope we're not keeping you up, Mr. Pickens," said Menzies pleasantly. "Been good of you to put up with our crowd. Still, I suppose it's been good for trade. Can't grumble, eh?"

He passed over his cigar-case.

The publican grunted, inspected the cigars with deliberation and finally selected one which met his approval. "Don't do the neighbourhood no good this kind of thing," he growled as he clipped off the end. He spoke as though the reputation of a high-class residential district had been ruined.

Menzies leaned an elbow on the bar and crossed his legs. "A pity, a pity," he said indolently. "Still we have to take it as it comes. Wonder what made those rotters pitch on this street?" he pursued speculatively.

THE MAELSTROM

"Talking about queer characters, Mr. Pickens, do you ever get any Chinese in here?"

"Not one in a blue moon."

"I was wondering if this dope shop hit you hard?"

"Y' mean opium, don't you? Naw, that don't touch me!"

"None of your regulars hit the pipe, then? There used to be a lot of it round here ten years ago." Pickens had said that he had only had the house seven years. Menzies could hazard the statement.

That so? The only bloke I know that touches it now is old Chawley Bates. Comes 'ome this way early of a mornin' sometimes, and regular swills cawfee. Reckon it pulls him together."

Menzies sized up his man. He wished now he had made a few enquiries about Pickens from the local men. "The Three Kings" was known as a resort of persons who had no great love for the police. Still, the keeper of a pub may have the shadiest customers and yet be an entirely straight man. The detective determined to chance it. He took some gold out of his pocket and slowly and absently dropped ten sovereigns from one hand to the other. Then he fixed his eyes on the other man.

"It's worth just ten quid to me," he said distinctly, "to find out where this opium shop is. No one will ever know who told me." He held the closed fist containing the gold out at arm's length.

THE MAELSTROM

Pickens' eyes glistened and he straightened himself out to full length. "I'm on," he said. "You'd better leave it to me. If old Chawley's at 'ome I'll git it out of 'im." He was putting on his jacket as he spoke.

He refused the detective's company and went out. Menzies did not rejoin Hallett and Royal, but reclining with one elbow on the counter smoked stolidly and thoughtfully till his return. Pickens was back within half an hour. He took a dirty scrap of paper from his waistcoat pocket and passed it to the detective.

"There y' are," he said. "I wrote it dahn to make sure. It's a little general shop kept by a Chink—Sing Loo. All you've got to do is to knock at the side door and ask if they can oblige you with a bottle of lime-juice and a screw o' shag. That's the pass-word. Where's that tenner?"

Menzies put the money into his hand and moved swiftly to where Hallett and Royal awaited him. In a little they were out in the, by now, almost deserted street. The chief inspector set the pace and they moved at a swift walk. No one spoke for a while. Once Menzies stopped a policeman with an enquiry as to direction and five minutes later they entered a short street bounded on one side by a high blank factory wall and on the other by a few small shuttered shops.

"That's the joint," said Menzies in a low voice, keeping his head straight in front of him. "Mark it as we go by. That one with 'Sing Loo' on the façia."

THE MAELSTROM

They swung by at a smart pace and took the first turning to the right. Not until they had walked for ten minutes did Menzies speak again. "Either of you chaps got a gun?"

Royal thrust a bull-dog revolver into his hands.

"Not for me," said Menzies. "You got one, Hallett?"

"Not here," said Jimmie.

"You take this, then; I wouldn't know how to hit anything with it, anyhow." He halted and shook a warning forefinger. "Don't get using it unless you've got to. I want Ling alive. Now, Royal, you'll have to hang about and use your own discretion once we're in ——Hello! What the blazes is a taxi doing in this quarter at this time of night?"

A taxi-cab whizzed by them in the direction from which they had come. It is not a mode of conveyance largely favoured by the inhabitants of the back streets of Shadwell, even in the daytime. In the small hours of the morning it is probably as rare as an aeroplane.

As though the same thought had simultaneously occurred to each of them, the three raced after the retreating vehicle. It was, of course, a hopeless chase, but there are moments when men do not stop to reason. Menzies was the first to pull up.

"Take it steady, boys," he said. "We're only wasting breath. The thing's a mile away by now."

THE MAELSTROM

"Likely enough it's nothing to do with us," said Royal optimistically.

"I've got a sort of feeling that it has, all the same. Well I'll be petrified! Here it comes again. Stop it."

They spread across the road, Royal flashing an electric torch as he moved. The three bawled fiercely to the driver. For a moment he slackened speed as though about to stop. Then, as if he had changed his mind, the vehicle leapt swiftly forward.

Jimmie had a scant five seconds of time in which to make up his mind. His hand closed on the revolver and it occurred to him that there was only one thing to do. The bonnet of the car was within a yard of him when he leapt aside and pulled the trigger. With a shivering rattle the vehicle stopped. Menzies was at the driver's side in an instant.

"Why didn't you stop when you were ordered?" he demanded in a blaze of wrath. "What's your number?"

"Why should I stop? Who are you? What business is it of yours anyway? If you've smashed my radiator——" The man's voice was less certain than his words.

"We're police officers," said Menzies curtly. "Why—what's the matter, Royal?"

Royal had opened the door and his cry now interrupted his chief. Menzies dropped back to him and followed the segment of light directed from the sergeant's pocket lamp to the interior of the cab. It fell full on the white lifeless face of a woman leaning huddled up in one of the corners. He gave an ejaculation of surprise. The driver had descended from his seat and was peering over the shoulders of the three.

"Good Gawd!" he exclaimed. "She's fainted."

"She's dead," said Menzies.

He wheeled and his strong fingers bit deep into the driver's shoulders. "Where did you pick her up?" he demanded. "Speak the truth or I'll shake it out of you."

The man gazed helplessly up at him. "Strike me lucky, guv'nor, I don't know nothing about it," he declared. "She was alive two minutes ago. There was a bloke with her. Where's he gone?"

Jimmie felt an eerie sensation along his scalp. He had gazed at the dead face, ghastly in the rays of the pocket torch which picked it out against the darkness of the upholstering and, like the others, he had recognised at once the features of Gwennie Lyne.

He had expected, he knew not what, when he peered into the cab—perhaps Ling himself. Certainly not that grim dead face with the staring eyes. He shuddered.

"Tell us all about it—quick," ordered Menzies. "We've no time to waste. Come on, out with it." He shook the man fiercely. "Everything, mind you, and get to the point."

"I don't know anything about it," repeated the man

again. "I was called by telephone from the cab rank in Aldgate—told how to get here and everything."

"Get where?"

"Why, to that Chinaman's place——"

"Sing Loo?"

"Yes. That's the name. There was a couple of fares there they said wanted to get to Shepherd's Bush. So I come along here. Seems like they were waiting for me, because directly I touched the bell the door opened and there was a tall bloke and her." He jerked his head towards the cab. "The bloke had his arm round her and she walked with him to the cab. He helped her in and then came round to me. 'The lady isn't very well, driver,' he says. 'I'm a doctor and I'm going with her to a specialist at Shepherd's Bush. Drive easy because I don't want her jolted more than can be helped.' With that he gets into the cab—at least the door slams just as if he had and I drive off. That's all I know about it, guv'nor, so 'elp me."

"You didn't know she'd been stabbed?"

He shook his head dumbly. Menzies released his grip. "Royal, you'll have to handle this for the time. Go to the nearest doctor first and have her examined. Come along, Hallett."

He caught hold of Jimmie's elbow and without another look at the cab and its grim burden started eagerly forward. "It looks to me," he said in a low voice, as though he was talking to himself, "that we're only just in time. Ling has struck a snag somehow. He must have intended to lie up just as I said and Gwennie and he have quarrelled somehow. If he'd meant to lay her out he'd have done it when it was less awkward for himself. As it is he was pushed to get the body away, or he wouldn't have sent for a taxi and left a trail right back to this joint. He means to vacate quick, and that cab would have gone, in the ordinary way, to the other end of London before we were on to it."

"You think we'll get him this time?"

"It's he or I for it now," said Menzies grimly. "Here we are."

He pressed the little electric button at the side **door**.

CHAPTER XXXI

THE door was flung candidly open and a young Chinese, clad in jersey, trousers supported by a belt, and his feet in carpet slippers, faced the pair. He gave not the slightest sign of astonishment or even of enquiry. His narrow eyes blinked once or twice as he stood, one hand on the door-knob, waiting for them to announce their business.

Menzies swayed a little and there was a touch of indecision in his voice. "I want a drink," he announced. "A drinka lime juice. Me an' my frien' both want a drink of lime juice an'—an' a screw o' shag."

"Come light in," said the Chinese, and stood aside. "You want Sing Loo. I go fetch him."

A second door barred the passage a few feet farther along and he glided noiselessly towards it. Menzies reached out to restrain him and then thought better of it. The young man—evidently a sort of hall-keeper—scratched lightly with his nail at a panel and someone opened a tiny trap-door and a face peered through. Jimmie realised that they were standing under the full glare of a gas jet and subject to the full scrutiny of the man behind the wicket.

There was a rapid interchange of words in incomprehensible language and then the click of a latch. An elderly Chinese with long grey moustache and wrinkled yellow skin came towards them and the door closed again. He spread out his hands in a sort of low obeisance.

"Solly, gentlemen," he murmured softly. "You want pipe?" He regarded them sideways out of his slits of eyes with an expression of artfulness. "Solly."

"Wot in 'ell you palavering about?" demanded Menzies thickly. "Wot are you sorry for? Me an' my mate 'ere wants a smoke. Just off the 'Themistocles,' y' know. We can pay."

The old Chinaman spread out his hands and lowered his head humbly. "Solly," he repeated. "You've made a mistake. My fliend six dolls up you get it. Not hele."

"W'y you rotten slant-eyed old 'eathen," said Menzies irascibly. "Wot ya giving us? You're Sing Loo, ain't you? We was sent to you."

Sing Loo made a gesture of acquiescence. "I've retiled," he said meekly. "My fliend up the stleet give you plenty opium."

It was evident that his suspicions had been aroused in some manner and that he was fully determined they should not set foot within the interior room. Meanwhile time was flying. Menzies took a sudden step and, whirling the Chinaman round, got his left arm in a strangle hold round his throat.

"Make a sound and I'll throttle you," he whispered tensely. "We want to have a look round this joint—

savvy? Get that gun out, Hallett. Show it to him. Put the muzzle right between his eyes so that he can see it. That's right. Now shoot the blighter if he makes an ugly move." He released his arm. "Now, my lad, get going. Where is the man and the woman who were here just now?"

Sing Loo's face was blank. If he was frightened he did not show it save by an almost imperceptible whitening of the yellow skin. "No woman has been hele," he stammered.

"Don't lie," said Menzies fiercely. "What do you call that?" He stooped and picked a hairpin from the floor and shook it between his finger and thumb in the Chinaman's face. "I wonder if you're deeper in this than I thought at first?"

His eyes narrowed and he surveyed the yellow face with fresh suspicion.

Sing Loo gave back a step, as it were, involuntarily and Jimmie followed him up with the revolver. He waved a long slender hand in front of his face as though to keep out the view of the menacing blue muzzle. "There has been a woman," he admitted. "She came to see a fliend and she went away in a cab."

"So. We're beginning to get at things at last. How did she come to be here? And keep your voice down. There's no need to shout."

"She came to see a fliend—Mr. Ling. He saw hel hele in this passage. They were angly—very angly.

THE MAELSTROM

Then she fainted and he asked me to send a boy to get a taxi to fetch hel away."

"Sounds as if you might be speaking the truth for once," said Menzies. "Now listen to me, Sing Loo. Is that man here still?"

"Yes, in the back loom. He's going soon after he's had one mole pipe."

"Ah. He's got the craving in his blood, has he? Very well. We're new customers of yours, see? You'll lead us in to where he is, and if you get gay remember my friend's gun is liable to go off, and I'm a bad-tempered man myself."

"I undelstand," murmured Sing Loo. "Come this way."

Jimmie slipped the weapon into his overcoat pocket and kept his hand on it ready for instant action. Menzies edged up close to Sing Loo and twisted his hand into the other's sleeve. The inner door opened in response to the Chinaman's summons and they found themselves in a passage lighted very dimly in comparison to that outside.

Jimmie's heart was pounding with excitement. He was glad that the chief inspector had permitted him to carry the revolver. He had acquired a certain amount of respect for Menzies, but he also had views about Ling and he was resolved at the first hint of trouble to shoot fast and to shoot first. The legal question of his justification could be settled afterwards.

THE MAELSTROM

Menzies, if his face was any index to his feelings, was as unmoved and impassive as though he was about to take a seat in a theatre. Ling was to him merely a piece in the game that was so nearly played out—a piece he intended to remove from the board and then to forget, except as something that had played a prominent part in a well-fought game.

They descended a couple of steps into a gloomy room lit by two or three tiny gas jets and a glowing fire. As his eyes became accustomed to the darkness Jimmie saw vague forms about the room, the majority lying on a series of platforms with tiny glass lamps by their sides. They were mostly smoking, one or two cigarettes and others opium. A few were asleep.

The atmosphere was no new one to Jimmie. He recognised the usual paraphernalia of the *inyun fun*. Each smoker had a tray with his apparatus from the pipe itself to the *yen hock* used for smoking the opium over the flame of the lamp.

Most of the customers were quite apathetic to the entrance of the new arrivals. Menzies in one rapid glance gleaned the fact that there was no window and that the only other egress from the room, except that in which they stood, was at the opposite side of the room. In the dim light it was at first impossible to make out the identity of any of the smokers.

He relinquished his grip of Sing Loo's sleeve and bounded across to the other door. Someone raised himself on an elbow. "That you, Menzies?" drawled a lazy voice. "I'll give you credit for being a hustler when you get on the go. Take that, you swine."

A streak of flame split the darkness and a bullet smashed against the wall. Jimmie's pistol was levelled and almost in the same instant his shot answered. There was a groan, immediately stifled, and then a short laugh.

"Bull's-eye—five," said Ling in the monotonous chant of the ranges. "That's one I owe to you, Master Hallett. You've smashed my wrist. Good shooting in this tricky light."

The place was filled with a vague vision of crawling forms, all of those who were not too far under the influence of the drug being anxious to get out of the way of the bullets. Jimmie's muzzle was full on the dark figure of Ling.

"Drop your gun—drop it, I say," he ordered peremptorily.

Ling laughed again. "All right, sonny, I know when I've got enough. Don't I tell you you've smashed my wrist. I aren't worth a cent at left-handed shooting. Say, your friend Menzies seems to have got his medicine."

The chief inspector had collapsed at the first shot, and though Jimmie was too wary to take his eyes off the master crook he had an impression of his great bulk lying motionless at the other side of the room.

THE MAELSTROM

"Stand up," commanded Jimmie. "Put your hands up. My God, Ling, I'm only looking for a good excuse to plug you." He remembered Peggy and all she had suffered at this man's hands and his blood boiled.

"Tut, tut! Let not your angry passions arise." Ling might have been remonstrating with a petulant child, but he stood up nevertheless. "I told you I'd got a bullet in my wrist, didn't I? How can I put my hands up? I'll put one up if that'll suit you. You're a smart boy, Hallett, but if you'd been alone I could have handled you."

"Shut up!" said Jimmie. "I want to think."

It was a position not without its difficulties. There would have been a dozen solutions of the problem had Menzies not been laid out. That had been a piece of most execrable luck which had made all the difference. So long as he held his back to the door and his weapon on Ling Jimmie was in command. To remain like that was, however, impossible. Something had to be done, but what, it was hard to decide. For all that he knew the place might be teeming with friends of Ling only waiting for that steady muzzle to waver a second before rushing him. At the best he was confident that five out of every six of those present were crooks and blackguards who would stick at little if it came to the point.

Ling crystallised his dilemma with a sneer. "Say, bo, you've got hold of a tiger's tail, haven't you? Don't know whether to keep hold or let go. You take my advice and run home to your mummy."

Jimmie never answered. His lips were firm-pressed and his dogged chin jutted out. Even if he had been able to rush Ling out at the point of the revolver until he found a police officer, he could not leave Menzies. Moreover he had an idea that in any case Ling would not calmly submit to such a programme. He lowered the pistol muzzle a trifle and his finger hovered indecisively over the trigger. An easy, simple way would be to maim him so that he could not get away. A bullet in the leg would do it.

Yet, when it came to the point, Jimmie could not press the trigger. It was too cold-blooded to shoot down an unarmed man. He wished Ling was not so cool—that he could give him an excuse for an attempt at violence. Otherwise it seemed a stale mate.

Of course there was Royal. Sooner or later he would be back or would send aid of some sort. But then Royal had his hands full for the time and he might believe that they were capable of coping with the situation without assistance. It might be hours before relief was to be looked for from that quarter.

"Well, what are you going to do about it, sonny?" asked Ling coolly. "Seems to me that you'll have to do a heap of thinking before you take me. Meanwhile, if you don't mind my saying so, my arm's getting tired."

THE MAELSTROM

"You'll keep as you are—if you're wise. I can keep my tiger one way—if he puts temptation in front of me."

"Right you are," acquiesced Ling cheerfully. "I'll try to endure it, only I just hate to hear your brains creak under the strain."

Jimmie could have sworn he had come nearer, yet he had not noticed him move. He strained his eyes and what he saw made him tighten up. The one hand held by the crook above his head had the two middle fingers and the thumb closed. The first and little finger were extended right out. To a man not aware of the trick it might have seemed insignificant. But Jimmie had seen it before—seen it carried out. Ling was manœuvring to get within reach of him. Then these two fingers could be used with deadly effect in a leap—one in each eye, and in his blinding, agonising pain he would be at his opponent's mercy.

"Go back," he said crisply, "back three paces. I like you better at a distance."

As Ling obeyed Jimmie turned his eyes for the fraction of a second to the place where he had seen Menzies fall. There was nothing there. Forgetful in his surprise of the importance of watching Ling he stared blankly, wondering if his eyes were playing tricks with him. Menzies had certainly gone.

His distraction was only momentary, but it was the chance for which the other had been waiting. Swiftly and noiselessly as the tiger with which he had compared himself Ling moved. Jimmie fired wildly and knew instinctively that he had missed. Yet Ling had crashed forward headlong and was cursing as he squirmed on the boarded floor, struggling to free himself from someone who had gripped him as he fell.

Then Jimmie understood. Menzies had not been hit at all. He must have foreseen Ling's purpose and dropped just the fraction of a second before the bullet sped over his head. Then he must have wormed his way silently across the floor towards the crook, his progress unnoticed among the recumbent forms in the half light.

After his first vitriolic outburst Ling fought in grim silence. Jimmie dared not leave his post by the door to go to Menzies' assistance and he watched breathlessly, wondering if he dared risk a second shot. He could hear the harsh breathing of the two men, their shuffling on the floor as they manœuvred for the top position, and now and then the thud of a blow. It ought, he thought, to be a fairly easy thing for Menzies if Ling's right wrist had really been smashed. Then he remembered that the detective also had a left hand injured. In that respect the struggle was nearly equal.

Once there was a gasp that was almost a groan; once a fierce epithet punctuated the laboured breathing. Though he strained his eyes Jimmie could not make out in whose favour the struggle was proceeding—he could only see a bundle of twisted, straining forms with first one man on top and then the other. They rolled over one of the drugged smokers and he paid no more attention than if he had been a corpse. Then, silhouetted against the gas flame for a tithe of a second was an upraised hand and below it the fantastic reflection of light on steel.

Jimmie focused his weapon, but before he could draw a sight another hand grasped the wrist and wrenched it down. The knife dropped with a little musical tinkle and the two forms became obscure again. Then he became aware of a man's head slowly rising into the dim light and he saw that it was Menzies. The vision was like a badly focused cinema picture. Menzies' hand was at the other's throat and he dragged him slowly, relentlessly upwards and then suddenly flung all his force downwards. There was a crash as Ling's skull touched the boards and the chief inspector got shakily to his feet. He passed a dazed hand over his forehead and laughed a trifle shakily.

"I'm getting a bit too fat for this sort of work," he said.

He spoke as though he had been engaged in a football match rather than a life-and-death struggle. Hallett laughed too, the overstrained laugh of relief. "Bully for you," he agreed. "I thought you were down and out."

"A close thing," admitted the chief inspector, mopping his brow with a big handkerchief. "He had the pull of us. His eyes were used to the light. I just caught him pulling the gun in time and dropped. I concluded in the circumstances I'd let you play the hand until I got a chance to chip in."

"How about him?" asked Jimmie.

"Him! Oh, he's all right. I've not killed him. Only a little tap on the head to knock some of the deviltry out of him. You keep on holding up this room full of toughs. I'll be back in a minute. Don't let anyone in or out."

He slipped by Hallett into the passage. Presently Jimmie heard from without the shrill series of long and short whistles which in the Metropolitan Police is a call for assistance. In two or three minutes Menzies was back, though outside the whistle was repeated.

"We're all right now," he said casually. "There'll be a regular little army here in no time."

Jimmie looked at him in astonishment. "Well, you take it," he said. "You come to this place practically single-handed, you lay out Ling, and now he's there for you to do what you like with, you go and call up help. What do you want more than one or two constables for, anyway? We could have run him up ourselves, for that matter."

There was a twinkle in Menzies' eye. He swept a hand round comprehensively. "And leave this nest behind me, eh? Don't forget I'm a policeman, laddie. If I'm engaged in a forgery case it's no reason I should shut my eyes when I see your pocket being picked."

THE MAELSTROM

In an incredibly short space of time, as it seemed to Jimmie, the place was swarming with policemen. They were prompt and businesslike, and there was no unnecessary fuss. Sing Loo went off protesting and tearful between a couple of stalwart constables and a similar escort was provided for most of his clients who were able to walk. On the others a guard was placed.

Menzies walked over to Ling and, lifting his head, forced a flask of brandy between his teeth. The crook sat up and opened his eyes. Then with a sudden movement he knocked the flask away and scowled on the detective.

"You got me," he growled deep in his throat. Then with a sudden spasm of energy, "By H——, Mr. Policeman, you may think you've got the odd trick, but the rubber isn't played out yet."

"You don't want to talk for a minute," said Menzies placidly. "Better have a drink."

CHAPTER XXXII

THE scar on Ling's temple was flaming blood-red against the whiteness of his features as they brought him into the cold, businesslike atmosphere of the bare charge room of the police station. His ordinary clothes had been removed when he was searched and the suit temporarily substituted hung loosely about him. His injured wrist had been bandaged and he had had doctor's attention since he had been brought from the opium joint. He looked ill and worn, yet his eyes flamed indomitably as he glanced from one to the other of the little group of men who were awaiting him.

"We're all here, ain't we?" he snarled. "Why don't you get on with the séance?"

The beast in him was still at the top, but to the men there his words did not at all matter. They were content to know that he had been run down and they were only concerned to see that he was held in safe-keeping till the mechanism of the law had been put into operation. No one resented his manner so long as it did not go to physical violence. He was impersonal—a piece of merchandise that had to be dealt with. When they had done with him he would be put back in a cell like any common drunk and disorderly, and be more or less forgotten when any reasonable physical wants had been attended to.

THE MAELSTROM

That was the impression Jimmie had of these men in his mind. And partly he was right. Yet Menzies at least, though his nonchalant manner did not show it, had a sense of triumph, of work in great part achieved that made him view Ling with a more personal interest. Ling as Ling did not matter to him, but Ling as a symbol of the forces which he had defeated was of mighty interest.

The whole scene struck Jimmie as something unreal —like a badly stage managed, badly acted scene in a play. The spectacular, the melodramatic touch was absent. The grey dawn was filtering through the skylight, yellowing the electric bulbs, yet Menzies did not stalk to the centre of the stage and with outstretched arm denounce the villain of the piece. He was not made up for the part.

Instead, a bare-headed police inspector—Jimmie thought he looked singularly unreal without his cap and sword belt—sauntered casually to the tall charge desk and leaning one elbow upon it lifted a pen. Ling was standing a few paces away between a couple of policemen but not even in the dock. Menzies moved over to the desk and leaning both arms on the back of it talked to the inspector. Jimmie caught a word or two here and there, but even then he did not realise at first that the charge was being made.

" . . . wilful murder on the night of. .   I charge him. . . ."

THE MAELSTROM

The inspector's pen scratched busily. Then, putting the pen in his mouth, he used both hands to blot what he had written and read it critically before inviting Menzies' signature.

"Thank you," he said politely. "Now——" He raised his head and looked at the prisoner.

"Stewart Reader Ling, you heard what the chief inspector said. You are charged with the wilful murder of John Edward Greye-Stratton. No. Keep quiet for a minute——" He raised a placatory hand as Ling opened his lips. "If there's anything you wish to say you may do so, but I shall take it down in writing and it may be used as evidence against you."

"You think you can prove that?" said Ling.

"There are two other charges of murder I may as well tell you will be brought against you later," said Menzies, ignoring the question. "One is in connection with the death of a fireman in Levoine Street——

"Here. Hold on a minute, Mr. Man. What fireman's this? I never killed any fireman. There was one knocked out for a while, but he wasn't killed by a long way."

"He was killed when the building burnt out. We call that murder. The third case is that of the woman known as Gwennie Lyne whom you are believed to have stabbed to-night."

Little wrinkles of profound amusement appeared on Ling's face "You seem to have got it right in for me," he laughed. "I reckon you'll wish you'd been a bit smarter by the time you get through. It's mournful to see you struggling. You don't mean that Gwennie got past you with that fake. I didn't believe she'd pull it off even against you bone-heads." He chuckled again as if intensely entertained.

Several pairs of puzzled eyes were centred on him. All had a suspicion that he was trying to work some new kind of bluff. Menzies alone guessed what he was driving at. He clenched his fist tightly but kept an unmoved face to the prisoner.

"Gwennie's not dead," said Menzies crisply.

There was not a man in the room who was not startled at the words so casually uttered. Ling's mouth remained open in ludicrous astonishment and he would have taken a step towards the chief inspector had not a touch on his sleeve reminded him of his guard. Then his face relaxed as his keen wits began working.

"You're a hell of a guesser," he retorted. "You got me for the minute. I reckon Gwennie is far enough away by this time. *She's* not murdered, anyway, and I don't believe I'd have stayed and waited for you if I'd had anything to do with the killing of the others. Gwennie's the one you want to get. She fixed up the place in Levoine Street, and it was she who did in the old man. You write that down, Benjamin." He addressed the inspector at the charge desk.

THE MAELSTROM

"So you're going to lay it all on to her now?" said Menzies with a note of scorn in his voice.

"You'd better bet I am, sonny. Gwennie can look after herself. You've kept us on the run pretty hot for a day or two, but to-night's been the limit. The only fault with you as a sleuth, Menzies, is that your imagination doesn't go far enough."

A retort rose to Menzies' lips but he suppressed it. He was too old a hand to taunt a prisoner.

"Yes, sir," went on Ling. "That's what you want—imagination. I'll own I didn't expect you to smell out that opium joint as quick as you did or we'd never have gone there. We were surprised some when you and the other two walked down the street. I'll make you a present of that. Your imagination didn't rise to us having a lookout. If you'd have walked in then you'd have found both the little birdies at home—Gwennie and me. It isn't exactly a place for a lady and she had already sent for a cab, not feeling that she could be real homelike there. If we'd known there were only the three of you we might have tried a run in the other direction, but we thought that you'd got the place shut off tighter than you did Levoine Street.

"So we fixed a little stunt for your benefit. You'll have got the idea by this time. You see she'd got more at stake than I had—me being innocent of all these things you've accused me of—so we had to see to her get-away first. It was her stunt all through—a fake

THE MAELSTROM

quarrel in the passage, some flour well rubbed into her face and a touch of brown paint on her dress just above her heart. She looked real ghastly when the cab came up and I helped her in.

"We reckoned you'd rise to it," went on Ling drily. "If the cab did get through well and good. If it didn't, why you wouldn't keep as close an eye on a corpse as you would on a live woman and you could trust Gwennie to light out when she saw her chance. Anyway it was the best we could do in a hurry. I stayed a little longer than I ought. Guess I thought there was time for one more pipe. Anyway, if you think you can touch me for murder you can't—you've got to get her. She's away by now, so my telling won't hurt her."

He grinned maliciously as he finished. The station officer calmly put down his pen.

"Done?" he queried.

"That's all I've got to say just now. My lawyer'll do the talking if you go on with this."

"Take him below," ordered the inspector and began to gather up his papers.

Jimmie eagerly turned to Menzies. "What do you make of it?" he asked. "How did you know about Gwennie? I've been with you ever since and——"

The chief inspector smoothed his sparse hair. "Didn't know," he said shortly. "I guessed. We were too pushed to judge except by appearances and he's probably right about it's being a fake. No good worry-

THE MAELSTROM

ing till we hear from Royal. He may have tumbled to it, but you see he'd go to a hospital and then to the local station and then perhaps on to the opium joint. We don't know what sort of a rumpus he may have had. We came straight on here to Kensington to charge Ling. If she's got away he'll have done everything necessary to head her off. We can only wait in patience."

"But he won't know where you are," remonstrated Jimmie.

Menzies smiled. "He knows that I'd have brought Ling here, and if he didn't he could find out in ten minutes by putting in an all-station call from wherever he happened to be. There's the tape machine and the telephone to every police station in London and you can't lose an officer unless he wants to be lost. No, the question of Gwennie isn't going to upset me yet. In our business you can't often run a one-man show. You've got to trust your colleagues. Royal's keen enough, and if she should bilk him the wires would be alight mighty quick." He pulled out his watch "I shall give him another five minutes and then go home. I'm fairly worn out."

"Do you think there's anything in that guff of Ling's? Whether he's bluffing or not, it seems to me you've got your work cut out to prove any murder against him if she does get-away. She had as much motive as he did."

"Yes. It sounded plausible, didn't it?" said the

THE MAELSTROM

chief inspector serenely "There's only one little legal point that he as well as you missed. I'm dead sure that Ling killed Greye-Stratton but it wouldn't make the slightest difference to him if I couldn't prove it—which I think I can. It doesn't matter a button who fired the shot—all those in the conspiracy are equally guilty of murder—even if they were a million miles away at the time. There's the motive, there's the fact that Ling (or someone wearing clothes of exactly the same material, which would be an extraordinary coincidence) was in the house; there is Greye-Stratton's pistol, which you will have to swear you took from him, and—oh, there's a dozen things."

The swing door of the charge room clattered noisily open and Jimmie wheeled to confront Royal. The detective-sergeant's clothes were torn and smothered in mud and there was an ugly black bruise on his face. Deep encrimsoned scratches were on both cheeks and his eyes were bloodshot. He laughed unsteadily as he saw them.

"What a night we're having!" he said. "*What* a night we're having! You got Ling?"

CHAPTER XXXIII

MENZIES was at his side in an instant and had slipped a supporting arm round him.

"Got him tight," he answered. "You look to have been in something, old chap. Much hurt? All right, don't trouble to talk now." He raised his voice. "One of you people call that doctor up again."

"I got Gwennie," muttered Royal feebly. "Slippery Jezebel she is, too, but I got her. She wasn't dead at all, Mr. Menzies. She."

"That's all right," said the chief inspector soothingly. "You shall tell us all about that later." But he drew a long breath of relief.

It was half an hour later that Royal, pulled together by the skilled ministrations of the divisional surgeon, was able to tell his story. He grinned apologetically at Menzies.

"Sorry to have made an ass of myself like that, sir," he said. "I wanted to come right on and tell you all about it so I didn't stay to be patched up. I never thought I'd get the worst doing I've ever had from an old woman."

"She seems to have mucked you up and that's a fact," agreed Menzies.

"She did that," explained Royal. "I was too busy cursing my luck at being left to look after a deader

THE MAELSTROM

while you were on the warpath with Ling that I never stopped to consider she mightn't be dead after all."

" I made the same mistake," said Menzies. " You aren't to blame there."

" Maybe I was in a bit of a hurry," confessed Royal. " I didn't think a corpse required much watching. I was thinking of the driver. He might have been all right and again he mightn't. So when he patched the engine up I took my seat alongside of him and we started off for the hospital at quite a respectable speed. We'd just turned into the main road when I heard a click behind me and it flashed across my mind that I'd been careless in taking the old girl so much on trust. I bent round the side of the cab to take a look through the window and there was a hand fumbling with the door handle. I'd had to twist like an acrobat to get a fair look and I suppose I was a little off my guard. First thing I knew the cab gave a lurch and I was rolling over and over in the mud of the roadway. It was a mercy I didn't break my neck, but I wasn't thinking of that. I just picked myself up and there was the cab a hundred yards ahead putting on steam for all it was worth.

" It came to me then what a damn fool I'd been. If you'll believe me, sir, I hadn't even taken the number of that rotten cab, and it was too far away to see it. ' This about puts the finish to your career in the C. I. D., Royal, my man,' I thinks to myself and pulled out my

THE MAELSTROM

whistle. Of course I knew there wasn't a chance in a million of that doing any good. She'd got too big a start.

"I'm not much of a believer in miracles, but I'm blest if one didn't happen then. As I'm alive a great big touring car came sliding along towards me. The chauffeur was bringing it back from Southend or somewhere, I learned afterwards. I jumped to it and pulled him up.

"'You noticed a taxi-cab that you've just passed,' I says.

"He looks me up and down and you can guess I was in a pretty pickle of mud from head to foot. If I hadn't pulled myself up into the seat alongside of him and took possession I reckon he'd have gone on without me.

"'You've got a devil of a cool nerve,' he says. 'Get off this car or I'll fling you off and call a policeman.'

"I was getting over my shake-up a bit then, but there wasn't time for argument. 'For God's sake don't chew the rag with me,' I says. 'Turn her head round and get after that cab before it gets a chance to dodge me.'

"Well, that chauffeur was a sport. I will say that for him. He jerked that big car about in double-quick time and we began sliding after Gwennie. I felt my luck was in.

"'Now what's it all about?' he says as soon as we

got going. 'If you're having a game with me, my lad, you've got the biggest sort of hiding you ever had in your life coming to you.' He looked it, too.

"'I'm a detective officer,' I says, 'and in that cab there's a woman wanted for murder. Now bust your car or catch her.'

"He nodded and let the car out. You know the Whitechapel Road's fairly straight in stretches and we had a view of the cab before it took one of the bends. There'll be some summonses out against that car this morning for exceeding the speed limit unless we put in a word. That chauffeur was quick to take a hint and you can bet we shifted. The road was fairly clear at that hour and we came up to the cab as if it was standing still.

"'What do you want me to do?' asks the chauffeur.

"'Get alongside and yell to the driver to stop,' I says. I hadn't any plan very clear in my own mind and that was the best I could rake up at the moment. It was just silly, too, because if he'd stop for a demand like that he'd have stopped when I tumbled off.

"Anyway we tried it, and then I got an idea of what was happening. The driver's face was like dirty white paper and he was hanging on to the steering wheel like grim death. Inside Gwennie had opened one of the windows—you know some taxi-cabs have got windows that open straight on to the driver's seat—and was leaning forward with a little ivory-mounted pistol in her

THE MAELSTROM

hand. He told me later on that when I tumbled off he started to pull up and the feel of the pistol muzzle in his ribs was the first thing that woke him up to the fact that Gwennie was going to have a say-so. He thought she was a ghost at first.

"As we came level I yelled to the man to stop. He just took no notice. She had him too thoroughly frightened for that. All his mind was on his steering and that wicked little pistol that was behind his back.

"Then she saw us and swung the pistol round towards us. But she never fired. She must have understood what kind of a fix I was in, for, while she kept the cab going, it seemed impossible that I could get at her. She just smiled and then kissed her hand towards me.

"That got my goat. I passed the word to my chanffeur to drop a little behind and then I put it to him.

"'Can you cut a wheel off that thing for me—smash the blighting thing up?'

"It didn't seem to appeal to him. He looked grave. 'I wouldn't mind so much if this was one of the guv-'nor's old cars,' he says, 'but it isn't. It's his pet and I wouldn't risk a smash for anything.

"'How much petrol have you got?' I asks, thinking we might shadow the other car till it was forced to come to a standstill.

"'I don't know exactly,' he answers, 'but it isn't much. We may get to the bottom of the tank any minute. Whatever you're going to do you'd better do

THE MAELSTROM

quick. I'm game for anything that won't do in the car.'

"I looked at the road sliding past and it gave me the shivers. We were fairly hustling. However, I wasn't going to let her have the laugh at me.

"'You put us level with that cab again,' I says, 'and hold as close and as near the same pace as you can. I'm going to board it.'

"'You'll be killed,' he says.

"'That's my business,' I tells him. 'I've got to stop that woman and I'm going to do it.' I was pretty well strung up. Perhaps her kissing her hand to me had something to do with it.

"Well, he eased up to let me get on the footboard and I held on with one hand. I knew I had to be mighty quick in pulling open the door of the cab and grabbing Gwennie and I didn't like the idea of her pistol a little bit.

"That chauffeur knew how to handle a car. He swung out a bit a little behind till he had gauged the pace and then he edged till as we drew level again there wasn't three inches between the two cars. I tore at the door of the cab and wrenched it open somehow. I hate to think in cold blood of how I did it. There wasn't much time for thinking and I went for her hell for leather before she could get to work with the shooter.

"I got her wrist as she turned and smashed it against the side window. It cut us both about a bit, but she dropped the gun, and that was the great thing.

THE MAELSTROM

They say it wasn't two minutes before the cab stopped then. It was just about the busiest two minutes I ever spent. A tiger's cage would be a peaceful spot compared to the inside of that cab. She may be a woman, and an old woman at that, but she's got muscles like whipcord.

"Once she got her hand at the back of my neck and I saw forty million stars as she flung me up against the side of the cab. Then I got my arms around her and tried to force her down, and she used her ten commandments on my face. I thought my cheeks had gone. And all the while that door was open and I'd got a kind of idea that at any minute we might both go through it.

"But we didn't, although we must have been near it once or twice. I'd got my arms locked round her and I wasn't going to let go, though I was half tempted to take a chance and smash her one under the jaw to lay her out—especially when she got her teeth into my shoulder and bit right through coat and all. She was all animal just then.

"At last the cab stopped and my chauffeur comes to my help. The driver was too paralysed to do anything but sit staring, goggle-eyed. We dragged her out into the roadway and managed to get the cuffs on her—a nice job that was, too—just as a constable came up.

"Things were easy after that. She saw the jig was up and didn't make too much trouble. I shipped her down to the local station and left her there without any charge, and when I found you were here came on straight away. I thought you'd like to know. Shall I make out my report in the morning, sir?"

Menzies nodded complacently and let a hand drop gently on his subordinate's shoulder. "You run away, laddie, and get some sleep," he said. "That's all you've got to think of now. There's no urgency about getting to the office to-morrow. Let me know when you turn up, that's all. By the way, did you ever pass the Civil Service examination for inspector?"

Royal's face glowed. "Yes, sir."

"Then I wouldn't wonder if you got called before the C. I. Board sometime. Good-night. Which way you going, Hallett?"

"Back to the hotel. What time will you be off duty to-morrow?"

The glance the chief inspector shot at him had a mixture of questioning and amusement. "To-morrow looks like being my busy day. Why do you ask?"

"Oh, nothing." Jimmie was a trifle confused. "I've been taking a little interest in gardening lately and I thought I'd like to have a look at some of your roses again—if you'd let me come over to Magersfontein Road sometime."

"H'm." Menzies surveyed him doubtingly. "I don't know. Honest Injun. Now do you know a Captain Hayward from a Caroline Testout?"

"I was hoping to learn something from you," said Jimmie humbly.

"I'll bet you are," agreed Menzies. "You turn up at the Yard at six to-morrow evening if I don't send for you before and we'll see."

CHAPTER XXXIV

TRULY, as he had said, this was Menzies' busy day. He sat bending over his desk, going over the piles of papers which were the evidence of the minuteness with which Scotland Yard, aided by other great police organisations, had ransacked the world for the smallest facts. Hundreds of men had spent days and money in compiling these reports—and nine-tenths of them were useless.

Before he met the Treasury Solicitor, and the counsel who would have charge of the case in court, it was his task to have his evidence at least roughly sorted into what was material and what was not material, if he did not want to have it straightened out by the legal advisers of the Treasury.

More than once the door opened noiselessly and Foyle peeped in, took one look at the industrious figure at the desk, and as noiselessly vanished.

As he arranged the reports, Menzies sent for the officer responsible for each one and went through his statement with him with deliberate care. Sometimes a man would be sent out again to further verify an important point which had appeared of no great value at the time the statement was taken. Gradually things began to fall into shape. The chief inspector began to pack the documents and exhibits into a despatch case.

THE MAELSTROM

For the fifth time Helden Foyle poked his head inside the door and then the rest of his body followed. Menzies looked up and nodded.

"Just finished," he said.

"How does it look?" Foyle asked.

"Fair. Very fair indeed," said Menzies cautiously.

"Heard about Ling?" demanded the superintendent.

"What about him? I was down at the station on my way here and there was nothing much fresh then."

"Nothing much. It's interesting, though." Foyle kicked an obdurate coal with the toe of his brightly polished boot. "It happened after you had gone and they've just had me on the 'phone. You know they put a constable in the cell with him? He offered the man one hundred pounds to smuggle him out."

"That's interesting. Looks as if he doesn't fancy his chance overmuch" The detail did not appear to greatly stir Menzies.

"Yes, but listen to this. The blame fool, after refusing it, seems to have got into conversation with Ling and asked him if he really did shoot Greye-Stratton."

Some sign of consternation flickered over Menzies' face. "You don't say," he exclaimed. "The cabbage-headed idiot!" . . . Words failed him.

There is one unforgiveable blunder in the Metropolitan Police, the hideousness of which no layman can adequately plumb. To question a prisoner, to coax or bully him into an admission of guilt is one of those things that no zeal, no temptation can excuse. It is not merely that it is against the law. It is not playing the game. The slightest suggestion that such a course has been pursued has before now secured a guilty man's acquittal.

Foyle kicked the coals again and the action seemed to afford him some relief. "And Ling admitted it. The chap was so proud of what he'd done that he took a note of the conversation."

"I don't see what we can do," said Menzies slowly. "We can't put the constable in the box. The only thing to do is to let it slide. If we don't use it the defence won't make a point of it."

"What I'm wondering about," said the superintendent, "is if your evidence is water-tight as it stands. You see, even if Ling should make a voluntary admission now it's tainted. He's been seeing that shyster Lexton and I wouldn't wonder if all this wasn't a carefully put-up trap."

Weir Menzies drew his brows together and began eating his moustache. "There might be something in that," he agreed. "Lexton's a good lawyer and it's like him."

"See." Foyle demonstrated with a forefinger. "If we could be tempted into putting an officer in the box to say that Ling had confessed he'd have us by the short hair. We'd have to admit that at least one of our men had questioned him and "—he snapped his fingers—

" there you are. The whole police evidence tainted. We're so anxious for a conviction that we've applied third-degree methods in England. Why, he'd be acquitted if he'd committed as many murders as Herod."

" I quite understand, sir." Menzies was a little peevish at having the i's dotted. " If he makes a thousand confessions we won't use them."

" I only wanted to put you wise," said Foyle almost apologetically. " You've got to rely on a straightforward case. Got it mapped out?"

" I think so. There's the direct case against him. There's plenty of evidence to indicate Gwennie Lyne's association, and we've got Miss Greye-Stratton's story. Big Rufe was caught, so to speak, red-handed, and I rather fancy when he sees how deep he's in he'll turn King's evidence. We don't want that, though, if we can help it."

" No. I should think not," said the superintendent quickly. He had all the prejudice of the trained man against calling the assistance of one guilty person to convict others. King's evidence is never suggested by Scotland Yard officers except as a last resource.

" The weak point," said Menzies, " is Dago Sam. Except his threatening Hallett, and what Cincinnati Red can tell us about him, we've got little to connect him up.'

" Well, see what the lawyers say," said Foyle. " After all, it's their funeral now."

THE MAELSTROM

Menzies nevertheless had a doubt rankling in his mind, and before he left for the consultation with the legal lights he had put into motion again all the machinery that he could bring to bear to find out whether any part of the case as affecting Dago Sam had been overlooked. He held no animus. He would cheerfully have volunteered any statement in favour of a prisoner, but equally he had that stern sense of duty that impelled him to make sure he had every accessible fact.

Many difficulties had been brushed away since all the main persons of the drama were in his hands, and it not infrequently happens that evidence of vast import is picked up after arrests have been effected. It is then possible to go over the ground more at leisure and with an undetached mind.

Congreve, with a big Gladstone bag and an air of jubilation, was awaiting him when he returned from Whitehall. He had been assisting in the search of the opium house, and, though he suppressed it well, it was plain to the inspector's keen eyes that he was labouring under some excitement.

"Having a birthday, Congreve?" he said. "You look happy."

The other was diving into the bag. He stood up with something wrapped in tissue paper in his arms. "We went over that place as you said, sir. Mostly old pipes and lamps and all the old junk that you'd expect. I left it in charge of Hugh. There was one room,

THE MAELSTROM

though, that had apparently been lived in by a European, proper bed and washstand and everything. The mattress looked rather uneven, so we undid it. Found this suit of clothes stuffed in it. Shouldn't wonder if we found that they fit Ling. Here's the jacket. Look at the stain on the left sleeve and breast.

"Don't be in a hurry to jump to conclusions, Congreve," said Menzies calmly.

"It's blood, all right, sir," asserted Congreve confidently. "Look." He pointed as Menzies spread the jacket carefully over the desk. "You'll remember how the dead man was lying—on his left side with his face towards the fireplace. Anyone approaching the body would naturally come from behind and use the left arm to support the head. If the wound was bleeding freely then the jacket would be soaked exactly like this one."

Menzies opened a penknife and removed a hair from the breast of the coat. "Go and get me two small pieces of glass," he said.

He placed the hair between the small glass slabs which Congreve secured and tied a piece of tape round them. His lips were pressed together tightly.

"Does it strike you, Congreve," he said quietly, "that if you're right and this is the suit that was worn by the murderer it queers my theory? I was relying on the thread of cloth I found to show that it was Ling. Now this material isn't in the slightest respect like that.

THE MAELSTROM

It means that we've got an entirely new angle to look into."

"Yes, but——"

"Never mind about anything else for the minute. Take the coat round to Professor Harding's and make sure that it is human blood. Before you do that 'phone through to Mr. Fynne-Racton and ask him if he'll oblige me by coming on here as quick as a motor can bring him. Tell him to bring an instrument. It's very urgent or I wouldn't trouble him" He opened the breast pocket of the coat, wrote a few words on an envelope and passed out, carrying the hair in its glass shield.

He held a brief conversation with Foyle in the latter's room and left the hair with him. Thence he walked to the Home Office, from there took the tube to Kensington, and thence returned to a certain tailoring firm in the Strand. From the Strand he took a taxi to Buxton Prison.

He had entirely forgotten his appointment with Jimmie Hallett and that young man's reproachful face peering out of the waiting-room was one of the first sights that he encountered on his return to the Yard.

"Hullo, Hallett, old man. Sorry. Hope I haven't kept you waiting long?"

"Only a matter of a couple of hours," said Jimmie. "Don't apologise."

"Lucky you're a man of leisure," grinned the de-

THE MAELSTROM

tective. "Another ten minutes won't hurt." He swung into the superintendent's room.

It was nearer another sixty than another ten minutes before he emerged and carried the impatient Jimmie to the electric cars opposite the Houses of Parliament. "That's another good day's work done," he said thankfully. "I clean forgot all about you, Hallett, or I'd have left a message. I've had a hundred things to think about."

"And I," mourned Jimmie, "have only had one. By the way, how is Miss Greye-Stratton?"

"As fit as could be expected, all things considered. Ninety-nine girls out of a hundred who had gone through what she has would have been knocked out. I told her I should probably be bringing you home to dinner."

"Things been all right today? No hitches of any kind?"

"One or two little points," admitted the chief inspector. "I'm expecting a telephone call when I get home. Perhaps I'll tell you then."

They had the top of the car to themselves. Jimmie laughed. "Still as cautious as ever. I'll begin to have doubts soon whether you're as wise as you seem."

"I've begun to have doubts myself. We're none of us infallible. If I was I should be on the Stock Exchange, not in the C. I. D."

Although Menzies lived in Magersfontein Road, Upper Tooting, the dinner that had been arranged

THE MAELSTROM

smacked little of the suburbs. Jimmie felt that he had eaten many worse at Princes and Delmonico's. Perhaps a difference was made by the slim black-clad figure that sat opposite to him. Some of the melancholy had gone from the blue eyes, though she was still sober and subdued. Mrs. Menzies, discreet and tactful, watched her closely, and Jimmie noticed that the conversation was never allowed to flag.

"I don't know how many years we've been married, Hallett," said Menzies reflectively, as he poured out a glass of claret, "but this is the first time I've ever taken my wife into my confidence on a professional subject—and the first time she's ever asked me."

Jimmie's eyes dwelt on the smiling, genial face of his hostess. "Effect and cause," he murmured. "If Mrs. Menzies ever wanted to know a thing you'd have to capitulate."

"Don't you believe that, Mr. Hallett," interrupted Mrs. Menzies. "He's like a bit of stone sometimes—a most aggravating man to get on with. Don't you ever marry a detective, Miss Greye-Stratton."

"She won't," said Jimmie promptly, and watched the rich flood of colour that surged into the girl's cheeks.

"One minute," said Menzies, standing. "Fill your glasses. I'm going to propose a toast. Oh, da—bless the telephone" With an apology he hurried to the instrument.

"Yes   yes. This is Menzies speaking. . . That

you, Mr. Foyle. Oh, yes, yes. . . . I see, that clears everything up. . . . Yes, I'll be along early in the morning. Good-night."

He returned to the dining-room. "To break another professional rule," he said quietly, "I don't mind telling you that my mind is perfectly at ease for the first time since Mr. Greye-Stratton was killed."

CHAPTER XXXV

JIMMIE presented a French roll sternly at Menzies, pistol wise.

"You don't get away with it like that," he warned. "Look at him. Cold-blooded isn't the word. He's got a perfectly clear mind and he can sit down and eat and drink in our presence as though we didn't matter."

The chief inspector brushed his moustache with his serviette. "Plenty of time," he murmured. "Let's have some coffee in my room, my dear." His eyes twinkled at his wife. "I must try to satisfy this insatiable young man, even if I get broken for betraying official secrets."

"If you betray any secrets to Mr. Hallett you betray them to us," assented Mrs. Menzies definitely.

"But, my dear"—a series of humorous wrinkles formed around the corners of his eyes—"you know you don't like smoke in the drawing-room. How can I talk——"

"Oh, very well." Mrs. Menzies spoke in laughing resignation. "You may smoke there—but not a pipe. Mind, I totally forbid a pipe."

Menzies winked at Jimmie. "It shall be my very Sunday best cigars," he said. "Come along."

In the drawing-room he took up his favourite posture

with one arm on the mantelpiece and a foot on the fender. He lit his cigar with deliberation and drew silently at it for a second or two.

"You know pretty well as much as I do about this business up to last night," he said to Jimmie. "If you had to guess who would you say was the actual murderer?"

"Ling?" said Jimmie promptly. "Why, you told us yourself——"

"That's what comes of talking before a case is complete," said the chief inspector oracularly. "If I'd kept my mouth shut and said nothing you wouldn't have been able to convict me in my own house of being a liar. I was too quick with the cockadoodledo act, though," he added quickly. "I was right in my main facts. Ling is certainly a murderer—legally all of the gang are murderers, and I don't doubt that they'll all receive the same punishment. But even so, there's something more than an intellectual satisfaction in clearing up the last fragments of doubt. Ling is not the murderer. He was present in the house when the shot was fired, he was the man who, posing as a doctor, knocked you out, but the real assassin was Mr. William Smith—otherwise, Dago Sam."

"The gentleman who wanted to persuade me not to say anything."

"That same gentleman. Funny, isn't it, that he should have been under lock and key all this while and

THE MAELSTROM

we never dreamt of considering him anything but a subordinate—which in point of fact he is, although he killed Greye-Stratton.

"In one way or another we've now got roughly the life of the five persons involved in the conspiracy since its inception in the brain of Gwennie Lyne. Pinkertons and the New York police have helped us a lot on that. I won't burden you with a lot of detail about that. Big Rufe was brought into it by Gwennie because she didn't want Ling to boss the show, and Rufe, though he's got no brains, is a handy man in a row. Dago Sam was the man who originally knew Errol and he seems to have slid into the scheme because he wouldn't be left out.

"Now about the murder. Mr. Greye-Stratton did not seem in any hurry to die naturally and the gang of course found expenses running up. There was every probability that Errol was right and that he had left his fortune to you, Miss Greye-Stratton, but there was no certainty—only Errol's word. Now Dago Sam was an expert burglar. There wasn't one among them who objected to the idea of making certain. Errol had spoken of the safe. The chances were that if the old man had made a will he would not have confided it to his lawyers—I am answering their line of argument—but would keep it in his own safe under his own eye. If it was in Miss Greye-Stratton's favour, well and good; if it was not the scheme was that it should be

THE MAELSTROM

destroyed and a dummy substituted. Then she would automatically inherit."

"Hold on a minute," interrupted Jimmie. "Is this a hypothesis or——?

"It's concrete fact. I'll tell you how we got at it in a moment. Very well. Dago Sam was delegated to do the burglary on the first convenient night. It so happened that when the fog came down he decided that his chance had arrived and set off without confiding in anybody but Errol. That was the night, Miss Greye-Stratton, that you got the cheques.

"After missing you in the fog Ling went on to the Petit Savoy, where he met Errol, who spoke about Sam's decision. Now Ling, it seems, wasn't quite certain that Sam hadn't some game of his own to play. Crooks rarely trust one another entirely—and what must he do but start off to Linstone Terrace Gardens himself to keep an eye on things. He must have acted just on general principles, because, unless by accident, he hadn't a ghost's chance of getting into the house. You see, he's no burglar.

"The accident happened. While he was kicking his heels outside the door opened softly and old Greye-Stratton, a pistol in his hand, looked out. To a man of Ling's acuteness it was obvious what had happened. He walked casually by and was, of course, stopped. 'There's a burglar in here,' says Greye-Stratton. 'Will you fetch a constable?' 'It's not much of a night to find one,' said Ling. 'I'll come in if you like. The two of us ought to manage him.'

"They went in—Ling taking the pistol and—it proves what his nerves were like—putting up a play of holding up Dago Sam, who was hiding behind a curtain. 'Bring him into the other room,' said the old man. 'There's a telephone there. I can send for the police.'

"That took them both aback for the minute. It is to be supposed that the old man had not telephoned in the first place because he was afraid the sound of his voice might alarm the burglar. He crossed the dining-room, leaving Ling to look after Sam, and that was how it happened. Sam impulsively pulled the weapon out of Ling's hand and fired. Possibly if Ling had realised what was going to happen he would have stopped it. However, he had no chance and he must have realised instantly that now it was done he had to sink or swim with Dago Sam. He took the revolver away and put it in his pocket. Sam went round the table to inspect the shot man. It was at that moment that you, Mr. Hallett, knocked at the door.

"Now, whatever may be against Ling, he never lacked courage or resource. Your knock must have staggered the pair of 'em. It might simply be a casual caller, though that was unlikely, seeing what sort of a man Mr. Greye-Stratton was, or it might be someone who had heard the shot. When your second knock came they had either to open the door or risk the possibility of an alarm being raised. Ling had taken the precaution to switch off the whole light when they came through. He started for the front door. Sam quietly called him back and passed him a small sandbag. He had that spiel about being a doctor all ready to loose out on you. If the caller had happened to be an acquaintance of Greye-Stratton's it would explain what he, a stranger, was doing there. You fell for it, were lured inside and laid out and the cheques taken from you. Then you were locked in. It occurred to Ling that something might be traced home to them if any trace of the forgery was left. That was why they cleared out all those bankbooks and things. It only seems to have occurred to them next day, after they had had a sleep on it, that you might have seen Ling and be able to recognise him again. So Dago Sam was put on that fool idea of trying to terrify you."

He lifted a cup of coffee, took a sip and replaced it.

"It is an old truism that every criminal makes mistakes. So if you come to it does every detective. We're all human. But there's this difference and it explains why the world is not overrun with crooks. A detective's mistake is not necessarily disastrous. He can retrieve himself. A crook who is being hunted by the whole resources of civilisation hasn't often much time to repair an error, even if he knows he's made one. The shooting of Greye-Stratton was an accident in a sense and looking back you will see how inevitable it was that at least the main persons in the conspiracy should be brought to justice—and the personality of the man in charge of the search scarcely mattered a button to the ultimate result. It was merely a matter of common sense and organisation. Every step is obvious. Here is Greye-Stratton killed. Obvious first enquiry: Who and what are his relatives and friends? That leads us to Errol and Miss Greye-Stratton, and through them we get on to Ling, and systematic enquiries about him would have certainly resulted in the discovery of his accomplices. It is one of those cases in which it was as certain as sunrise that a corps of disciplined, intelligent men could not be unsuccessful. We've had luck—but that only hastens things—the end would have been just the same now as in three months' time."

"It's perfectly simple as you expound it," said Jimmie. "But you haven't told us how you got all the detail which you have told us about the murder. You aren't going to tell us you had a dictaphone there?"

"Not much. That is one of my short cuts in which I did the Sherlock Holmes act—with the help of several other people. Today for the first time we found out where Dago Sam had been laying up."

"The opium joint?"

"Which will you have—cigar or cocoanut?" asked Menzies smilingly. "Like Ling, he is fond of the pipe, and Sing Loo had found him a room. When that was searched a blood-stained suit was found and I happened to notice a hair when it was shown to me. Now, most of the rest was plain sailing. There was the tailor's name and date and a reference number on a label sewed in one of the breast pockets. I went to the tailors' and took their fitter down with me to Brixton Prison, where we had Sam paraded with a dozen other men and picked out as the customer who ordered that suit of clothes. Meanwhile I had got a Home Office order for the exhumation of Mr. Greye-Stratton's body. A piece of hair was taken from the corpse and sent to the Yard, where I had persuaded an expert microscopist to bring an instrument. Already one of the medical experts associated with the Home Office has pronounced the stain on the jacket to be human blood. Then when Fynne-Racton declared that the hair of the murdered man corresponded with the hair I had found I had the last link. I got that result from Mr. Foyle over the telephone just now."

"I can follow that all right," declared Jimmie, "but where I go off the rails is how you fixed the respective rôles of Dago Sam and Ling. How'd you get at what happened at the house?"

"That is where the human factor comes in. So long as Sam thought the only case against him was a minor one he was determined not to say a word. The fear of being hanged is a wonderful incentive to secrecy. When

THE MAELSTROM

he was stood up for identification today it was clear to him that we were close up on the facts and it didn't much matter what he said. He was rankling apparently under the idea that his pals had deserted him when he was arrested and he sent for the governor of the prison and made a statement pretty well as I've told you except that he asserted Ling fired the fatal shot. He was a little confused about that part of it and on reflection admitted that he himself snatched the revolver. It doesn't matter a pin, anyway. They're both murderers. The four of them will be brought up in court together to-morrow morning."

He emptied his cup and moved towards the door. " And now if you'll excuse me I'll drop a line to the vicar. He'll think I've been neglecting church affairs lately and there's something I want to ask him about the organ fund. Have you got a minute, my dear? "

Husband and wife went out together.

A prolonged fit of coughing heralded their return. Peggy, scarlet-faced, was turning over some music on the piano. Jimmie Hallett was lighting a cigarette. He interpreted the twinkle in the chief inspector's eyes and met the situation boldly.

" Menzies," he said, " do you happen to know how long it takes to arrange an international marriage in England? "

THE MAELSTROM

Menzies produced a yellow-covered book from under his arm. "I thought you might need Whitaker's Almanac," he chuckled. "Pure deduction, without any fake. I told you I was your fairy godfather, didn't I?"

THE END

BOOTH TARKINGTON'S NOVELS

May be had wherever books are sold. Ask for Grosset & Dunlap's list.

SEVENTEEN. Illustrated by Arthur William Brown.

No one but the creator of Penrod could have portrayed the immortal young people of this story. Its humor is irresistible and reminiscent of the time when the reader was Seventeen.

PENROD. Illustrated by Gordon Grant.

This is a picture of a boy's heart, full of the lovable, humorous, tragic things which are locked secrets to most older folks. It is a finished, exquisite work.

PENROD AND SAM. Illustrated by Worth Brehm.

Like "Penrod" and "Seventeen," this book contains some remarkable phases of real boyhood and some of the best stories of juvenile prankishness that have ever been written.

THE TURMOIL. Illustrated by C. E. Chambers.

Bibbs Sheridan is a dreamy, imaginative youth, who revolts against his father's plans for him to be a servitor of big business. The love of a fine girl turns Bibb's life from failure to success.

THE GENTLEMAN FROM INDIANA. Frontispiece.

A story of love and politics,—more especially a picture of a country editor's life in Indiana, but the charm of the book lies in the love interest.

THE FLIRT. Illustrated by Clarence F. Underwood.

The "Flirt," the younger of two sisters, breaks one girl's engagement, drives one man to suicide, causes the murder of another, leads another to lose his fortune, and in the end marries a stupid and unpromising suitor, leaving the really worthy one to marry her sister.

Ask for Complete free list of G. & D. Popular Copyrighted Fiction

GROSSET & DUNLAP, PUBLISHERS, NEW YORK

KATHLEEN NORRIS' STORIES

May be had wherever books are sold. Ask for Grosset & Dunlap's list.

MOTHER. Illustrated by F. C. Yohn.

This book has a fairy-story touch, counterbalanced by the sturdy reality of struggle, sacrifice, and resulting peace and power of a mother's experiences.

SATURDAY'S CHILD.

Frontispiece by F. Graham Cootes.

Out on the Pacific coast a normal girl, obscure and lovely, makes a quest for happiness. She passes through three stages—poverty, wealth and service—and works out a creditable salvation.

THE RICH MRS. BURGOYNE.

Illustrated by Lucius H. Hitchcock.

The story of a sensible woman who keeps within her means, refuses to be swamped by social engagements, lives a normal human life of varied interests, and has her own romance.

THE STORY OF JULIA PAGE.

Frontispiece by Allan Gilbert.

How Julia Page, reared in rather unpromising surroundings, lifted herself through sheer determination to a higher plane of life.

THE HEART OF RACHAEL.

Frontispiece by Charles E. Chambers.

Rachael is called upon to solve many problems, and in working out these, there is shown the beauty and strength of soul of one of fiction's most appealing characters.

Ask for Complete free list of G. & D. Popular Copyrighted Fiction

GROSSET & DUNLAP,   PUBLISHERS,   NEW YORK

UNIVERSITY OF CALIFORNIA LIBRARY
Los Angeles

This book is DUE on the last date stamped below

INTERLIBRARY LOANS
REC'D LD-URL
AUG 20
OCT 01 1986
Due Two Weeks From Date of Receipt

INTERLIBRARY LOANS
OCT 15 1986
Due Two Weeks From Date of Receipt
NOV 10 1986

Lightning Source UK Ltd.
Milton Keynes UK
UKOW05f1106130217
294258UK00002B/492/P